CALVARIA FELL

STORIES BY
CAT SPARKS AND KAARON WARREN

Meerkat Press
Asheville

"Witnessing," originally published in *The Canary Press Story Magazine,* Issue 6, The Canary Press, 2014

"68 Days," originally published in *Tomorrow's Cthulhu: Stories at the Dawn of Posthumanity,* edited by C. Dombrowski and Scott Gable, Broken Eye Books, 2016

"The Space Between All Possible Ways," originally published in *Phase Change: Imagining Energy Futures,* edited by Matthew Chrulew, Twelfth Planet Press, 2022

"Air, Water and the Grove," originally published in *The Lowest Heaven,* edited by Anne C. Perry and Jared Shurin, Jurassic London, 2013

"Dreams of Hercules," originally published in *Relics, Wrecks & Ruins,* edited by Aiki Flinthart, 2021

"Everything So Slow and Quiet," originally published in *The Art of Being Human,* edited by Tehani Croft, FableCroft Publishing, 2022

"In the Drawback," originally published in *The Grinding House,* edited by Donna Maree Hanson, CSFG Publishing, 2005

"Hacking Santorini," originally published in *Dark Harvest,* edited by Ian Whates, Newcon Press, 2020

Lyrics quoted in "Gardens of Earthly Delight," from *Many Mansions Up There* by R.F. Lehman, Public Domain

ISBN-13 978-1-946154-82-8 (Paperback)
ISBN-13 978-1-946154-83-5 (eBook)

Cover and book design by Tricia Reeks

Printed in the United States of America

Published in the United States of America by
Meerkat Press, LLC, Asheville, North Carolina
www.meerkatpress.com

CONTENTS

WITNESSING

KAARON WARREN

The gang rolled like a pack of dogs, dust rising around them. Hound pulled his shirt up over his nose, trying not to breathe it in, but he hadn't had clean plastics in months and his stink made him choke. The wheels of his skates were smooth along the road and that was something.

Someone woofed up front, and the gang howled in response. They liked hanging their identity on dogs. Dogs were good and loyal. Dogs were brave and they made noise when they wanted to. Hound liked all that. Better than the Waterboy gang, cleaner than the rest of them but angry, or the spike-hair, split-tongue Lizards.

"Here, Cur," one of the boys said, and he tossed Cur a shiny coin. "Just found it. Back there."

Cur spun the coin, flipped it and let it fall back in his palm. "Every little bit helps."

Hound watched the coin fall, wanting it in his own hand.

"You need to pay attention, loser," Pooch said, and she waved her long, sharp nails in his face. The gang rolled on and Hound could not pull away from her. She sliced his cheek, but gently, lovingly, and he wondered for a moment if he had a chance with her. He reached out and tugged one of her curls then let it fall back. Pooch snapped her teeth.

"Which finger don't you want?" she said. Hound's cheek stung where she'd cut him.

Around them the city writhed. People everywhere, other gangs, lovers with their dark miasma of stink, the rattle and hiss of the street cleaners, patrolling, waiting to wipe up the filth left by citizens not willing to follow the law.

They rolled on.

—

Music reached them. There weren't too many songs played in the public arena. The one's that were came from some government studio. This song got stuck in your head even if you tried not to listen. Your legs flew along to the tune, the rhythm just the right pace to make you glide. "Keep on moving, keep on watching, we're always watching, you're always moving."

In an alley to their left, the Waterboys had formed a huddle, all bent over an old man. He clutched a bottle of water, glugging it down before they could take it from him.

They left him bleeding and still thirsty.

Cur led them over to the old guy.

"Fuck off," he said. "Fucking thieves. I got nothing for you to steal."

Cur cocked his skate at the man.

"Watch it," Hound said, but his words were lost in the great rumble of traffic going by. He sucked air, fighting for it. Enclosed on all sides by people. Hound felt an elbow in his back, shook it off. You didn't turn; you'd get something worse in the face if you did that.

"Let's roll," he said. "Come on." The Waterboys would be back.

"Roll on, you all," the music played. "Move on."

—

They rolled down a city street, shouting for attention. They quietened as they passed one of the techo buildings, with its massive cameras following them like eyeballs.

Blocks away now, they tossed rubbish through windows, aiming at the Homebodies sheltering inside.

"They're scared of us, scared of us coming upstairs to rape and take them. Fucking Homebodies. Look at them, hiding in the walls. Not me," Cur said. Hound saw shadows up there. The Homebodies wouldn't show their faces, not with a gang about.

"Homebodies are evil," Cur said. "Every last one of them. Soft, evil, warm-loving arseholes."

Hound couldn't breathe, so he pushed his way to the outside of the pack. It was almost as bad there, but at least there was some room, fingers of space between him and all the people going the other way.

From high up there came a shout.

"Fuck off, you lot. Keep moving. This is our place. We see you! We see every one of you!"

Cur wound his arm back for a huge throw. "I'll brain him! I'll splatter him!"

But the Homebody tipped pebbles on them, a bucketful, and they came down like hailstones. The gang ran. Mutt was hit, crack on his skull, and he went down. Other windows opened and missiles flew out; tins, rubbish, pebbles, shoes. The fire escape shook down the side of the building and Hound thought he wouldn't want to climb down that way.

He thought they should drag Mutt's body to safety, but he didn't want to be hit.

They all hid until the rain-down stopped.

"Give it a while then we'll roll out and collect any good crap," Pooch said.

"And Mutt," Hound said. But as they watched, another gang rolled through, swooping on the treasures and away before anyone could react.

"I'm too tired to chase," Pooch said.

"We have to get Mutt," Hound said, but Mutt, too, had been taken as treasure.

"They should have left the crap there. See those Homers explain rubbish on the ground," Cur said. "We need a new Front Roller . . . you do it, Pooch."

"Come on, roll with me," Pooch said to Hound, grabbing his shirt. The thin plastic tore a little, and she poked her finger in to widen the hole.

"He's always bad moodish after we've dealt with Homers. Have you noticed?" Hound said.

Pooch poked his forehead with a finger. "You think too much," she said.

Hound knew Cur would love to have a home, that he hated the street, hated the constant movement of living there. To Hound, the idea of being closed in by the walls was frightening. Pooch rolled up front as if Mutt never existed.

It was easier to breathe out there and Hound wanted to prove how good a lookout he was, so he elbowed his way forward. He stared till his eyes watered, lifting a finger in the hope of pointing at something worthwhile. He could do this, he knew what was expected. Spot rubbish disposals to empty their belly bags. Spot food outlets not mobbed. Spot treasures dropped and forgotten.

He could do all that.

"There!" he shouted. "Rubbish disposal."

"Not that hard to find," Pooch said, pointing to the huge sign. *"No Unauthorized Disposal."*

Hound didn't care. He was the one who'd found it.

—

The gang stopped suddenly.

"Keep rolling," Cur said, but they were surrounded by techos in their fresh clean plastics, their Government ID demanding attention. This could mean anything. The gang didn't want to be broken up, though Hound looked at the techos, space between them, and he thought it would be okay to have that space for a while.

"Who're they after?" Hound whispered.

"You," Pooch whispered back. She pushed at him.

"One of you has been witnessed witnessing," the techo said. "Which of you is Frank Ragula?" The gang howled with laughter. No one liked their real name.

"Told you," Pooch said.

"I am," Hound said. He stepped forward, and they checked his face against the disclist they carried.

"Can I have a turn of that?" Cur said, reaching for it.

"Get your own," the techo said. The gang laughed. They would never have enough to buy one of those things.

—

"I bet you'd like a wash," the techo said, entering the cubicle. He led Hound down a silent corridor, and motioned him into the vacuum cleaner.

It had been months since he had bathed, that last time he'd snuck in through the back entrance of the local hospital and stepped quickly into their vacuum cleaner. Then, he had to put back on his filthy plastics, and the effort was almost wasted. His face and his hair though, clean for days.

Hound undressed and hung his belly bag on a hook, then stood with his head tilted back and let the cleaning work. It was an odd yet glorious feeling, to have the dirt sucked off. His skin tingled and he found it hard to breathe, but in less than a minute the noise subsided and he was clean.

"Put on your pajamas, Witness," the techo said.

Fresh throwaway pajamas waited for him, and Hound slipped them on, sniffing the collar. New. New. No remnants of anything else.

The door opened and Hound stepped out. He could not stop smiling.

"Better?" the techo said. He led Hound down a white hallway to another room.

"Sleepy?" The techo dressed the wound on Hound's cheek without mentioning it.

Hound nodded. Inside was a bed. With sheets. There was equipment all around but Hound wasn't bothered by that; he whooped and leapt onto the bed, bouncing on his knees. He didn't feel claustrophobic here. The air was fresher, cleaner, and there was an emptiness he loved.

The techo watched him for a moment, smiling.

"You've got a lot of energy, haven't you? Let's get you strapped in and we'll see what you can do."

Hound knew how witnessing worked; they all did. But he had no control over what he dreamt. He hoped it wouldn't be shameful. He climbed off the bed, hugging the pajamas tight around his body.

The techo said, "Don't worry. We're professionals, trained to see the true witnessing. We don't record the dreams, only the flashes of reality in between."

"But don't you watch the dreams? I would."

"Dreams are very dull if you're not in them yourself."

Hound was not convinced. "What about sexy dreams? You watch those, right?"

The techo shook his head. "We're professionals. We've seen it all."

Hound wondered what it would be like to have seen it all.

"Which thumb do you favor?" the techo asked him. Hound lifted and wriggled his right thumb.

The techo strapped him in and attached an IV to his left arm.

A coldness began to seep into Hound's wrist and he shivered. The techo pulled a blanket up his shoulders. It wasn't new; Hound could smell a faint sweatiness in it. Then warmth. Sleepiness. Hound yawned and closed his eyes.

—

"You've done well," the techo said. "Very, very well. Keep it up and we might be able to shift you somewhere better. A new gang, indoors, even."

Hound lay still, loving the comfort of waking in a bed.

"Would you like to see? They don't mind us showing you afterward. Most witnesses like it. They say it gives them a sense of satisfaction."

Hound nodded, and the techo led him into a room of monitors where images flickered. They saw a man leaving via a fire escape, a child dropping a piece of fruit, a woman adjusting her clothing, two men crossing the road dangerously and many more scenes. The detail of it surprised Hound. "I don't remember any of it."

"That's good," the techo said. "It's better for everyone if you don't see these things consciously. That way there is no interpretation, analysis or judgment. The witnessing is unchangeable. We have no effect on it. It is pure. It's just what you see."

The techo flicked on his time chart. "This is you here," he said, pointing at a cluster of eighteen flashing lights amongst dozens.

"I saw all that?"

The techo nodded. "Like I said, some of it appears to be so minor you would never think it worth mentioning. But look, see here? The man climbing down a fire escape?" The techo put his finger on one flashing light. "We have a dozen other witnesses giving his movements before and after. Another witness saw him jump the last step and hurt his ankle. We see him hobbling across the street in this person's witnessing, and here, you see?"

The techo ran the footage for Hound. "Here he is buying some pain medication. He'll use that as his defense, I imagine. That there was a chemical reaction which caused his behavior."

The techo shut the screen off. "We'll track the batch, of course. Trace it through witnesses to its production. We could trace the raw materials before that, but it may not be necessary. I imagine he will not last long in the system."

"What did he do?" Hound could not remember seeing the man but there it was, straight from his own cortex.

"You've done good service, here."

Hound could tell the techo was proud of his position. "So now what?"

The techo shrugged. "We won't know until we make our interpretations. They'll gather the witnesses you witnessed and input their information. Witnesses see everything. Nothing escapes the witnesses."

Hound stretched. "I meant with me. What happens with me? Can I sleep here again tonight?"

The techo shook his head. He unstrapped Hound's arm, disconnecting him from the reader. "They've got all they need from you for now. If you want to come back, my advice is to keep moving, keep your eyes open. Be vigilant. Don't think too much about what you see, because conscious thought damages the witnessing."

Hound rubbed his wrist. It ached with a cold stiffness. He wriggled a finger and pain shot up his arm, causing a spasm in his shoulder muscle.

"The chemical we used to immobilize you during sleep will take about two days to be excreted," the techo said. He handed him a small packet of nuts. "Nibble on these when you get a bad taste in your mouth."

"Thank you."

"No, thank you. All information received will be judiciously used in the pursuit of criminals."

"Will they catch that man?"

"They probably already have. If something comes of it, you will be credited." He passed Hound a card. "You keep hold of this. Check it every couple of days. If something comes of your witnessing, you'll be rewarded."

———

Hound walked onto the street. It was different, being clean, with fresh, new plastics. People noticed him; they gave him space to move. You weren't supposed to judge people by their smell but who could help it? That was how you assessed a person's worth. His gang would find him soon, but for now, just for a while, he wanted to stand alone.

Hound closed his eyes and tried to imagine space, vast space. He tipped his head back, opened his eyes and stared at the sky. He wondered if it was quiet up there, or if the clamor of the earth reached as far as that.

Someone chopped his throat with a hand edge and he fell forward, choking.

"Dreamer," Pooch said in his ear. "Dreamer dreamer, can't be a breeder." She winked at him but he ignored it. He'd never breed with her. He reached out to squeeze her belly bag, feeling a knife hard and sharp in there, and for a moment he was tempted to zip open the bag, steal the knife and use it on her, slice her up and be done with her teasing. Then he glanced over and saw a woman blinking at him, not reacting, just watching, and he knew she was a witness. Next to her, a child, and beyond that, a rolling gang of old men, staggering, blinking, shouting.

Witnessing.

"So, how was it?" Pooch said. "Because you kinda stink."

Hound smiled. "I slept in a bed. I had a wash. They fed me. It was okay."

Pooch shook her curls at him. "They should pick me!" She narrowed her eyes, staring into the distance. "I see everything. I'm good at it."

"You can't look on purpose. They told me it has to be subconscious. They said the witnessing is damaged by conscious thought. They can't use it," Hound said.

Cur cuffed Hound on the ear. "Shut up about it, all right? We're going back to those Homebodies who killed Mutt. We're gonna leave a message for them." He held up a bag. "I've been collecting shit."

Pooch turned her head away in disgust. "That stinks, you creep. It's disgusting."

Cur shrugged. "It's meant to be. I'm not gonna give them a birthday cake. Let's roll."

—

Things had changed. Hound saw that as soon as they turned the corner. The Homebodies sat out the front of the building, piles of belongings at their feet. Others entered the building, carrying ratty boxes or torn bags. New residents?

Cur called a halt. "Looks like they've got theirs for killing Mutt, anyways," he said.

Hound knew that his witnessing had affected this. He'd seen it, and it had been seen. Pooch rolled up to a woman with two children clinging to her legs.

"What's happened?" Pooch asked her.

"Water violations. Someone witnessed it. So we're kicked out."

Pooch came back and winked at Hound. "Your work, I believe." Hound noticed pipes down the side of the building, water dripping beneath. He didn't remember seeing the pipes before, but he must have.

———

Two days later, when they passed a news screen, Hound saw a face he recognized. His foot tapped as he watched, "Keep on moving, keep on watching."

Damn song.

The guy he'd witnessed on the fire escape had been arrested and charged with the rape and murder of eight women. The report said, *"The man was caught through witness accounts, once again showing that every piece of information, no matter how small, can help to track violent criminals, terrorists and other lawbreakers."* The man claimed his innocence. He said he was a good man. *"The witnessing doesn't lie,"* the report said.

"I did that," Hound said. Pooch didn't care; Cur didn't. But Hound felt important, as if he had a say in the future. The gang's existence achieved nothing. He could see that now. It was the power of his witnessing that lifted him, gave him strength.

Hound found an outlet when they paused for food, and entered his card. Credit in there. Enough for a night in a home. Enough for a week's food.

He tucked the card back into his skate and kept on moving.

Kept on watching.

SOME KIND OF INDESCRIBABLE
CAT SPARKS

When Aloha Joe strolls through the gates, Mila takes him for an apparition. More practical than a blessed virgin, but folks round here aren't as picky as they once were. Signs from heaven, signs from hell or signs from one of those *things*—whatever. With biological landscape patterns so distorted, you take your cues wherever you can find them.

Not *him* specifically, Aloha Joe—or whatever his name turns out to be. His type. Shufflers, travelers, moochers, spongers and freeloaders drifting from clave to clave, taking chances ordinary folks are no longer up for taking. Spreading gossip, knowledge, intel, edges of which have long past blurred and fused. Aloha Joes can tell you what they've seen—or think they've seen. About valleys cleft in two by impossibly big machines. Or cities melting into thick gray sludge. Other phenomena they don't have *adequate capacity* for describing. Clave 53 is doing pretty well by contemporary standards. Clave 53 has, in fact, got its shit together. They grow food and they draw water and they make stuff and they have shelter, but perspective, well now. Perspective is something else entirely.

The big lug saunters in with his nekkid lady shirt and ratty dreads. Ukulele, flute and sturdy boots. Army issue—no armies anymore, but plenty army gear still in circulation. Heavy stitching suited to harsh terrain. He raises an open palm and fires aloha, namaste and greetings in a scattering of languages, waves to the ones on balconies and others scooting in and out of doorways. And they lean over, waving back because what the hell else ever happens out this way? Drifting freeloaders bring small treats along with their half-baked bullshit. Ganja, chop-chop, sugar candies, seeds. Leads and rumors of crisp fresh pharma trails. Trusty volumes for the pride-and-glory shelf. Older the book, the more valuable its words. Back in the days, predigital, was the time of checks and balances, when any old junk did not get printed. Inked words were verified and trusted. People got paid for writing them. Post-Net, well now, there's no words at all aside from the spoken form in all its glory. Folks who sketch and scribble notes are the most unreliable of all—and the less said about ukulele songs, the better.

Mila stares at his nest of knotted, sun-and-salt-scoured dreads waterfalling down broad shoulders. She's not tripping—dude's a traveler all right and he's seen some salty sun, not just the cruel, relentless scour that comes from meandering through parched and burnt-out scrublands; the wind scored decades of dusty topsoil leached and drifted barren. This man has stood at the ocean's edge. Could have picked the shirt up from a station—threadbare palm trees, faded girls in grassy skirts—but his stance? The casual slanting leaning swagger, strolling in like he's trying to remember where he parked his shaggin' wagon. Maybe last night or the night before—try thirty years, mate. Thirty years too late.

Ol' 53 don't get too many visitors—and the ones who come aren't encouraged to hang around. Most are running away from something; often someone too. Others are on the lookout for a score. But this clave has its secrets and firm policy of avoiding broad spectrum attraction. They've all heard stories of other claves well-situated and packing heat and smarts. Of what goes down when one of those big old Saints comes rolling in, law enforcement summoned by some hapless idiot or other who decides we all might need help sorting our problems. Our problems being the fleshy, human sort.

Aloha Joe knows what he's doing, settling down on a dusty mat. Little kids tug on his hair. Laughing at tinkling bells embedded in waxy dreads. Digging a ukulele from his pack, threatening to sing 'em up a storm.

On the first few notes, Mila flashbacks with a shudder to a

different place and time, when half the guys she knew looked just like him. Only younger, leaner and with fuller sets of teeth. Wave riders. Sunchasers. Losers anyplace but on a board, hypnotized by pounding ocean rhythms.

And before long Aloha Joe's serenading loud about the perfect, longest waves and the water moving underneath and being healed and mended by the sun. About gnarly landings and insane swell and ocean people baptized in the barrel and how it's all *some kind of indescribable* and man, *the ocean's only place I feel alive.*

Kids who've never seen an ocean laugh and squeal and clap and cheer as Jed and Kina drag the biggest keg. And Mila smiles because Aloha Joe is right on point, about here now being the *only thing.* She is going to seize the goddamn moment—a moment she's been waiting for since she let the last one pass, too scared to make her move and take a stand.

Aloha Joe chugs a mug of their fermented finest, fires up his uke again and sings some ditty she's never heard before:

Moonlight shivers on the silent sea
Baby, baby, swim with me
Smell the sea and drink the sky
Adrift amidst the ocean's gentle lies . . .

———

Acoustic thrum washes through the courtyard as the scent of ganja wafts and permeates. Night's coming down, tools are packed and stacked and fires stoked and the courtyard fills with tired clavers hungry for tunes and company and news as much as beer and stew and bread.

Cross one new face with a couple of hours and pretty soon they'll all be baked and slaked and powered down with nobody minding anybody else's business. Simple three chord synergy; smooth blues with Aeolian grooves filling the gaps in between here and tomorrow.

Not the first time Mila's grateful for the two small rooms she and Lily are allotted, close and quiet on the ground floor to the back of the residential slats. She could never have gotten Lily down a flight of stairs in secret.

She shoves aside the beaded curtain. Whispers, "Tonight's the night, baby girl—it's right now or never."

Lily gives no answer, as expected. Hasn't spoken for well over a year and Mila has moved on from counting days. From the point her daughter's particular affliction presented clear and evident, there seems no further point in charting time. Time has nothing to do with their predicament. No cures, no answers and not much hope, save for the slimmest, craziest, most dangerous. Hope that will probably kill them both, but hell, it isn't like Mila has all that much going on in the living sense. Not much to look forward to. Stuck out here in the middle of nowhere, keeping clear of *things* they don't understand. *Things* that baffle more than threaten. Not with her only child in this condition.

The human spirit and the will to live, to fight on in the face of bleak adversity, turns out those things aren't as *evenly distributed* as folks used to consider—or have been told it is supposed to be by gods and angels and fools and blessed virgins. All those books and make believes, all those heroes on their journeys, fighting dragons, saving babies, waking princesses, kissing frogs, rebuilding on the burnt and battered earth, rising from calamity and ashes. Happy endings scream for happy lands to live your ever afters in and whatever lands are these days, they sure aren't happy. Nor are they obliterated. Uncertain is the word she picks if ever she's called to pick out words. Uncertain times and uncertain ground. Land that changes from week to week, resculpted by unseen, unknowable forces into structures claves like theirs can only guess at.

Meanwhile, Mila has been busy building too, cannibalizing a monstrous old wicker chair, a bicycle and small wheels from a busted pram. *Bath chair* is the name that fits her rough construction best, something she's seen in one of their precious top shelf books, but also in a black and white movie she remembers vaguely from her childhood daze. An old man with rugged-up knees in a greenhouse atrium, his drunken daughter flopping all over, telling some suited man how he was cute.

Nothing cute about her darling Lily's cramped and stiffened limbs which will never fit into a regular wheelchair—the Clave has three of those in working order—thank you Brenda, dearest heart, who has the knack for repairing anything human mechanical ingenuity once came up with—or has come up with so far, so good, touch wood, toss a pinch of salt over your shoulder. This bath chair is bicycle wheels and padded wicker, Mila can make that work all on her own. All she needs is Aloha Joe's loud-mouthed distraction. Couple hours of drunken Beach Boys oughta do it.

She charted the pathway to the Dispensary half a year ago and walks it through—or almost through—once every month, making sure nobody tails her, that the trail is wide enough, kicking stones out of the way and slashing back the ever-growing scurvy weed and other hardy vines she's never seen the point to recognizing— not natural foliage, that's for sure and that's enough. The final push over the crest leading down to the Dispensary doors—well, they'll have to cross that bridge when they roll up to it. Just like they'll have to deal with whatever barrier defense mechanisms the Dispensary facade has built into its structure. If any. And you never know—perhaps it is a harmless, good old-fashioned building proper, not just something that resembles one. A honey trap as Bern would say—*yeah, well fuck you, Bern. Your daughters are alive and well and you don't get to tell me what I can't do.*

"Now, come on girl, let's hit the road!" She tries for cheery, unanswered questions hanging in the dusty air. Lily loved bright, shiny things, had a box in which she stored her treasures: flattened beer bottle tops, pink lipstick cases, coins and buttons and cicada wings. But it's her singing Mila misses most, sweet melodies that linger in her head.

Not a whimper from her fragile daughter as Mila swaddles her in blankets and lifts to place her gently in the wicker. No whimper doesn't mean she isn't hurting. So hard to tell with no hints or clues. She hears of claves where folks who catch the plastic cancer get put down swift with deliberated mercy before it has a chance to spread. All very well, perhaps, but Mila cannot do it, cannot not go there, cannot even think of such a thing, which leaves the Dispensary her one and only recourse.

They slip out through the shadowed gardens, a near full moon drifting in and out of cloud. The handmade bath chair bumps and rattles. More than once, Mila swears she hears her Lily calling out *Mama! Mama!* Each time she stops and bends across, readjusting blankets, double-checking. Each time disappointed at the stillness of a face that does not change, day in, day out, has not changed and can never change—not without a cure. And there is no cure.

Nothing left to try, except what she is trying now with the help of Aloha Joe, unwittingly, in his own sweet stoned and addled way.

—

The Dispensary is one of those places that wasn't there before. That formed itself from a bed of coral—coral being the best word they can think of. A hard white bioceramic ooze that spills like lava from the broken ground to take on any shape it seems to fancy. She touched a bloom once, back in Civic, when she'd been a child and didn't know. Touched it without consequence, only now maybe it's Lily who's paid the price. Or maybe not. There are no answers. No clear clues why or how the plastic cancer seeds.

The ground is stony, the bath chair difficult to push. Lily used to skip along the trails when they'd take the young kids out for exercise, thrilled by birds, rabbits and kangaroos. Collecting leaves, then tossing them into the air, so easily distracted.

Moonlight vanishes behind a patch of cloud and when it frees, she spies the unmistakable inevitable. Bern, Young Grigor and god-damn-not-you-too-Brenda, spaced evenly in silhouette so there can be no doubt. Blocking the path's last bottleneck—the chair won't make it through that choking scurvy weed. Must have left the clave ahead of her, must have known her intentions all along.

Bern sniffs, wipes his nose along the length of his sleeve. "Now Mila . . ."

"Don't you *now Mila* me you sack of—"

"We can't let you—"

"What gives you the right to try and stop me?"

He sucks on his teeth "You do know what happens if—"

"Of course, I bloody know," she growls. "Go in and we don't come out again. Got it. Bingo. Hole-in-one. A risk for sure, but I can't take it anymore. Lily's out of choices. *And I'm out of my fucking mind.*" She grips the wicker with hands like claws. Shoves. Expects him to step out of the way—or shuffle back, but Bern doesn't move and he doesn't blink and he's not showing any signs of quitting. He stops the chair with a well-placed boot. Not army issue, she notices.

"Why are you picking on us?" Words tumble out of Mila, loud and sudden. "Why can't you just fuck off and leave us be? Me and

Lily never did you or 53 or the council any harm. We just want to get on with our business."

"Can't let you chance your luck in there now Mila—you know I can't." He turns his face, gestures with his chin. The entranceway, so bright-lit, glossy as lemon butter, only artificial light for miles. A different hue to their solar charged clave lights which tend toward a muddy, dirty ochre.

Birds call from somewhere far beyond the charcoal trees. Bern transfers the weight of his gaze to Lily, bundled cozy and indifferent in the wicker. Seventeen and dead to the world in all the ways that matter. He sniffs, shoulders drooping as he thrusts his hands into his pockets. "Push that girl in there, you'll upset the balance. That's why you're creeping up here under cover of thieving darkness. A crime, no matter how you frame it. Stir them things up and you'll set these lands a shifting and shaping—and we might not be so lucky as last time. And, it won't help your poor girl any. You don't know what their kind might do to ours."

"You don't know either!"

"Nobody knows!" cuts in Brenda, both hands raised with fingers splayed for emphasis.

Mila's steely glaze adheres to Bern's shadowy form. "It's a *dispensary*, Bern. Says so on those letters above the door."

"Used to say something like that. Ten years ago, maybe. More like twenty. Hand painted before things shook and settled and mountains started moving by themselves. But there's no . . . if you take a closer look. No letters—more like blackness thick as tar that leads to god-knows-where. Or what. We done all right, Clave 53, nestled in between the rocks but don't want to push our luck—I'm afraid that's final."

A blast of cool wind sets the bushes shivering. Mila emits involuntary sound, a cross between a strangle and a whimper. "Get out of my way, Bern. Brenda. Young Grigor—your kind old dad will be spinning in his soil—this has nothing to do with you."

She yanks away the blanket revealing a good clear moonlit view of Lily's contorted form. "Look at her! She's not dead and she's not alive. She's plasticating and none of us can help her."

But the councilors hold their ground, hands thrust deep, eyes downcast, shrouded in a sadness thick enough to taste.

"She's my daughter, Bern—and she's all I've got."

"Not true, Mila—you know it's not. We've all had each other's backs for twenty years and some. Made a good go of circumstances. Not everywhere's come through so clean and clear."

He leers at her with big bug eyes ready to pop out of his face. "You take that sweet child into there and she'll come back—if she comes back—more than plasticated."

"Con-tam-i-nation," interjects Grigor, like he's spelling something out for an idiot. Takes a few steps, leans in close till she can smell his lavender gin breath. "Shane Brady's kid went into one of them . . . empty spaces. Was supposed to be a dispensary and his kid come out again with an extra arm."

And sure, you can believe all kinds of crap. Extra arms could very well be true. *Stranger things*, as people say when they pass each other on the track under a sky that doesn't look like any sky our grandkin might have recognized, although the stars are still there. Most of 'em.

Stranger things, as if within these words lie explanation, or perhaps excuses for the lack. The absences of whys and wherefores that have plagued this land since the last good, regular years. A time when people understood their world. Hell, they ran the damn place. Or thought they did—and perhaps this is the underlying point. A time when folks felt in control, when they could name the men or women at the top. When they could read about them in the news. When news was stuff that might have really happened.

What passes for news these days is pitiful, a contaminated trickle of autogenerated bumf extruded by degrading algorithms abandoned by whatever corporate corpse had spawned them. The Dispensary is Mila's last best hope and now it's sunk. She will never get another chance and she knows it.

"I'm sorry about your Lily, Mila," says Brenda in hushed tones. "Sorry as it's possible to be, but we got to be thinking about the whole before our individuals. You know how it has to be. You're one of the ones who voted for it."

Gently, Brenda nudges Mila aside, swivels the bath chair in the opposite direction. When she pushes, Mila follows, with starlight humming and Bern leading and Grigor bringing up the rear in case she decides to make a break for it. *A break for where? There is no place to go.* Bern's lantern swings from side to side, footsteps crunching out of time with squeaking wheels never intended to spin together over such uneven stony ground.

"My Lily never voted for this," says Mila through gritted teeth.

Nobody alive voted for any of this.

Walking in silence, surrounded by insectoid thrum and the calls of creatures they've never seen; cricks and hoots, pips and squawks, chirrups, coos, rattle and scratch, vibrating madly through the raven dark.

—

The guitars back at 53 sound heavier than when they left. No more surf and sand and sun but a rip and pull into deeper waters. Turgid tides of love and loss and broken hearts and dying dreams. So half-familiar, mashing all the words together till you can't tell one song from another, when one begins and the other one leaves off. Doesn't matter who wrote what, such things have mattered less and less as the claves push out from the urban fringe occupying spaces people didn't used to live. Not white folks anyway, nor Chinese, black, or other names that no longer seem important. Claves seed and stick where the soil still blooms and the floods aren't too intense and the fires few. And there's plenty of talk about how soils like this should be impossible out here—impossible by natural means, that is. Can't sift conspiracy from truth with the whole world spun and scattered on its head, not once but over and over and over until, honestly, anywhere half-safe and seeded strong is good enough for claves like this one and their neighbors. They keep to theirs and away from *other things* and for the most part, other things are keeping distance too.

Brenda seems to sense it's time to stop pushing the chair and back away. Looks like she wants to speak but changes her mind. Bern and Grigor junior vanish into the comfort of the fireside and Mila wonders if they'll let her keep the bath chair and use it round the clave, now they know of its traveling potential.

She turns her back on the rest of them, guiding the chair inside, lifts and settles Lily in a nest of cushions with a view of their small window. Lily can't look out, but the window is a pretty thing. She lights candles, listens to the tap and swish of the beaded curtain settling into place. Beneath it all—their rooms, the clave—sludgy currents of decaying freeform jazz, all lyrics siphoned off and dissipated.

She's on her third big swig of gin when the beads start up their clattering, pushed aside and in walks Aloha Joe in all his blue-eyed, half-baked dreadlocked glory.

"What the fuck do you want," Mila snaps, wiping blurred tears with her wrist. Checks out his tatty pants and knobbly knees, which might have borne him across a slab of continent, from crusty cliffs just as he claims. Or maybe he just trekked over the Brindabellas, making up every piece of shit he sings about—the whales and sharks, mermaids and serpent dreams.

"Take your bullshit nostalgia traveling freakshow and fuck back off to where you came from."

"Hey—hey lady! No need to be so harsh! I just want to talk a while. Saw you pushing that contraption. Thought I might provide a little company." He unshoulders his ukulele and smiles.

"You thought wrong," she says. "Now get on out."

He pauses, nods, then looks to Lily amidst her mound of colored cushions.

"She's got the cancer," says Mila bitterly.

"What kind of cancer?"

"*Their kind.*" Mila nods at an imaginary horizon. "The lamination spreads under the skin."

She strides across to tug the blanket from her daughter. "There now—are you satisfied? Once it's set in good, you can't take food nor water."

He stares into the girl's lightless eyes. "She turning into one of *them?*"

Mila snorts. "How would I know what she's turning into? You've had a good gawk now so get out—"

"Lady, I don't mean you any harm . . ."

She snorts again. Louder. "None of us meant any of it, and yet, here we are."

Aloha Joe doesn't leave. He drags a small stool over to position himself between Mila and her daughter, places his bedroll and uke gently on the ground.

Mila watches him, wide-eyed. Too outraged to speak as he closes his.

"Each wave is a lifetime," he tells her. "It has a beginning and an end." He blinks and stares at her directly. "Pain is a shortcut to mindfulness. When I'm out there in the lineup and there's a set coming in . . ." He fumbles in his pocket, then begins to roll a spliff. "When that set comes in, we can look at it with joy. Move away from the past, move away from the future and stay present and remain human. Reaction is our only control. I might get pounded but I'm gonna get back out again."

He lights up, takes a deep drag on the joint. "I surfed 'em all, back in my time. Bells, Treachery, Prevelly, Crescent Heads, Noosa, Exmouth, The Pass. Black Rock. Rennies and Peregian."

"Well, you certainly talk the talk, I'll give you that."

"Still go to sleep dreaming about surf." He clamps his lids again. "Out into the lineup, losing perception of where I am, with seagull screams and crashing waves. The energy around me. All the parts moving together. So stoked I don't even know what to say.

"Kicking out and then everything starts like . . ." He opens his eyes. "Thing is . . . It's all gone."

"Hell yeah, along with civilization and everything else."

He stares at her hard. "Lady, I'm talking about the entire and actual ocean."

She blinks a few times. "What do you mean the ocean's gone?"

He licks his cracked dry lips. "Ain't no ocean like the oceans we once knew. Just rocks and wrecks and fallen things and a heaving slurry made of . . ." He takes another drag before continuing. "Yeah, well I don't know what. Used to be fish, I guess. Maybe. Seaweed perhaps? Salt stands in crystal pillars, raw meat pink like something bled all over it. All through it. A fucking offshore cathedral of bleeding salt stretching for miles and miles."

She squints as she tries to picture what he's telling her. "What about the blue?"

He shakes his head. "Not blue, not green, not brown, not steel hull gray. Not water neither. Not anymore. Just a solid mess of gelid, fleshy . . . kind of like stewed tendon woven through with rotting gristle. I dunno man, poked it with a bit of driftwood and it kind of quivered. There was stuff alive in there. Under it. Flipping and squirming. Becoming part of it. Digested maybe. I don't even know . . ."

He shivers as she feels a queasy wave wash over her.

When he passes her the spliff, she takes it.

"So, where you from?" she asks after a time. "You know . . . back when. Sydney?"

"Started in Eden, walked along the fringe of places I used to hang in, once knew like the back of my hand." He rubs his knuckles absent-mindedly. There are letters tattooed on his skin, but she can't read them.

"Walked a way to Pambula Beach, to Tula then on to Tathra. Stayed with folks at Cuttagee till it was safe to move again. Couple of years, maybe. National Park was dark as death, man. Evil and dark as fucking death. Lost a couple of real good friends in there. And my dog. Don't see dogs much anymore—have you noticed?"

She's noticed. Everyone has noticed. Just one of a long list of things folks don't like to talk about.

He stares at Mila, sharp and sudden, fire blazing in his eyes. "Gimmee the girl. I'll take her." Nods at the beaded curtain and she knows exactly where he means.

"No! You're not taking my daughter anywhere, matey. Aloha Joe. Whatever the hell your name is."

He traps her stare within his own and, with a fluid motion, yanks up his sleeve with his tattooed hand, then thrusts his exposed forearm forward so she can get a good clear look in the dim light.

Mila stares. "Jesus . . . is that . . ." She swallows dryly.

"Can't keep on living like this," he mumbles with great solemnity and purpose while staring past her to a distant place only he can see. "Can't keep living in the cracks, skirting around fast blooming land corals, bleeding seas and mountains that move like . . . like . . ."

She nods. She's never seen a mountain move and yet she understands. "Used to be our world," she says. "We made those things. Those machines, or whatever they are."

"No, we didn't," he says slowly. Thoughtfully. "We made the machines that made those things. Not the same thing at all."

Her gaze flicks from his plasticated arm to her daughter's expressionless face. "And now they're making us. Remaking."

"We need to strike a dialogue," he nods, lowering his arm and his sleeve falls down to cover his changed skin. "Came all this way in search of *connectivity*. Bern says you call the portal-doorway a Dispensary, but I've heard different names in different places." He clears his throat. "Gonna find ourselves a way to talk."

"With my Lily too?"

He nods again. "With them and with your Lily too."

Out there in the courtyard, guitar and other instruments have petered out completely. Mila says nothing for a long time, listening to familiar sounds of the clave's evening shutdown. Slams and drags and heaves and straps, checking everything one last time just in case. Night music overtakes, gradually asserting. Rustling, the wind and then silence.

"Hell, I might even play 'em a couple of ukulele numbers," he adds, face cracking into the ghost of a smile.

And finally, eventually, Mila nods with grim pressed lips. Spoken human words might still be good for something. Aloha Joe nods, stands, steps across, bends to lift the girl in his strong arms and heads out through the beaded curtain into darkness.

68 DAYS

KAARON WARREN

Matty said no way was I going camping with them unless I saw a doctor and got my rash cleared up. He didn't care about my headaches or my sore eyes. Never looked at my eyes. "There's something wrong with you and I don't mean just in the head. I mean you're fucked in the head but there's some weird shit going on as well."

So I booked in to see Mum's doctor, because at least he knew all the background stuff and I wouldn't have to start at the beginning.

I had been feeling weird, as if my blood was made out of chocolate. My mum used to say, "You're slower than ever. What's up?" whenever she was mad at me. If she wasn't mad she'd say "You all right? Cos you look a bit off." Then she'd be hugging me, breathing in deep like she did. She reckoned she could tell when I was spiraling down. Feeling bad. But she was already in the pit herself and all she could do was drag me down.

They asked me in court why I'd lost it the way I did, smashing car windows up and down a dozen streets.

"My mum killed herself and I'm the one who found her," I said. "It's like the broken glass helped me forget for a minute at a time."

My lawyer did her job, and the judge was a kind person; I got off with time served. The months I'd rotted in jail, waiting for trial. So luckily I didn't have to go back.

The damage was done, though. I was already sick.

Already dying.

The doctor knew where I'd been, what I'd done. Mum told him all my secrets when she was alive and I told him the rest.

So when he said he thought I had something he couldn't fix, I believed him. It seemed right. Inevitable, although he was almost crying telling me. He gave me a script for antibiotics and painkillers and a great pile of brochures. Everyone gets a showbag like this when diagnosed with a terminal disease. Self-help, diet, counseling, and a brochure about the Mars Mission and medical research. That was like a disc, showing where the stars are. *If you can see Mars, we need you. Call this number.*

I stuffed it all in my backpack.

The doctor told me to call him any time. He said, "You should talk to the counselors at least. Someone with your LE needs someone to talk to."

LE. He meant life expectancy. Didn't sound any better with only the letters.

He said, "You go home and make yourself comfortable."

I had no real home to go to. Our place had been a housing commission flat in Mum's name, so that went when she went. So I stayed with friends, and friends of friends.

I called Matty to tell him, but he was on the road. They'd left without me. His friends were all ten years younger than me but I passed okay. Only sometimes I noticed. When he called me back he said, "If you can get to the station I'll pick you up there. Did you get your shit sorted out? Don't want you dying on me." Laughter at that.

"You like it on the bottom, Matty?" I heard his passenger say. Giggling. Some girl.

—

First thing he said when he picked me up: "You look yellow as piss. And your rash is still disgusting."

I clung on to him. I didn't want to let him go for a minute. His friends called me limpet but I didn't have internet out there so I couldn't look up to see what it was.

Before long I was grubby, drunk and whining at him to have sex with me. They'll ask and if we didn't do it they'll say we're not together. He's like, "Keep it quiet, then. Don't make that noise you make."

Here I was, faking all that shit, and he doesn't even like it.

He went out to smoke bongs around the fire, but I was so tired I just wanted to sleep. I opened the tent flap and looked out at the stars, at the red glow of Mars, before I slept.

I woke late the next morning, covered with sweat. The tent was a hot box. I crawled out, desperate for fresh air. The sun beat down. Checking my phone, I saw it was past ten.

It was also dead quiet.

The other tents were gone. The cars were gone.

They'd left me.

I tried to call Matty but couldn't get a signal. Were they coming back? Surely. Surely.

Two hours later I realized they weren't and that I'd have to walk out to find a signal if I wanted help.

They'd left me the tent at least, and our used condom. I dragged the sleeping bag out, intending to roll it up. Then I thought, fuck it. Not carrying anything.

So I left it all there.

———

I walked till I got a phone signal. I didn't know who to call. I tried Matty first; no answer. I was pretty sure he wouldn't answer again. I didn't want to bother the police, and they hate me, anyway.

I called my doctor; his receptionist said he'd taken ill. I hoped whatever I had wasn't catching. "He did say if you called you should ring some of the numbers he gave you. They should be able to help. Keep us posted," she said, but there was already a bip on the line. Another call for her.

So I called one of the counseling services first, but all I got was "Call during office hours."

I tried another one and it was a wrong number.

So I thought about that red glow, that Mars in the sky, and I called them.

They were friendly, kind, like where are you? Stay there and we'll send someone.

They did, too. Within two hours, they had a prepaid taxi to pick me up and take me to their office. I read their brochure on the way.

It said, *Medical research is worth a fortune, especially when related to space travel.*

It said, *200,000 apply, only a few will get in. Will one of them be you?* I wanted it to be. I really did. So by the time we got there, I was ready to try out.

—

They were really nice. They gave me a comfy chair and a big test to do.

"Not a test!" they said. "A questionnaire. No right or wrong answers." There were, though. They were looking for particular answers. I didn't know what those answers were, so all I could do was be honest.

Question: What is your past job experience?

I'd had heaps. Right now I was working on a road crew. Loved that. In your gear you all looked alike, like a real team.

Question: Do you like being part of a group?

Did I what!

Question: What's the worst thing you've eaten?

I ate a rat in jail once, to prove a point. Can't remember what the point was, mind you. But it made them all leave me alone. Weird, though. After I ate the rat, even water tasted of it.

Question: What do you think of the Planarian Worm experiment? Obscene? Wrong? Worthwhile?

They let me use my phone to look it up and then my answer was It doesn't bother me. They're only worms.

Question: Do you eat meat? Do you have any ethical concerns or do you know that each creature has a place (for example)?

Love my meat.

Question: Are you looking for meaning in your life? Are you frightened of dying without purpose?

That was a tough one. I decided to tell them what my mum wrote in her goodbye note, about finding meaning and letting that make you happy.

—

And I got the job!

I had to sign an agreement:

No arguing.

Anything goes.

Eat what you're given.

Do your job.

Have fun!

—

I called to let Matty know I was training for Mars. He didn't answer so I left a message, and he called back, laughing at me until he choked. He said, "Jeez, you're a dumbfuck. And they must be too if they've hired you." I hung up on him and I thought that just getting the job made me stronger. Better. My parents never thought I'd be much and I'm not, yet. But I will be.

Day 1

The resort squatted in the distance, shadowy and huge, like an old giant from a fairy tale waiting for us to arrive.

I climbed off the bus, stiff and sore after fourteen hours traveling, watching the real world fade as the wheels of the bus rolled on. Everyone was quiet, mostly, with the occasional burst of conversation or laughter.

They'd told me to leave it all behind. That this was my second chance, my tilt at making a difference.

It's hard to imagine being so far away from anything but there we were. The bus driver and some others unloaded boxes and our stuff, then he took off. The only way out was to walk. It'd take days. Weeks.

So dry. Made me thirsty just looking out. And red. Someone said it was red like Mars which I thought was pretty smart.

Where we're staying is a deserted resort. It used to be for stargazing. Rich people would come here and get educated about space and all that. It has its own planetarium. The big sign at the entrance says Starstruck Resort and Planetarium but someone has made a joke and changed it to Starstruck Resort and Planarium. Not exactly sure but I laughed along with the others.

Wind blew so strong my hair flew around my head and I struggled to keep my skirt down. Someone whistled and said, "Hello, sexy legs." I was going to like this place.

—

They showed us to our apartments. Luckily we had guides to show us because I've never seen so many corridors, stairs, elevators, more corridors. Like some huge maze. We all have our own place, spread out over the whole resort. I couldn't believe how much room I had.

My apartment looked out over the dried-up swimming pool. It was the quietest place I ever slept.

Our corridor was called Olympus Mons. They said it was named after a volcano on Mars. All the art, in the rooms and along the corridors, was spacy. Stars and planets, that kind of thing. So beautiful.

—

I got totally lost trying to find the dining room, so I called for help. Stay put, they said, just like when I was deserted in the bush. One young guy came to find me. He was so good-looking I was glad I'd put my makeup on, but wished I'd worn one of my sexier tops.

In the end I was one of the first to arrive; everyone else got lost, too.

I sat at a table with four other newbies. I felt a bit overdressed but better over than under, I say. It's all right when you're a teenager but as you get older you need to take more care.

It was awkward and exciting, complete strangers sharing a meal. My good-looking helper (his name turned out to be Tony) sat elsewhere but the guys at my table were cute, too. They gave us a list of "conversation starters," which we were supposed to go through in order to get to know each other. So lame! I could just imagine Matty going, "Fuck that shit."

That night we had lasagna. It was pretty good. Meaty and saucy and heaps of cheese.

Day 2

They told me to go to room 821. I had no idea. Lost again, but someone showed up and rescued me. No way was I ever going to figure it out.

They sat me down in front of a wall of equipment. What the hell? I had no idea. I just sat there for an hour, hoping I didn't have to figure it out in order to stay. They did tell me that they just wanted to see what could be achieved in 68 days. Didn't matter what I did, just that I did it.

Then someone came and got me and we all went to have dinner in the bar. It was meatloaf tonight, best I've ever had. I sat with a different group and already it felt as if I knew them. All of us were in the same boat; a diagnosis we didn't want to think much about. Most of us were on our own.

Day 3

By the third day, without anyone telling me a thing, I'm working those knobs and buttons as if I was a rocket scientist. Wish people at home could see. My teachers. My mother. Matty. They'd be seeing a different me.

We had movie night; an old classic called *Braveheart*.

I don't know what the others are dying of, but we all are. All expenses are paid, even the medical stuff. They're giving me no questions asked painkillers and my head and eyes feel better already.

Day 5

I'm treading paths I've never trod before. It's a compulsion; a weird familiarity with something I know I don't know.

And I realize I'm treading paths I've never been taught.

We booze up every night. Beer, champagne, cocktails. Wine and beer. I don't know if it's that, but already the conversational starters are weird; we all know each other's answers.

Day 10

Every night we'll go out and look up at the stars.

"If I was living on Mars now, I'd have 687 days left. Not 365." We all said that, doing the maths.

We had spaghetti and meatballs for dinner. I had two servings and no one cared less.

Day 15

There are so many good-looking guys here. Tanned and carefree. Most gorgeous of all is Tony.

Tony and me, we click together. Just a perfect fit. His skin is so warm. I don't know what he's got and he doesn't know what I've got and neither of us know how long.

Day 20

Tony took a bunch of us for a hike, out to this huge meteorite which is meant to be from Mars. We placed our hands on it. He said, "One of the things that draws us together, and to Mars, is the ability to go against the rules. She spins back on her own orbit, does a twist."

He twisted as if he was on the dance floor. "That's us. Rule breakers. Well, not sensible rules like we have."

We all laughed at this.

"But the ones in place for no reason."

We loved every word he said. "The only way forward is to choose to go forward to your next existence. This is for humanity. For the future." The big rock glowed warm and felt magnetic. We asked him how it got there.

"Legend says Ancient Ones on Mars threw rocks like this at Earth, trying to get our attention. It's finally working!"

Day 25

Movie night was *It's a Wonderful Life*.

Day 29

We trekked out to the rock again. It buzzed, slowly warming up, and we all put a palm on it. We've never felt so connected in all our lives. Around it, mounds of small rocks. Some of them painted. An art project, maybe? One of the guys said they were ancient burial mounds.

Day 30

Part of what they're figuring out is how to beat depression on the Mars project. It's the isolation; you know Earth is far away. And you know you only have a small number of days left. You'll die out there.

That's what we're helping them with.

How do you stay motivated to achieve, not for yourself, but those who come after?

We've never felt better.

Day 32

We all wake up around the same time now, in the early hours of the morning, and all end up out around the empty pool. Looking up. Someone brought out armchairs that people weren't using and we'd laze about, watching the sky and talking while the sun rose.

Sometimes we'll go into the planetarium but the place needs fixing. It smells bad.

Every step is familiar.

We talk about the ancient ones who might be waiting on Mars. "Imagine!" we say. "They'll wake up and there we'll be!"

Day 38

No post went out and none came in. Where would we send things to? We signed to say we wouldn't tell anyone we were going. Mostly no one cared. Mostly we didn't get reported missing. I would have been surprised. My brain would have exploded. But it didn't happen.

We were better than anyone else because we were the ones with absolute freedom. We were the ones who could do whatever we wanted.

Ironic, given how close we were all becoming. Like a merged brain, with merged feelings. It was nice.

Movie night was a cartoon thing called *The Iron Giant*.

Day 42

There's something comforting about being in a commune full of people who are dying. All of us strangers, so there's no past to contend with, no long-term emotions.

All we have are the 68 days.

And we're all fucking each other. You couldn't do that outside. No one will fuck a dying person. But seriously if you had weeks to live? Why not feel pleasure while you still can? No one cares about my rash. It's better mostly, anyway.

We're lost in a fog of sex and booze.

Lost in a fog of déjà vu. It's not just that we have a routine: work/eat/play/sleep. More than that. A deep sense of this has happened before.

Day 50

Counting down the days. I don't want to leave, but no one stays beyond the 68.

"Stay any longer and you'll start to suffocate." That's what they reckon.

Setting/emotions like one mind. Meal. Meat. Always. 'Lucky there are no vegetarians here," someone joked, and we all laughed, although it felt like we'd heard it a dozen times already.

Day 52
People like me here. We feel at home. At one with each other.

Day 60
Just over a week until we're gone and the next group comes in.

"Look what we've achieved," they're telling us, and I can't quite believe it myself. We built a dome that works like a greenhouse. We learned how to cook and operate machinery. We fixed the planetarium. We grew to love each other. "You are such a cohesive group," they said. "So positive."

—

The sun burns hot here. It's like it's a different sun from the one anywhere else. Here it's free, unbridled, like we are.

We'd sit naked but our poor boobs would burn and the skin would peel and no one wants that.

The idea makes us laugh and once we start we can't stop until we're so weak with it we're in the sand and someone carries us inside.

"It's a side effect we're working on," Tony said. They were figuring out ways to stop the Sads on Mars, because the Sads don't make things happen.

But it made us laugh too much, at too little. It felt good. Like Tony does. Not like Matty did. Nothing like Matty.

Day 67
Serious fucking partying going on. Swapping of fluids. Swapping of contact details, none of us wanting to go back, but 68 days is what they're testing so 68 days is what it is.

We were all together. Ten of us. Sometimes felt as if we were one. Other times there was just me and Tony.

—

I liked it when he took me out onto the roof or way way away from the resort. He was quiet out there and we could just hang. He showed me Mars through the telescope and I swore I could see movement up there.

"It's incredible to think people will be there in a generation. And that we're helping them get there."

Day 68

We wake up on the last day. Tony brought me breakfast, the tiny spicy sausages we have every few days. They are so good and hothouse tomatoes and mushrooms with butter and parsley, and champagne. I still felt drunk from the night before.

He sat on the end of the bed, watching me. It felt weird. Like my mum used to do. It's one of the things I miss most about Mum. When I was in my early teens, before things went to shit, she'd come into my room in the morning and sit on the end of my bed and we'd chat. I was still a bit sleepy so not as defensive as I'd be later. I remember those talks so well. In those sleepy times, we both thought it would be all right.

—

He made me get up, and we walked to the meteorite. I loved it there in the early evening, when it was so warm. So familiar.

"Do you really want to go back to the city?" he said. I felt a surge in my heart; was he saying I could stay?

"No! I want to stay here!"

He shook his head. "That can't happen. But to be honest, they're nervous about sending you back."

"Just me, or everyone?"

"Mostly you. It's a couple of things." He made me drink a glass of champagne. "It's your LE, for one." (he was the same as the doctor, thinking that calling it LE will make it easier to take) "You're looking at weeks once you go back home, they think."

"But I feel fine."

"That's the beauty and the curse of it. You'll feel like that until suddenly this happens."

He showed me the worst photos I've ever seen, of people in dying stages of my disease. Pus and blood from every orifice. It was horrendous.

"You're so beautiful the way you are. It would break my heart to see you like this," making me look at the photos, every single one of them. "Have you got anyone to look after you?" He knew I didn't. "You can make it worthwhile. Don't waste all you know. All you have up here." He tapped my temple gently, then stroked his cool hand on my forehead. "You know what you've been eating."

I had known. I just didn't want to think about it. I didn't want to be sent home for complaining about it. And everyone did it. No one seemed concerned. You wouldn't tell anyone outside, but it tasted fine. Human meat tasted fine.

"The knowledge you have came from the one before you. She got hers from the one before her. On and on, and the knowledge improves each time. It's brilliant; each person doesn't have to retrain. We don't have to waste time. Complex tasks managed in a day or two. Relationships remembered. Finding your way without being lost. Every day, every hour, is critical." He's still stroking me. Under my clothes, now.

"It's totally groundbreaking and will be part of the future of us. It will literally help the survival of the human race."

It made perfect sense.

"You'll join others who went before you. You'll be a proud member of an elite team. You'll be remembered. This moment is perfect. You are perfect. It is all downhill from here."

I said, "What about the others? Are they doing this, too?"

"What do you think? See if you can feel the hive mind."

I closed my eyes. "I think yes."

—

He left me there. It was warm, perfect, and I had champagne and the smell of strawberries.

He gave me a pill. One. It would be enough.

I took the pill and laughed and laughed and laughed to think of what would happen next.

THE SPACE BETWEEN ALL POSSIBLE WAYS

CAT SPARKS

Present

The drones come first and then the war machines, lumbering like beasts across crags and dirt, twenty-inch radial tires chewing rocks. Compact, stocky vehicles, blast protected as they bounce and glide, bullet-riddled ballistic paneling draped with tangled, dusty camo, 50 caliber machine guns mounted high and proud.

Trucks mean business: high mobility variants with v-shaped armored spines once used for deep battlespace reconnaissance. These days after whatever they can get. Women, alcohol or water; forgotten caches from bungled supply drops half a decade past or even longer.

Lately they've been chasing rumors of a magic tree taken root in inhospitable terrain. A wonderous bloom, scraping filth from empty air, returning it as gold and gems and car parts. From diesel to the finest liquor, make your wishes and the tree provides. Refugees have gathered, attracted to its bounty.

And there it is, a speck of nothing nestled in the valley. Children playing outside the settlement abandon games to watch; first drones and then the dusty trucks laden with men shouting through speakers, enhanced and crackling electronic demands in

English, French, Arabic and Hausa, faces wrapped against the sun's relentless cruelty.

Trucks slam to shuddering halts. Everyone wants to watch how guns are made. How the tree-that-is-not-a-tree sucks bad dirt from the air, rendering it solid and functional as metal. Trees-that-are-not-trees are rumored to be blooming in many troubled places: Ukraine, Yemen, Uzbekistan, Mississippi, Abu Dhabi. Perhaps the guns extrude from branches to drop down into waiting hands? If they're quick enough, they can catch them when they fall.

But the so-called trees look nothing like expected. No bark, no wood, no jeweled oasis, no sprays of lemon morningstar around their roots. Arrays of peculiar, scaffolded contraptions, half buried, half exposed to open elements.

Engines idling, distracted by the bright weave of children's garments, stark as petals against the pale, dry sand. Nearby cluster candy-colored domes, textured formations of earthen peaks and bulbs. Tethered goats, scattered dogs and chickens, same as everywhere.

Drones whine and mass above like angry insects.

The trees perform no magic tricks and soon the men are bored. Staring as panel after panel realigns and another sound; a shrill and purring engine coupled with a semimuted growl, perhaps like the stomach of a dog who has eaten garbage poisonous and rotten.

Gunshot splits the sullen air. An angry storm of men turn on the shooter, swear and strike until the man's knocked to the ground. *Do not fire upon the magic. Shoot the ones who would keep it for themselves.*

Random, interrupting sounds, distracting from the swirl of heat and dust. A grind distinct from whining truck emissions, metallic, crisp and sharp. Treetops shift and realign before unfurling extra struts and shapes.

Shouting starts again and then the engines, veering closer, turning sharply, testing mettle, taking chances, one eye on those angling panels that might be leaves in case they shape-shift into weapons.

More gunshots as the convoy circles closer. Angry voices

amplified: Give us your magic tree or we will burn your huts and kill your children. There's nowhere to run, nowhere to hide.

The pulse hits, swift and clean and bright, dislodging drones from dizzy orbits, slamming them to sand like broken birds.

The tree-which-is-not-a-tree morphs form into something like a giant seedpod. What happened to those playful children; the women in their brightly woven wraps? No time to bolt for cover. Even the chickens, goats and dogs have vanished.

The pulse has frozen all the trucks, engines jammed and stagnant, men furious and shouting, firing what weaponry still functions, vomiting as a queasy timbre reverberates around the granite spars and shards. One man calls out he is blind, another cries of witchcraft, djinn and demons swirling in kaleidoscopic shapes and colors.

Two are dead from collateral damage bullets.

Where has everybody gone? No place to hide out here in the open desert, except, perhaps, within the tree itself, although that too seems impossible. One moment forty people living, working, visible and blatant. A well-played trick. Furious men take aim at artificial roots thickened into shields against which bullets slam and clang. Chunks and shards of green-gray spray and scatter.

The angry men power down to wait it out, for the magic pod to unfurl and reconstruct. For the tree to make the parts to fix their ancient, ailing trucks and for the bounty harvest of grenades and ammunition, raining to the sand like acacia blossoms. Others have spoken of seeing such things with their own eyes all around the world, the digital traces shared from phone to phone.

Beneath the ground, in a bunker made from concrete chemically bonded with air-siphoned carbon, Cray stares intently at a bank of screens, heart thumping. Uncertain that the tech would work the way it was designed to. Relieved they haven't lost so much as a chicken.

"Gonna wait us out," he says.

"No, they won't," she answers.

"They'll be back in bigger numbers."

"Not that either. The story they'll report will not be one their masters can believe. It won't fit the evidence."

Cray sniffs, considering. "There's drone footage and coordinates."

"Hacked and scrambled."

"Lakesha, why should I believe you?"

"Have I ever been wrong so far?"

The man shrugs.

"They'll leave," she says. "Already they're questioning their eyes."

"Perhaps," says Cray, unwilling to commit. Around him, families and travelers are settling in to wait, laughing at the chaos of chickens, squabbling good-naturedly over which games to play, which foods to prepare for dinner. The bunker is well-stocked. They have sheltered here from storms and only the children are curious to watch the screens revealing what the shouting men are up to.

Come first light, no longer shouting, the deep desert men abandon useless broken vehicles, heading back the way they came, winds rapidly obliterating any trace they'd ever been there.

When All Clear sounds, the pod disassembles and reverts to forest form. People emerge from the hollow cavern beneath the tree's broad base, calling to each other as they right the mess the trucks have wrought, warning children not to touch the drones—they might be booby trapped. *Dogs are trained to smell such things, let them get on with it.*

A dying bandit slouches, propped against a ruined truck, galabeya stained with thick brown blood much more of which has leached into the sand. He's mumbling prayers, or maybe words to songs from old times past.

He's dying but the children bring him water, sit with him so he won't die alone. Cray moves fast, but already light is leaching from the bandit's eyes.

Eyes that widen at the sight of Cray.

"I recognize you, brother," he rasps through sun parched lips. "Brother, you can't hide in a magic tree."

Glassy eyes slip in and out of focus, stare past Cray to the metal forest, branches unfurling, extending, realigning. Nubbins sprouting solar flowers expand to lock on to the sun's trajectory. Thin flat banks of concertinaed membrane reasserting, repositioning. *More things on heaven and earth*, a narrowing of the space between all possible ways.

A mighty, wonderous creation, reaching up, unfurling and unfolding exaltations. *God is great*, the bandit comprehends, as the bonds that tether him to this world slip and loosen. Last thing he sees is a tree praying to the sky.

Cray stands, steady, but uncertain, unsettled by the dying man's last words. *Recognize me or recognize my kind?* A world of difference between those options.

Relief spreads rapidly amongst the settlers—precious sandcasting molds have not been damaged. Big tires could have made short work of them, but the men with guns didn't even notice, or if they did, did not comprehend the inherent magic of wind turbine parts and blades manufactured from carbon harvested thin air, casting shapes for fixing broken infrastructures. Designing new materials required to fill the gaps. That their tree's specific reputation is for aerofoils with high lift to drag ratio and hand crafted, specialized tip geometries.

The settlement knows much about kinetic energy and subsequent velocity, power coefficients, downwash and wake effects. Following on from seven hundred years of windmills turning, powering a future with no limits.

Cray goes to find a shovel for burying the dead, the words *I recognize you, brother* turning over and over in his head.

Past

The dog tags say his name is Cray, strung around his thick and sunburnt neck. Cray would rather be anywhere than in this baking hell and desolation. Not that he remembers anywhere. Holds his arm up, seeking faded traces of tattooed imagery, clues to who he might have been before.

They say Refurb requires consent, that you choose your new life and new chance in some harsh and blasted foreign wasteland. That such a gift cannot be forced. That you have the right to turn it down and thirty days to make the call for a Chinook to airlift you back to prison or whatever else you're running from.

They say you will come to love the tree like a sister or a daughter, but words are meaningless without memories of loving anyone or anything. They say a third of new Refurbs plot escape before the capsule seeds, stripping salvage from the small encampment, bartering it for passage with the gangs and warlords staggered throughout the mountains. Taking chances in the new free zones, drawing on embedded repetitions; the kinds that got them dumped here in the first place. Mind memory being one thing, muscle memory something else, those grooves scored deep and fierce and lifetime strong.

Such thoughts flit and niggle, irritating as the sticky flies as he hammers, drills and welds the base together with hands that, for all he knows, are killer's hands.

Sunset glints off distant drones, followed by deep night satellites that arc and trail through silken voids as meteorites hiss and scream and blow their loads.

Animal, mineral, forgettable, disposable. No memory means there's no one left to blame, not even your stupid, lonely self. No past means nothing to replay, no way of etching hate into the bone and gristle.

No one to remember his true name if the desert kills him.

No way to prove he's not already dead.

The abomination in the tub is not a tree but part of one mixed up with parts of other things besides. His mission is to protect the growing mess like you might a baby while it unwinds, unpacks and plants itself within the airdropped, prefabricated creche. None of which is real until it happens. Nothing grows in this barren place, nothing but thin and reedy scrub; lovegrass, thyme and tamarisk. Nothing since the mines dried up, the people forced off lands by drought, migrated toward far-off urban spokes and hubs in search of something. Anything but here.

Damn thing's not even a half-tree yet, just a scratch and scrape of component parts; seed and root and gelid heart embedded in a soup of nanoparticulate enhancements. There's a movie if he wants to watch. He doesn't. Cray has all the smarts he needs embedded, imprinted, implanted, same as the tree.

Should he walk away to take his chances, they'll just airdrop another sucker, some poor sap who dreams he'll save the world or another ice-hearted man with strangler's hands.

Can't be sure of his own name, but implants jabbed beneath his skin will guide him through establishment procedures. Machinery programmed to dig, embed and stabilize, some controlled by signals from low orbit.

An ankle tag, but he won't be staying. Just time enough to craft a plan for on the lam survival. To learn precisely where he is, how far to the nearest town or settlement. No memories, but he's worked out how to hack into encrypted footage. Forewarned and saddled up for the next step.

The weather station he erects over the ridge does more than monitor key situational parameters. Coupled with a scanner rig, it sifts the radio spectrum for electromagnetic dialogue: VHF through UHF and far beyond. Active frequencies leaking helpful hints and clues and targets.

Less than an hour away on foot he establishes his secret cave cache. Things he'll need when he decides it's time to split this lonely blast of denied terrain. This slab of nothing littered with the trails of fallen souls. Lifers, loafers and last-chancers, bleached bones strewn beside the wrecks of burnt-out vehicles. Plenty of ordnance scattered for the taking.

And he won't be staying. Not to babysit a tub of AI tree soup.

His name and past exchanged for a crate of vacuum-sealed machinery, biorefineries and point-source capture, solar cells and anionic exchange resins.

Peers at the strange hybrid thing printing and assembling itself, module by module, encouraged by a bloom of solar flowers. A beast worth millions, whereas he knows he is worthless. He could so easily crush it beneath his boot.

As he lifts his foot, testing the thought, embers of a memory flicker, dream whispers of a creature, small and helpless, cupped in his callous workman's hands. A flush of certainty, whatever it was, back then, he didn't kill it. Whoever he'd been before was not all bad. He's examining his trembling hand when another voice kicks in. Female. Indistinct, and without accent.

"You had choices and you still have choices," she says.

"Fuck off," answers Cray. "Leave me alone."

A trick, implanted to control him.

He's not falling for anything.

The voice doesn't speak again for several weeks. Not until he's working on the thermal reactor column following a blast of sudden rain, checking to see the foundations aren't subsiding. A festive bloom of desert flowers, her voice kicks in gently naming each variety. This time he doesn't tell her to fuck off.

Future

Saharan air layers travel fast, with winds up to eighty Ks per hour. Force enough to shred through storms and raise temperatures above seas. Hot, dry air downdrafts, preventing cloud formation, upsetting thermal wind balance and messing with meridional temperature gradients.

The sandcast blades are small, but strong and word of them is spreading.

"It'll all go to hell, you know," says Cray. "Everything always does." Three years on the ground and he's still trying to bait Lakesha, trying to force her into pointless argument. Sometimes she takes it, other times she doesn't. Today is one of the many times she chooses not to answer, so he gets on with checking interface circuits for corrosion.

The Tuareg camped alongside the dome village are heading off, saddlebags loaded with machine parts, bespoke items difficult to source. Sturdy shapes formed from biocomposite foamed plastics.

They turned up after word spread of the wind turbine blades installed at Ouadane.

"What did they bring us this time? Anything of value?"

Beneath the shade of resin-coated leaves, a group of women with babies strapped upon their backs unfurl bolts of brightly colored cotton.

A little further out, three young girls kick a soccer ball between them while a group of smaller children squeal, chasing dogs and frisbees across the sand.

"The kids really love that spotted dog."

"OK, so they brought us a few dogs."

"Ordnance sniffers amongst the mongrels."

"Nobody doesn't like dogs."

The tree has become a microforest, twenty-eight units and still counting, a triumph of polyethylene backbones, anionic exchange membranes and polymer morphology, puffing and hissing to their own internal music. Trees breathe in and trees breathe out, perpetually adjusting to variants of wind speed, temperature and humidity.

The forest whispers, expanding and contracting, sinking deep beneath the sand, depositing payloads of dirty air to be extracted and set by solvents and resins.

Cray dozes in the hottest parts of daylight. Come afternoon, in his office—a shack until the weavers tricked it out in ocean blues and jungle green—he assists doubtful travelers with their uploads. Never part of the job description, but so many arrive knowing what they need, yet unable to describe their wants in detail.

Some bring broken parts that need replacement, wrapped up carefully in faded cloth or yellowed newsprint, torn and dusty, inscribed with stories that no longer matter.

Other times, clean paper folded: white or pale blue, rough sketches enhanced by measurements. They sit for hours on woven rugs beneath whatever shade is spare, boiling tea or sharing coffee, dark and bittersweet from all the miles it's traveled. Talking of the things they've seen. The world is changing, they can all agree on that. Warp and weft microgrid tapestries knitting communities together, powering lights and conversations, heating furnaces and seeding dreams. Enabling security on ancestral lands while others without permanent address are free to wander where challenge and desire might take them.

Beyond the colored domes, a stretch of recent tents has birthed into a quarter, the first mud bricks for a coffee house; next up, communal kitchen gardens. Two healers announce the choice to stay; one tends to people, the other goats and camels. A family of weavers running from some distant, violent feud thatch roofs from refuse blown in by the wind. A mix of wires, branch and plastic reinforced with dung and mud gives the place its own eclectic style.

Between himself, the weaver mother, father and the tree, new looms get dreamt up, drafted and printed. One of the daughters, whose face Cray has never seen, lectures in poetry and some obscure branch of economics via satellite. Keeping different hours to the rest of her family.

And then there's the tower. Who knows who's building it, or

why. A carbon-infused brick structure on its own, with a view across the desert to infinity. Perhaps a place to observe the traveling crescent dunes migrate or keep an eye for dronesign or accumulating storm cloud.

Once it's built, Cray stands for hours watching convective storms whip arid ground, lofting particles of silica, iron and phosphorous as high as 20,000 feet. Fog-like, laden with sparkling minerals, bacteria, fungal spores or toxic heavy metals, triggering carbon soaking phytoplankton blooms in distant, synoptic scale dust events.

All very well until the ghosts appear. Screaming shapes of falling planes, scorched steel trailing into smoke tailed spirals, slam dunks with blinking, helpless lights, turbine powered plummeting through clouds, gust buffeted, twirled and tossed in mad panic before kissing dirt in a ballet of crumpled fuselage, tangled slats and flaps and spoilers, screeching wheels aflame.

Pretty sure he's the only one who sees them.

"You'll be leaving soon," interrupts Lakesha. "I can tell."

Cray ignores her, leaves the tower for his office shack. Tugs the bug out bag from behind the couch. Walks the winding trail leading through the domes.

"Don't run. Stay a little longer. Strong arms are always useful."

"Says you who has none."

"Strong hands and a stronger heart. You are so very welcome here."

"I'm not running." Cray stops to hold his hands up to the sun, squints and turns his wrist until the faded tattoo is barely visible. "Hands of a killer, I'm pretty sure. Hands that have held a gun or two. Close my eyes, I can feel the weight. The resonance, you know?"

Lakesha has no answer. He's right, of course—she has no hands, nor imagination, and was not designed to conceptualize such things.

"That mark near your wrist. Reckon it's a bird."

"You see birds everywhere you look."

"Don't you?"

It's true. He's keeping tally of the firefinch and desert sparrow, coursers, larks, and the spectacularly ugly lappet-faced vulture. Nice to know there's creatures out there uglier than him. Tough and grizzled, absolute survivors. Not that he can compete with 165 million years of steady evolution, but at least he knows they're real—unlike the planes.

Implants tell him billions of tiny birds cross the Sahara twice each year, negotiating migration trajectories and optimum tail-wind components as they compensate for drift, dancing on predominant wind regimes. Swarming insects for fast fueling and favorable wind assisted flights. Knows more about the birds than he does himself.

Cray clears his throat. "Trees can't talk."

This time she's the one doing the resonating. "Trees rarely do anything *but*. We've always had a lot to say. You monkeys don't know how to listen—not even to other monkeys. Wars avoided had you latched on to Bonobo style."

What the tree never talks about is the skirmish that silenced 900,000 lives. A country close until no longer. The dirty bombs and dirty water; acid faded reefs and shattered skylines. Her sister trees stripped bare and blasted back to component elements, denied the basic chance to birth online. She doesn't talk about these things, but he knows she feels them, indicated by long, deep silent stretches.

Not leaving soon takes a chance he never will, which means Lakesha will keep talking in his head.

How he used to hate the tree in the heat and itch, the sweat and trickle, salt stinging his eyes. And hate this land, declared too hot for human habitation, which made him something less than human as he dug and stabbed, unpacking self-assembling machines, steering them as they hammered at the bitter, stony ground.

"Got some things I gotta take care of."

Heads toward his hidden cave cache, knowing she's known about it all along. Can she stop him? Neural failsafe mechanism implants? Explosive charges placed there for good measure?

If he hadn't died, the man who called him brother might have answered all his questions.

Crunch of boot tread on stony ground, perspiration clinging to his back. Each step, waiting for a bolt of artificial lightning.

The cave is shadow cool and smells of gun oil and desert rat.

The RPG is ancient and unstable, but the only weapon suitable for the job. Can't leave things the way they are. He made this mess and he's the one to fix it.

"Don't leave. You still have time to serve," says Lakesha.

"Gonna turn me in?" He hefts the grisly device onto his shoulder, slots the slender, bulb-tipped grenade into its place.

Silent standoff.

Lakesha says nothing.

A small black bird flies overhead, indifferent.

"I'll be serving for the rest of my life," he says.

Cray braces, aims and puts pressure on the trigger. "Better places suited to it than here." He squeezes. Recoil slams him staggering as acrid smoke spreads.

The entrance to his cave cache collapses in a rumble and crash of rocks, thickening the already tainted air.

"I'll keep my eye on you," she says.

"Don't I know it."

He bashes the weapon on rocks until the trigger breaks, tosses the useless thing aside. Shoulders his pack and walks up the gently sloping ridge, glances back at the spread of blooms and hues hugging the valley floor. Not flowers—there have been no recent rains—but domes and towers and assorted colored tents in many shapes and sizes.

"Your faded tattoo. A bird for certain. A swallow," she says. "I Googled."

He continues walking. Rendezvous point lies ahead in seventy-two hours. Eighty at the outside, but these people aren't the kind who wait.

He's watched shape-shifting swallow masses thicken air like dust. Dark morphologies of churning chaos, tides and pulses, enveloping coagulations waves and shimmers, pointillist blooms that expand, contract and scatter in a heartbeat.

But this trip he'll be winging solo, in imitation of the songbirds who predominantly fly at night, snatching strategic intermittent daytime rests in shadow on the ground. Like them, he'll be highly influenced by winds, circumventing barriers, conserving energy for the long haul.

Did Cray invent Lakesha or did Lakesha invent Cray? Only way to know for certain is to put some space between them.

"Come back some day," she says.
"I might," he replies.
And he means it.

THE EMPORIUM
KAARON WARREN

Chapter One

Things improved once the mattresses arrived. Before that they'd slept curled up in massage chairs or stretched out on couches that were too short for them and stained with old spills; drinks, food, body fluids, drips from the leaking roof.

They cleared out the secondhand furniture shop of everything except the bedframes, which mostly rested up against the wall.

That area had been a mess, anyway, filled with objects found over many years, the "miscellaneous," items no one knew what to do with. It was stacked dangerously high; boxes of picture hooks, crates of broken wineglasses, piles of true crime magazines. Things they no longer understood and could barely recognize. They moved the broken things upstairs, finding nooks and crannies in the old shops there, trying to keep some sort of order.

In the front corner of the shop, near the small register, were stacked boxes of ancient cat food. Maud said, "We should take that up to the roof. The birds might eat it if we spread it around." The other children all agreed, so they piled it outside the shop next-door, a newsagent still stocked with ancient news and magazines. They added the true crime magazines to that collection and headed back to the furniture shop.

Marty stood with his hands covering his face, his shoulders shaking.

"Marty! What's wrong?" Maud said. "You'll get a mattress, don't worry! There's enough for everyone."

"He's sad about the fish," Bean said. She was so short she could barely see over the counter, but she stretched her toes and pointed. At seven she was the youngest of the children in the Emporium and she hated that. She wanted to be old, like the rest of them. Yet she carried a sack full of soft toys and would bring them out for conversation and cuddles.

Maud looked. Revealed once all the mess was cleared away was a large fish tank. It was filthy, covered with moss and slime, with five centimeters of sludgy water at the bottom. Maud stepped closer. It stank; in the bottom were a dozen long-dead fish, their flesh mostly rotted off, their bones poking through. She sobbed as well, and that set all of them off, all of them sobbing over the starved dead fish. There was much they didn't remember but all of them remembered the pets they'd left behind.

Carlo pressed his head up against the glass. "Which one is which, do you think? Who is who?"

"You can't tell, once they're a pile of bones. They won't be able to know who's us when we're bones," Julian said.

—

They dragged the mattresses onto the bedframes and laid some in the spaces in between. Bean wanted to take hers into the entrance atrium, a glass-ceilinged dome, so she could sleep under the stars. Maud said, "You'll freeze to an ice block. Maybe when it gets warmer," so Bean crankily dragged her mattress into the furthest corner, tucked under an old counter.

—

The children collapsed, exhausted but happy, on the mattresses. They weren't very clean, though, so the next job was to traipse up to the first floor for new sheets and pillows. The Bedroom Bonanza store had been small but well-stocked. A lot of it had gone to customers outside (everyone preferred their bed linen unused) or in the looting, but there was one alcove the children had been saving for this occasion. They mostly used the stuff that came in through the dock in great mounds. They used the worst-stained bedclothes for other things, like an outer lining for the building as insulation, or they'd tear them up for bags of rags they'd leave outside in the delivery dock. They didn't get much in return for the rags: a crate of yo-yos (none of them had any idea what to do with them but luckily Julian found a book and that was fun) or a box full of broken, salty crackers, stale but still good for soup, a carton of books, all the same and with the front cover torn off. That sort of thing.

Julian pushed up the roller door of the Bedroom Bonanza and exclaimed. The smell washed over all of them; damp cloth and mold.

"Oh, no!" Kate said. She was the one most looking forward to the new beds. Somehow she remembered the comfort of climbing into a freshly-made bed.

Water had leaked through. They had buckets all over the shopping center and the rhythmic plink plink of water droplets calmed some of them, annoyed others.

The walls were damp and the alcove holding the sheets was inches deep in water.

"It'll be all right. They're still in their plastic," Julian said. He stepped into the smallest puddle and stretched out, passing the packages of sheets out one by one.

———

Carlo led Bean downstairs to the laundromat. It was dark; the line of high windows were dirty and cracked. The lights flickered on when he hit the switch and buzzed quietly; they would keep flickering until they were turned off.

Carlo organized the loads, saying, "I'm not doing it all." But they knew he would. Carlo used to run the machines alone, and he'd still help when any of them forgot which buttons to push. He got tired of the state of clothes and bedding. With someone else washing it, they didn't care about how dirty those items were. Once everyone had to wash their own, they took more care.

There were piles of washing in each corner and piled up behind the counter, way higher than the bench top. It had an odd smell, not bad exactly, but kind of meaty. Unpleasant.

Carlo timed it perfectly, filling the machines, adding soap (who knows how old, but it still smelled of soap at least) and closing the lids, then racing from one to the other pressing *START*. All six machines slowly filled with water and one by one most of the other children crept out. Carlo was mesmerized by the machines and their rhythm, hearing music that made him want to dance.

The machines followed one second after the other, and he spun around, click-spin rock and roll, not caring there was no one there except Bean.

"It's okay! I know it's loud! It's really loud! But the good thing is we know it will stop. Or maybe I'm magic and they will stop on my command."

Bean shook her head and giggled.

"You doubt the great Carrrlooo?" He rolled his *rrr*s until Bean joined in. She sat some of her soft toys on the machine and watched them vibrate.

When the machines stopped, Bean went to get the others while Carlo emptied each machine into a different basket. These were ones taken from the supermarket; the laundromat ones had fallen apart long ago or, perhaps, had been used to carry away loot when the shopping center closed suddenly.

The children weren't sure why it had.

Carlo gave each child a basket of wet washing and they all made their way to the roof. They didn't like to use the elevators unless they had to, for fear of being stuck between the floors. They told stories of ghosts, forever trying to get out.) The elevators worked before their time, but not since the children had been there.

There was the Very High Roof, but they rarely went up there at the top of the eight story tower.

The much bigger Lower Roof was only two floors up and was flat. The children had found ropes strung up here, with some aprons and workman's clothes, stiff from hanging in the weather for a long time.

This was where they dried their clothes, and where they hung the freshly washed sheets and pillowcases. They pegged pillows to the line as well, hoping to air them out.

Marty had grabbed a box of the old cat food and shook handfuls out to feed the birds. There weren't many (the manager had told them it was because the trees were too skinny) but sometimes they did come and perch on the cracked walls, perhaps on their way to elsewhere, somewhere greener. Two black birds and one that was a sickly gray came and pecked at the food, squawked, pecked again. Marty threw more and then the others did. Maud felt momentary joy in this, and she made sure everyone got a handful to toss.

For many miles around there were gray buildings, most of them less than four floors high. "Gravity Leaks," they called it, meaning tall buildings could not be expected to stay sturdy anymore. Beyond them lay the forest. And way beyond that was the water. From the high roof you could see the trees, or at least the concept of trees, way off in the distance; sometimes Maud would go up there, just to see something green. They didn't know what sort of trees they were.

Between the forest and the buildings, the Great Fire had laid waste to most everything. When the sun was out, you could sometimes see silvery trails through the black mess, left by people walking toward the forest, perhaps, or to the innumerable mounds that perhaps covered useful items.

Some of these items came as deliveries to the children: dinner plates, cake tins, barbeque grills, coats. Sometimes they were damaged beyond cleaning by ash and smoke, but most things they could wipe clean and sort, awaiting the next time someone needed garden chairs, or metal fence posts, or glass jars, or saucepans. Things the children didn't always understand, or had forgotten about. Before he ran away, the manager had tried to teach them stuff about the past but they forgot so easily.

—

They made the beds and snuggled down. Maud went into the supermarket and brought back some fizzy drinks and the oldest of the potato chips. If it was a really special occasion, they'd open a fresher packet. Like the birthday they all shared, or perhaps the arrival of someone new. Maud set her suitcase beside her mattress, laying it down flat so she could use it as a table or as a shelf. The others followed suit; they often followed Maud's ideas. Maud's suitcase was brown leather covered with stickers.

"No one is very hungry for dinner after all those snacks, are they?" Julian said. He had not eaten the snacks himself; that food made him feel sluggish.

"Me me me!" Bean squealed. "Sausages!" Bean always wanted sausages.

"It's not really dinner time yet," Josh said. The only clocks they had were the ones in the clock shop, broken most of them, and only one, which used sunlight for power, still running. Kate could keep time by the music that played, and she was teaching the others to do so as well. They didn't know the names of most of the songs and couldn't understand half the words, but they all sure knew the music.

"*Carry on*," Kate said. "It's time for dinner."

Izzy jumped up. "I'll do it," she said. She always did it.

There was no big oven in the kitchen, but there were salvaged burners and a toaster oven and a microwave, and with these Izzy wrought miracles. Most of the saucepans they received were only good for melting down, but they had gathered three good ones, still in their boxes, and these they used. They sometimes got fresh food delivered. Fruit and veggies. They didn't like that too much, preferring the frozen food. The old manager used to make them eat boiled vegetables. Disgusting.

Izzy made sausages (skinless frankfurts) from the can for Bean, then a big pot of soup. Tins of asparagus soup and asparagus pieces, a can of evaporated milk, a packet of herbs, and with some crackers it was a feast. They took their bowls into the food court and sat in small groups. They didn't always sit together but after the excitement of the mattresses, they felt like they wanted to be cohesive. There were old menus left on some of the tables, describing food long since forgotten. Sometimes they tried to cook by the menus, invent what they thought Spaghetti Carbonara was, or Eggplant Parmigiana. They'd say, *What should we have for dinner*, as if anything was possible.

The roof was leaking in the food court, so there were buckets everywhere. Over in the corner, one of them had a drowned rat in it. They'd all vote Julian take that away after the meal. Until then, they'd ignore it. He'd toss it over the dark side of the building. Below, a dozen cars sat rusting. This was where they threw all the dead creatures they found.

Josh gathered up the dirty dishes and dropped them down the elevator shaft. He was the first to do this when it was his turn, arguing that they had thousands of dishes so why waste time washing them? Now they all did it.

Bean was the first to jump from mattress to mattress, squealing with delight and the others soon followed, hollering and screaming with laughter as they jumped from one end of the large showroom to the other. Someone put a CD in the boombox. They sorted most sound equipment for sale but held one back every now and then when another broke. The broken ones were sold for parts and elements, like all the phones were. Carlo had the job of pulling them apart. Each of them took responsibility for something. They had to turn it up loud to drown out the playlist, but this way at least they felt they'd chosen what to listen to.

If the manager had been there he would have said, "If you've got enough energy for bouncing around, you've got enough energy to work."

But he had long since disappeared. He'd left with pockets full of salvaged (stolen) coins. Maud kept a list of all the things that came into the Emporium, as well as a tally of what went out, so she and the others knew what coins he'd taken. A lot of them were scrounged from the wishing well, but everything that came in was checked for money. He'd given them all lessons in value, but Maud was only fourteen then and remembered very little. That was a long time ago. She was fifteen now and thought she'd be better at learning if someone wanted to try. He'd stopped teaching them things; Carlo said it was because he didn't want them to know the value of what he was stealing, and that seemed as likely as anything else. Although he was very tired, always, so tired. He didn't say goodbye when he left but he did leave a map for them, directions to the stash of small, sealed cakes, dozens of boxes, that he was saving for a special occasion. They were stacked carefully on the third floor, in If It Fits, mixed in with the shoe boxes full of footwear that didn't, in fact, fit.

They hadn't seen that manager in a long time. It took a while before anyone outside the Emporium noticed. Julian took charge of the orders and Maud (after Rachel left to go to medicine school) was the boss of things delivered, so they didn't need a manager. It was only when the nurse came in to do the immunizations that the manager's disappearance was revealed.

Chapter Two

Irma had not been so far out before. The road was bumpy and she made a thing of that, bouncing up and down in her seat, to the enjoyment of the driver.

"You'll be popping out of your uniform if you're not careful," he said, one hand on the wheel, the other resting on the back of her seat.

"I'm just glad I packed the cargo nice and snug," she said. She twisted her head to check the back seat; the two refrigerated vaccine transport boxes were strapped in and steady. They were almost alone on the six-lane road, with only a large delivery truck, battered and scratched, following along behind them. On either side lay high piles of rubble and an occasional standing wall, glass long gone, window spaces letting through light and shadow. The last complete buildings they saw were the twin jails, known as the Factories, tall, clean buildings with tiny, high windows and painted green concrete surrounds. They'd passed a dark stretch of trees. Irma hated looking into that space. She imagined ghosts, and things hanging from the trees. There was something about the growth in there she didn't like.

Ahead, the shopping center loomed. It looked like rubble from a distance, a much higher mound, but as they approached she saw the sprawling building stood quite well. It was surrounded by a vast car park, now covered with dust and debris and potholes. There were small dark clusters of people, hiding under tarpaulins or sprawled out, baking in the sun. They'd either be moved on before long, whenever anyone could be bothered, or they'd starve out here for lack of food. Very few of them lived in the car park these days. Murder, rape and deprivation pushed them to find other places.

The driver had to focus in order to approach the main entrance.

"Can you see them yet?" he said. "The ghosts?"

"Don't be silly. Don't call them that."

He shook his head. "That's what they are. All the dead children come here because Heaven is full."

"Hell as well, I imagine," Irma said. She was a sucker for men like this; strong, confident, innocent in their ways and susceptible to theories beyond their discernment.

The building spread over about three and a half thousand

feet. Most of it was two storied, dirty concrete above, large windows below that. To the side, a tower rose eight stories, with a glass-windowed turret at the top. That was once a fancy place to eat, years ago, the driver told her. He said, "I woulda collected you, all dressed up and smelling of patchouli, and we'd ride the glass elevator right up to the top."

She said, "I'm gonna have to call you Patchouli from now on, you know that."

"Don't call me that!"

"Pat. I'll call you Pat." She shook her head as he tried to tell her his actual name.

Many of the lower glass windows were broken. Some were boarded up but most weren't.

She stretched her head forward to see. In her mind's eye she imagined it and felt a cool sense of calm with it.

Around the base was rubble and rubbish and mess. The stink of it seeped through the car windows; it wasn't the worst thing she'd smelled, but it had a steady hard rotting undertone that made her want to cover her nose.

Near the entrance hall, a very tall ladder rested up against the wall. It looked rickety and unsafe, and she wondered about the point of it. "You'll be able to sneak your boyfriends in there," the driver said. She smiled at the fact he used the plural, and she said, "If you're not scared of heights. You'll come visit me, won't you?" although her stay was only planned for a few days. "I'll need company."

"It's a shit job you've got, that's for sure," he said. That was annoying; it wasn't as bad as other jobs she'd done, no competition.

———

The entrance hall was boarded up. The delivery truck had caught up to them and drove around to the side where, Irma saw, a roller door stood open. The side of the truck read, "Children's Services."

He pulled up gently beside the delivery truck. "Have you got some sort of system here?"

She reached into her bag and pulled out her most recent memo. "To be honest it's pretty vague. I think I go in there, get myself set up, get to work. I should be done in two days, given their estimates." She waved the memo.

They climbed out of the car. It was hot out there, almost airless. The truck driver was emptying out his van as quickly as possible, aided by four helpers. Actually, Irma thought, squinting, they were younger. Maybe thirteen or fourteen, if that. They joked and bounced around, certainly not showing any signs of the flu she was about to immunize them against. That was a good sign.

The driver passed her the two vaccine carriers and her overnight bag. "I'd offer to come help, but they've got me on plasma delivery in an hour."

"I'll see you in a couple of days, then," she said, and she walked up the too-steep steps at the delivery dock.

Chapter Three

Marty, Bean, Izzy and Josh, the four children on the dock, paid no attention to Irma. They'd found a box of chocolate (it looked white and crumbly; who knows how old it was?) and were laughing and shoving as much of it into their mouths as they could fit. The delivery driver, a much older man, ("Call me Robbo") shook his head and smiled. "They love their sugar! They don't know how it'll rot them from the inside out." Bean picked out a scarf to wear, although she had one already, a purple and red threadbare number the others teased her about.

Irma suppressed a sigh. So many opinions she had no interest in . . . "Is there someone in charge here, do you know?"

"No idea, love. The kids do a fine job on their own, to be fair. They seem to know what they're doing."

His load looked completely random but then given the nature of the facility, that made sense. There were crates of old shoes, scarves, milk bottles, bottle tops, corks and movie flyers. She didn't want to put down her bags, but grabbed one small crate from the side of the truck to carry inside. She liked to be helpful and liked people to notice how helpful she was.

The four children helping to carry things still seemed barely to notice her. She didn't mind that; if they weren't scared of her, she'd be able to administer the medicine more easily. "I'm Nurse Irma," she said, smiling. "Would one of you mind carrying my little bag? There are some lollipops in there dying to escape."

Bean slung the bag over her shoulder.

"Introduce yourselves, kids," the delivery driver said kindly. "That's what polite people do." The children giggled.

"I'm Nurse Irma," she said again.

The tallest boy, almost to her shoulders, said, "My name is Josh Dior."

"Ooh, like the designer?" and his face lit up.

"This is Bean," he said, bodily lifting the youngest, a scrawny, scrappy little child of five or six, seven at the most, with a filthy face and piercing green eyes.

Irma resisted flipping through her notes to check them off. "Hello, Bean," she said, and nodded. A lot of adults would try to shake this kid's hand, but most kids hated that patronizing sort of behavior.

"I'm Izzy," the other girl said. She was about the same height as Josh and exuded a sense of calm. She had dribbled food all down her shirt front.

"Izzy Izzy always busy," Irma said. Sometimes she couldn't help speaking in rhymes. It helped her remember names and could put people at ease, sometimes because they were annoyed. The last boy hung back in the shadows and for a moment's fancy she wondered if the transport driver was right and some of these children were ghosts.

"That's Marty," Izzy said. "He'll be all right soon. He thought his dad was coming to pick him up today."

Robbo the delivery driver and Irma exchanged glances. The children, or this child at least, didn't seem to know where their parents actually were. It wasn't up to Irma to tell them; in fact she'd been asked not to answer questions, that there was a natural time for them to be told their parents or primary caregivers were in jail.

Having spent a month in one of those facilities a few years back (for public urination, something that still made her cheeks burn with shame) Irma felt sorry for the children who thought their parents were in a good place. "You could survive a nuclear holocaust down here. Along with the cockroaches" the driver said, as one went scurrying at their feet, followed by five more. "I'm going to leave you to it. All the best. Keep that ladder against the wall!"

Irma winked at him, then said to the children, "Lead the way!" and followed them inside, from the delivery dock through dank, mold-smelling concrete passageways.

As they walked, Irma said, "Thanks for helping out. I guess we'll see the manager once we get inside."

Marty said, "I'll run ahead and tell her you're coming," and before Irma could say anything, he took off, leaping over puddles of greasy water and piles of rubbish.

Izzy pushed open the double doors marked "The Emporium main foyer." Irma stepped through then stopped to take it in.

The air felt cool and surprisingly fresh. It was brighter than she'd expected; this part of the center had high windows, and the entrance had a glass-domed roof.

There were stacks of items everywhere, but organized, she thought. She could see shop fronts, most dusty and dark inside. The Gallery, with an easel in the window, holding a painting she'd try to check out later. There was the Young World Shop, its window full of tumbled, broken, burnt mannequins. Irma could see piles of new kids' clothes, looking undamaged, and running along the front, some half-sized train tracks.

"It's the mall train," Izzy said. "It used to work, take you around the mall. Not since we've been here. Everyone says we should fix it but no one knows how. Wouldn't that be cool? We wouldn't have to walk to and from the dock all the time. And they could send it back again all filled with stuff. Otherwise we have to carry it or trolley it."

Music had played continuously since Irma arrived, all of it familiar but at the back of her memory. She hummed along and the children did too; they had heard these songs many times. *"Am I young enough?"* they sang. It was a song she knew, but it sat just at the edge of her memory.

There was the Guest Services Desk, piled up now with egg cartons, jewelry boxes, piles of newspaper and dusty items she couldn't identify from a distance. Signs on the walls were cracked and dusty but she could read the old rules: No Congregating. No Skateboards. No Swimming in the Wishing Well. No Smoking. Keep Doors Closed. Keep Clear in Case of Fire. The place had only been abandoned for about ten years, but it could have been forty or fifty. It wasn't falling to the ground, but it was definitely grimy and unloved. Paint peeled off doors and walls, and those doors were off their hinges. The place echoed with silence. She could see in the corner one part of the flooring from above had fallen in altogether. She'd heard there was a lot of theft of floor and window coverings, and she could see this was true. Cardboard (some apparently wrapped in old sheets) provided insulation in some areas and covered broken windows in others.

—

Marty appeared at her side. "Here's Maud. She's the manager. She's . . ." here Izzy hit his arm, and when she saw Maud she knew why. He'd been about to lie about her age, or oversell the con.

Maud couldn't have been more than fifteen. She was all dressed up like a grown-up, with an ill-fitting suit and her hair pulled back into a bun. She had glorious curly hair, though, and this sprung out all over her head. She walked forward on high-heeled shoes, her ankles wobbling slightly.

"I'm Madame Maud but you can call me Maud. I'm the manager." Bean, the young one, giggled and Izzy put her hand over her mouth.

"Maud, Maud, married a Lord," Irma said. The children stared at her blankly which was frankly a relief.

Maud reached out to shake hands. Irma saw no reason not to play along. "And who else do we have here?" she said, because they were gathered behind Maud as if waiting their turn.

"This isn't everybody! Some of them like to stay upstairs or wherever. I don't know," Maud said.

There was Kate, about twelve, who carried a notebook with her. "*It's Now I Want to be Just Like You o'clock,*" she said. "This can be your song because it's what was playing when I met you."

Irma nodded, not really knowing what she meant. "I'll say Kate, Kate, you are great."

Kate smiled at that.

Julian told her he was sixteen, clearly proud to be the oldest. She wondered how much longer he'd be there; surely they'd call him up soon. She couldn't think of a rhyme for him.

Carlo was the neatest boy she thought she'd ever seen. "Are those creases in your pants?" she said. "Do you iron?" He nodded, ducking his head to the side like a little bird.

"And you've met Bean," Maud said. Bean hid behind Julian. "She's kind of shy but she also hates people." Everyone laughed at that, even Bean, although she bared her teeth like a dog when she did it. "She's only seven."

None of them were ghosts; all were flesh and blood children. Irma hadn't believed any of them would be ghosts, but at the same time was relieved. She felt foolish and determined not to be so brainless again.

Irma said, "You all look very well. Let's try to keep it that way." She held up her medical storage bag. "Let's get you all immunized. There are top up shots for most of you, and flu season is coming up, so we've added that to the mix."

"Where do you want to set up?" Maud asked.

"Is there a doctor's office? A chemist maybe?"

"A chemist!" Kate said, happy to help. "It's my favorite store."

"I'll need an assistant," Irma said. "Would you mind, Maud, if I borrowed one of your people?"

Kate hopped up and down. "I can help! I know where things are!"

"Is that all right, Maud?"

Maud had forgotten she was meant to be the boss. "Well, I'm not going in there. It stinks!"

"They don't like medicine smells," Kate whispered. "I do!"

She led Irma up a spiral staircase to get to the next floor. Irma was fascinated by what she saw. The shopping center had been avant-garde in its time and still retained some of its clever design gimmicks. There were long strings hanging down from the ceiling that glistened as she passed them. Fake marble columns that on closer look, revealed little pictures of people at work and play. Pets, too. Mosaics on the floor made of advertising tiles. And everywhere, there were motivational notices. You can be your Best Self, and Look in the mirror and See who you See, and Don't ever underestimate the Power of Kindness.

The door to the chemist was ajar and inside was a disaster. It had clearly been looted; shelves were tipped over, boxes emptied, glass bottles smashed.

"Let's get this sorted, see what we've got," Irma said. She recruited those gathered around to help; Kate, Julian, Carlo and Bean.

As they tidied, Bean asked a lot of questions. "Why do you have scars on your neck? Do you have any children and where are they? Where do you live?" Irma answered some, deflected others, and asked plenty of her own. She'd just been evicted and wasn't keen to talk about that; they wouldn't understand, not even Julian, she thought. She checked out the chemist, with its well-insulated storeroom, its small kitchen area. It could easily serve as a place to stay; it would do in a pinch. Her only option, if she left the Emporium, was to stay with someone, and there were always strings attached. She was tired of strings.

They stacked, they cleaned, they sorted. Irma noticed a box labeled isopropyl alcohol, half-filled with bottles. She took one out and shook it. She knew she couldn't drink it. Julian chuckled. "Rachel and me sniffed it once. So gross I nearly chucked it. But . . ." here he leaned close to whisper to her, "There's a big room at the top of the tower. It's got a bar. There used to be a nightclub there. Me and Rachel found it."

Maud hunched over in a bit of a sulk in the doorway, still refusing to enter. "I didn't like Rachel anyway. She should have given me her scarf."

"She loved that scarf!" Julian said. It was the print of an old oil painting, gorgeous pink flamingoes reflected on the water.

"I loved it," Maud said quietly. It was a rare showing of discontent for her.

Irma wondered why they hadn't decided to make Julian pretend to be the boss, given he was older.

"So a bar, was there?" she said. Already in her mind she was formulating an idea. She liked these kids, liked this place. She could stay awhile. Be the manager. Kate held up a teddy bear that held a heat bag. "Oh, here it is! I've been looking for this!" Irma looked at her, curious. It was clearly brand new, still with its albeit faded, damaged tag.

"Must be the one your mum gave you," Carlo said. "That time when you got a good mark at school."

Kate nodded, and the others, too. She tucked it into her shirt and later, Irma noticed her stash it in her suitcase.

"Lots of history here I guess," Irma said. "Lots of memories." She wasn't really sure what to say but this seemed to fit. "Who's first? Kate! You're a brave one. Come on then. And I wasn't lying about those lollipops."

Kate bravely took the injection. "Rachel's gone off to be a nurse did you know? She went to medicine school."

"Medicine school?" Irma asked.

"She went a few months ago." She broke briefly into song as music played. "*Everybody Wants the Same Thing*. She didn't really want to go but they told her there was a better life, where she could study and become a doctor. Or a nurse. I can't remember. I wonder how she's doing. Julian misses her a lot, don't you, Julian?"

Irma knew Rachel was not going to become a nurse, or a doctor, but they didn't need to know that.

"Who's next?" She was supposed to take their names and check them off and for a while she did, but they were having so much fun giving her fake names, ridiculous things that made them all cry with laughter, that she let it be. They were impressed that she'd figured it out, especially when Josh came back a second time. "Nope! You don't need two!" She had a couple of them still to go, and sent Josh to find Julian for his injection.

"Most adults can't tell us apart. Doesn't matter what we look like," he said.

She'd give them all basic health checks in the next few days, but for now she was done. She went out to the dock to have a cigarette; Robbo the delivery driver was still there, loading his truck. She wondered what he'd been doing for the last few hours; his ruffled hair told her he'd probably been sleeping. It wasn't up to her to judge him for that. She had no idea what hours he worked.

"Hey!" he said, happy to see her. They sat together on one of the solid metal boxes on the dock and smoked.

"I thought you'd be packed up and gone by now. Lost all your helpers?"

"Kids!" he said good-naturedly. "All gung-ho at the start then they lose interest and off they go."

"I may have distracted them," she said, laughing. He was not as good-looking as her transport driver, but strong.

"You are a distraction, no denying."

"They've got no manager here, did you know that? I don't know what happened to the other one. None of my business. And they seem to be doing okay. Funny kids."

"I suspected, to be honest."

"Poor kids. I feel for them. They all think their parents are coming back. That they're on holiday or something. They have no idea every last one of them is in jail. I guess it's okay they don't know. Well, I was told not to tell them so I guess that's the best. Hey, did you know there's a bar here?"

"I did not."

"Jesus, I need a drink. I tell you, I swear, I almost drank the chemist booze."

"That'll kill you," he said.

"Yeah. But there is a bar! I don't know if you like a drink or not."

He considered her then, summed her up is what she thought. "I do like a drink. I've lost a bit to it, though, to be honest. But I do like a drink."

She didn't tell him that booze had lost her pretty much everything. "So let's go sometime."

"Why not? But look," he said. "Look. I better let them know about the manager business. Just to cover our arses."

"Yeah. I was going to do it once I left, but you do it."

They finished their smokes and he gave her a good crisp apple. "See you tomorrow, most like," he said.

—

Early next morning, before she'd had breakfast, the dock bell rang. None of the children seemed concerned; a few of them wandered toward the dock doors, the others kept on with their business. Most were still in bed, enjoying the mattresses.

"Is there another delivery already?" Irma asked Maud. They were sitting in patch of sun in the atrium, Julian making coffee on a camp stove.

"We get them any old time. Sometimes we wake up and they've been overnight. We never know."

"Hey, gorgeous!" she heard. It was Robbo again. Julian handed him a coffee.

"Back already? Need a hand?" Irma asked.

"Some of the kids are on it. It's only a small load. Listen," he said, leaning close, taking her elbow gently, "Listen, I told them. I didn't want it on my head, not telling them about the manager going missing."

"Makes sense," she said. "I would've done it when I got back so thanks."

"But this is the bit you might hate me for. They've asked me to ask you to stay."

"For how long? I'm supposed to go back today," she said, but she thought *to what? What the fuck am I going back to?* Shitty job in the hospital, shitty two room apartment that she knew from past trips away would be musty and stink of spilled booze. And that, she remembered, she'd been kicked out of anyway. And, in the back of her mind, in the bit she tried to pretend was dead, there were some other issues. Things she'd done that perhaps she shouldn't have.

"Till they find a replacement, they said. What, a couple of weeks?"

She nodded. "They're the bosses. I don't have anything here, though. I don't suppose they got you to bring any of my things? They were holding them for me."

He looked horrified at the thought. "That'd be creepy as fuck," he said. "Going through your stuff? I can think of a much more fun way to get to know each other."

She liked the way he smelled, and the way she could see how strong he was, even through his company shirt.

—

It absolutely wasn't her fault no one told the transport driver not to collect her on the planned afternoon. She didn't even think of it and had no means of contact if she did. They needed to sort that out but they didn't, so he showed up to collect her as arranged. He came calling through the door, his voice flirtatious and filled with mirth. He was thirty minutes early through design or poor planning, she wasn't sure.

"Look at this fucken place!" he said. "It's a fucken miracle! Whoever designed it was a bit of a visionary, ay? No rush. We can hang for a bit."

Irma hadn't gotten a word in yet. "You didn't get the message? I'm supposed to stay another few weeks."

"No one told me. But hey, I get paid for the trip, not who's in my car, so whatever. Only thing is I was thinking we could go have a drink, you know? Just workmates, having a drink."

She touched her mouth briefly in case she was drooling. "Have a drink here," she said. "Celebrate my promotion."

He followed her up to the chemist, where she'd hidden some peach schnapps. She'd done a quicky reccy of the bar; Julian was right. There was some booze there, although most of it was vodka. A few of the older children had tried that but no one really liked it. Sweet drinks tasted better and didn't make you feel sick unless you drank a whole heap of them. They definitely preferred the schnapps and anything with butterscotch in the name.

———

Irma took Pat to the real estate office wanting the back room of the chemist to be hers alone, not sullied by memories or the scent of another person. One room in the office was set up like an actual lounge room, with fake TV and fake fire.

"I wish I could stay longer but I'm due," he said, looking at his watch. "We were supposed to jump on board and off we go."

She laughed at his unintended double meaning, tossing her head back. He smiled. "I could come back," he said.

"Yes! Do!" she said. She gave him a leather jacket she'd found; it fit him perfectly.

Chapter Four

It was over dinner (microwave pouches with your choice of packet curry) that Irma told the children she'd be staying a bit longer. She pushed a water bubbler lever, feeling thirsty, but just a trickle came out. "We don't drink that," Julian said. "I'll show you the tank later and you won't either."

"I'm not a fan of water anyway," Irma said. "But I am a fan of all of you, so guess what? I'm going to stay for a bit. I won't be the bossy one, but I will be here to help."

Bean hugged Irma's legs and the others gathered around, one big group hug. Julian did a little dance, as if relieved, and said, "Now we can show you where we hide the jellybeans. We only show people who stay." Bean started climbing Julian like he was a tree, landing on his shoulders. He didn't mind; he didn't mind anything. Bean tucked one of her many soft toys under Julian's arm and he carried that without question.

"I love jellybeans," Irma said. "Jellybeans for the Bean."

—

Irma quietly assumed the role of manager. She didn't say anything to Maud, who honestly had forgotten she was supposed to be pretending to be the boss.

The chemist, upstairs where she could watch down over the children if she stood at the railing, was a mess. Irma spent a day cleaning it up, with the help of Marty and Kate, who asked her many questions about the things they sorted. She told them about medicines, how some could make you feel better, some were for fixing illnesses, and some were for preventing illnesses. Kate found that fascinating. They sorted bottles (although many had been removed) and placed most things back on the labeled shelves. It was interesting the stuff that hadn't been looted. Bandages and antiseptics were still there, but all of the baby milk powder and nappies were gone. They'd left scented oils but taken the candles. There was plenty of stock left, although most of it was out of date. Irma decided that wouldn't matter, given the circumstances. She had collected some of the plastic plants and flowers from around the center, and she spent a few minutes dusting them off. She had to do this every day, wiping off strange gray-white dust that was possibly ash, but from where?

She asked Kate to gather up the last children for their immunizations. Maud sat on the bench, watching Irma, her legs swinging.

Irma had sharp cheekbones like some of the women did in the old movie magazines that came in. Her mouth was very thin but she kept it painted with lipstick. The shelves were still stocked with makeup, interestingly, and Irma and the children had fun choosing shades. Maud's lips were a dark purple at the moment, making her look gothic and pale. Irma didn't laugh at her though; she was a very serious girl.

Irma said, "I wonder if there's any hair dye anywhere?" because that was another thing gone from the shelves, and her mousy brown hair depressed her when it came through the dyed red.

Julian came in for his injection. "We can find you anything you need. There might be some in the supermarket, otherwise we've probably got a box somewhere. Didn't we get an order for some a while ago, Maud?" He was the one who knew where everything was. He had the sort of brain that remembered details. He could remember the color of books, if not their titles, and kept track of most of the good food they had. He flinched as Irma injected him but smiled; a joke.

Maud had been thinking. "We never did get a hair dye order," she said. Her voice stumbled a bit over words she'd never said before.

"Orders?" Irma said.

Maud and Julian showed Irma how the ordering system worked. The orders arrived, apparently, neatly handwritten on A3 paper. They were delivered in sheaves, forty or fifty at a time, with the urgent ones at the top.

"We never see who brings them, it's weird," Maud said. "Just in the morning, sometimes we find them in the old café, on one of the tables."

They walked there, past piles of rubbish, neatly sorted, past walls almost bare of paint, the peelings thick as autumn leaves on the ground. Past empty shops, doors ajar or off their hinges.

The Sunshine Express Café was made to look like a train. It must have been wonderful once upon a time. A train carriage ran all the way through it, and all the seats were train seats. Tracks ran up all the walls (not on the floor, which made sense. Imagine how many people would trip!) and the menu was written on a railway timetable.

"Sometimes we come and eat our meals here," Maud said. Irma could imagine a time when the café was full of life. Buzzing with food orders and kids, the sound and smell of coffee brewing, the hiss of the sandwiches toasting.

Julian helped Irma into the train. She was aware of how short she was as she stepped up, having to stretch out whereas Julian was comfortable but had no room to move.

Irma looked around the café. There was no food, not even stale biscuits, and no bottles of alcohol. She did find a hazelnut and a vanilla syrup, which would make the cheap, stale coffee here more palatable.

"Isn't it marvelous?" Irma said. "This would be a great place for a party."

"The bar's even better. You can see forever up there. I swear! You stand up there and you can see the future."

Irma laughed and Julian smiled, a gentle, kindly expression on his face.

Maud picked up a sheaf of orders. Instantly focused, she sat down at one of the tables and sorted them into piles. She told Irma, "Big, small, medium. Then I'll sort got, haven't got, don't know. The ones they say they want first go on top when they come in but I just do it this way."

Irma looked into the backroom, hoping for supplies of some kind. A massive freezer rested in one corner, with shopping bags, boxes and empty glass bottles on top of it. "Anything good in there?" Electricity hadn't been an issue to the area, so it might still be.

Maud and Julian shook their heads. "Nothing," they said. There was a handwritten sign (adult writing) saying, "Do not open, human remains inside."

"Are there?" Irma asked, fascinated.

"We don't know. That sign's been there forever. We were told not to open it. We were told it was a customer who wouldn't leave, who wanted to eat everything and they died, and no one wanted to deal with the body so they put it in there and forgot about it until the ghost came out and said help me; but no one wants to look in there. What if they are still alive? Preserved or something?" Maud shuddered.

Irma lifted a box labeled "rice crackers," and dozens of cockroaches skittered out. All three squealed and ran from the storage room, jumping up to sit on the bench, hoping to avoid the awful creatures. "I guess there must be food somewhere," Irma said.

Julian made a face. "They'll eat anything. Cardboard, mold, bodies; anything."

Josh found Irma a suitcase. Bright orange, fake leather, with a tag still on it, "George Crowins, Bondi." It was heavy and Irma felt anxious about what might be inside. She couldn't cope with anything too sad.

Julian clicked the latches. Inside was someone's silver collection, stolen or preserved? it was hard to say. It was dull and quite ugly, but worth keeping track of, she thought.

"We'll stack that in Cool Jewels," Maud said.

Josh arrived with an armful of clothes. He'd done a great job, got the right sizes and nothing too dramatic. It was all about ten years too old for her, but kids thought anyone over twenty was old. He'd chosen flared trousers, a few tailored shirts, some funny t-shirts, some well-made dresses. She'd never worn designer gear before and enjoyed the textures and the colors. She packed some in her suitcase, stacked some on the chemist bench.

Kate flicked through a stack of photos, handing one to Irma. "That's you and your boyfriend who died in the war," Kate stated. Irma laughed; the woman obviously wasn't her and the man not her type. But the children were very serious. They were giving her a new past. Kate gave her a photo of a baby, clearly taken at least a hundred years earlier. "And that's you."

"How old do you think I am?"

"Teasing! Hahahaha. That photo is actually one of our ghosts. She isn't too bad if you're nice to her."

"How do you be nice to a ghost?"

Kate farted. "Not like that!"

They fell about laughing. Then they all picked photos out for themselves. Marty picked one of a child of about six, proudly holding a blackboard covered with scribbles. "That was my next-door neighbor. He used to steal all of the pictures I drew and give them to his dad, and now his dad is a famous artist."

Bean and Josh showed a photo together. It was of an old caravan, incapable of going anywhere. "That was our holiday," Bean said. Josh nodded. "And Josh and I would ride on the top of the caravan and catch birds for dinner with a big net. Except we fell off and no one noticed and that's why we're here."

Everyone nodded solemnly.

Carlo read off the back of his photo: a lovely pool but a bit breezy for my hair. The photo was of a pretty young woman with a neat haircut being blown in the wind. Carlo stared at her, shook his head. He didn't want to tell a story.

Julian shuffled through and found another one for Bean. It was of a middle-aged woman, kissing a baby on the cheek. "Helen was godmother to Baby," he read. They didn't really know what a godmother was but they'd read fairy tales.

"I'm not baby, I'm Bean," Bean said, outraged. Julian hugged her. "Of course you are!"

Kate launched into a long story about hers, which was a school photo. She had a story to tell about every person in the picture, but the rest soon lost interest.

Izzy showed them one of a pet bed. A soft purple blanket filled it, a clear dent where the animal had been. She turned down her mouth. "That was my little doggy's bed. He died because we didn't give him enough to eat. I fed him all the time, every time I made the dinner, but the people I was living with said he wasn't allowed that kind of food."

Irma recoiled, shocked. She was only in part convinced they were inventing these stories; surely that had a basis in truth?

Maud showed them her photo; two old ladies, a man, and a young lady leaning on a black car, with the ocean in the background. Maud envied the easy familiarity of them, the "Taken at Dunbar by George" by someone who knew where Dunbar was, and who George was, and was so familiar with the people in the photo they didn't need to be named. She said, "That's my grandma, the pretty lady. Her name was Maud. They named me after her because she died the very night I was born."

Kate said, "They're all ghosts now, anyway."

Over the next few days, the children helped Irma fill her suitcase with clothes, toiletries and other people's memories.

Chapter Five

Maud pinned the sorted orders up on a wall outside Young World. There were dozens of orders already pinned there, and boxes under all of them. Collected were shoelaces, green plates, blue glasses, henna shampoo bottles, eyeliner, funeral dried flowers (all with RIP ribbons) and much more. A lot of the boxes delivered when Irma arrived sat still unsorted in the general area, and Julian told Irma she should tell the children to get to work. "They won't do it unless you tell them. We all like being lazy." So she did tell them, in the nicest way she could, and she handed out lollipops as a sweetener.

"You can help too if you want," Maud said kindly. Irma got the impression Maud felt sorry for her, that she thought she was a lonely old lady.

"Good idea!" she said.

"Do you want to call out the new orders?" Irma shook her head. It was clearly something Maud relished doing.

"Forty small frames. Twenty pairs of slippers, new. Five work-bags." No one knew what they were. "Three black covers for beds. Sixty stirring spoons." The list went on. As far as Irma could tell, no one took much notice of the lists, although every now and then an object would be added to one of the boxes. Mostly, they added things to their own suitcases. They'd tell stories as they did so, stories that proved this item belonged to them.

The things that scored them fresh food and juice were coins, high quality clothing, unworn shoes, copper wire they wound into skeins, that sort of thing.

Julian set Irma up to unpack a large, torn box. She did that one, finding little of interest, then another two more, before, in the fourth box, she unearthed more enticing items. Glass inlaid mats, for plants, she thought, but that were decorative in their own right.

"Ooh, look!" Kate said. "Look what I found of yours, Irma!"

Irma knew that nothing of hers could be here, but still she paid attention. It was a sash with lost regalia. Thick silk, the material felt cool to the touch and was quite heavy. It lay satisfyingly flat on her shoulder. There were pin holes and the faintest trace of rust where the regalia once was, so it hadn't been removed all that long ago. Had the children stripped it before giving it to her or had it arrived this way?

"This sash belonged to the man who murdered my great-grand-mother," she began. She knew they liked murder stories; there were true crime magazines everywhere.

"Why did he murder her?"

"The best question is how. You see how the important bit is

missing? The bit that pins on? If you stick that in far enough, in the right place . . . the police won't even know what you've done." She remembered how that felt. He'd deserved it, that foul old man. He would say she'd deserved what she got, too (that short stint in jail) because of course he hadn't died. You couldn't kill an old bastard like that so easily.

"Oooh, look! A tennis racquet!" Irma swung it around, the children watching her. She guessed none of them had played or even watched the game; for her it was a distant memory. "So . . . this belonged to my great-grandmother. And this will tell you the why. Why she got murdered. She was better at tennis than the man who killed her. Some men hate that kind of thing."

"That's pathetic," Julian said. He stood close to her, as if physically wanting to protect her from something. "What sort of man does that? What sort of man thinks that?"

"I'm not saying it's a good reason!" Irma said. It surprised her how deeply they engaged with stories they must know are not true. "And yes, he's one of the bad guys." It was clear Julian had no idea what his own father had done. She wasn't going to tell him. Perhaps he'd find out one day, perhaps not. How he didn't remember, at least in part, seemed astonishing. He'd been four when his father slaughtered his mother and two sisters, leaving Julian tucked up in bed. She followed the news, like everybody else did, and there was much discussion about this. Some even thought Julian must have been involved, but clearly he hadn't. He was just a very good sleeper. Irma felt a small sense of power, knowing so much about these children. They had no idea their cases were written about, discussed, argued about. That they were a matter of public interest.

Izzy sang along with the music (*Waiting for the dinner bell ring*) then said, "Hey, guess what we got?" A food delivery had arrived but they had yet to look through it. They liked to save that treat up. Izzy had done a quick inventory though. "We got fried chicken!"

"WE DID NOT!" Josh shouted, jumping up and down, and the other children, excited too, joined in. They all ran for the kitchen.

It was frozen.

"It won't take long!" Irma said. "Come on, by the time you all wash up it'll be nearly done. What else did we get?"

There was fresh orange juice, and there were bananas. There

was cream in a squirty tube. Maud said it must have been for all the silver (Irma checked; it wasn't her silver they gave away).

"Let's do dress ups!" Josh said. "What goes with fried chicken?" None of them had any idea. They wandered off, leaving Izzy and Irma to prepare the meal.

—

They all ate together in the childcare center. There were lots of little chairs there, and the floor covering was still quite comfortable, not yet caked in mold or insect trails like elsewhere. There were plastic plants and flowers everywhere, some a bit dusty, but most still shiny and real-looking.

They made a big pile of chicken bones in the center of the room and Julian began poking them into a bottle. He gave it a shake and laughed; it was almost like a musical instrument and the rest of them made one too, dancing around the room to *Jitterbug* and then *Feel my way*, before they tired of that game. Then they took their plates to the elevator shaft and threw them down.

"What's that about?" Irma said. "We should wash, dry, put away!"

"Have you seen how many plates we have? So so so many." They showed her, in the back of the department store. Many thousands of chipped, cracked and crazed plates. "We've got more plates than dishwashing liquid!" Maud said, which made them all laugh, even though it was true.

Chapter Six

A new delivery had arrived. Irma was annoyed; she missed it, missed the chance to see the driver. There were a couple of different ones and she liked them all, really. Liked chatting to them. Maud said, "Don't worry, he'll be back in an hour to pick up stuff and take it away."

The delivery was a couple of hundred shopping bags, crammed full of belts, power cords they'd strip the copper out of, paper clips, notepads. Those they'd tear off the used pages and stack them in a box. They filled a big order and it was ready to go, neatly packaged.

"It's like a sausage machine. A mess of stuff comes in, neat packages go out."

"I like sausages," Bean said.

"Fresh sausages are really tasty," Irma said, "but I can't even remember the last time I had one."

"I like them from a tin," Bean said.

"How about when you die we turn you into a tin of sausages?" Julian said, squeezing his cheeks together with his hands. Irma was horrified, but Bean laughed till she fell onto the floor.

———

They tipped out another bag and found dozens of flea collars. The ruined ones they'd take the buckles off, but others they could sort. They'd had hundreds of these collars but an order came in a while ago and out they all went, cleaned and sorted into sizes. They got a carton of condensed milk in exchange, and some comic books, although they had a lot of those already.

Marty held one to his chest. "This belonged to my little pup Perry. He was so cute, you should have seen him!"

The others all grabbed at collars too.

Marty said, "He used to sleep on the end of my bed even though he wasn't allowed to, so when . . ." He paused. He hated to talk about his parents. "When someone came in, Perry would curly up in a tiny ball, and he looked like a cushion! They didn't even know!"

"That's like me!" Izzy said. "This collar belonged to my little cat . . . Walky. Because I found her when I went for a walk. And I wasn't allowed to have her, but she loved me so much they let me keep her after all. I wish she wasn't dead."

Maud said to Irma, "Do you have a pet at your house?"

Irma said, "I used to. I had two rabbits who lived in my back-yard. It was a really small backyard but big enough for them. They lived off lettuce and carrots and whatever food I had leftover."

The children didn't know what she meant by leftovers, and she found it hard to make them understand. "Anyway, the thing is, I had this special friend. And he was so special that I forgot about all other things, even my friends and even those little bunnies. So . . ." there was no way she was confessing she'd let them starve to death. "So they dug their way out of their little house, and under the fence, and off they went. They're having adventures to this very day, you watch!"

The children all looked at her, horrified. They somehow knew the truth of it, or found the story as she told it awful enough.

A song came on, Irma started to dance to *Bad Dreams in the Night*. Most of the children joined in, laughing, but Julian wasn't impressed. "She's drunk," he said to Maud.

"Doesn't matter, she's fun!" Maud said. They danced around until Irma fell over, taking Bean with her. Bean landed on her wrist, bending it, and then there were tears.

"See?" Julian said. He remembered nothing of his family, but he remembered how a drunk adult made him feel.

I've Been Waiting played, and Kate said, "Hey! That's the lunch song! Should we eat?"

They were having so much fun unpacking the stuff they decided to have a picnic-style lunch.

While they ate, Maud showed Julian an envelope. It was red, stamped "Urgent," and they both knew what it was. An envelope like this had come in for Rachel, letting her know a place had opened up for her at medical school.

"Who's it for, do you think?" Maud said. It wasn't always the oldest who went next. Children as young as seven had been pulled out to go to school. There was an excitement about it but also a fear of the unknown. If they were sent to school together it would be better. This way they never saw each other again, although who knew what happened out there? Maud was tempted to hide it again; she'd put it underneath a pile of material, ragged at the hems but still colorful and not moth-eaten. She didn't want anyone to go.

"We have to open it some time," Julian said.

It was Julian, being called up for training. It didn't say school, it said training. It said he could be an engineer or a carpenter. He wasn't sure what either thing was, but he said, "Oh well! Next thing!"

Maud went into a sulk, not wanting him to go. Kate, Carlo and Marty gathered around him, asking him questions he didn't know the answer to. Bean joined Maud in her sulk, adding as many hmmmphs as anyone would listen to. Josh said, "Let me find you your going away clothes," and Izzy told Julian she'd make him food for the trip. Bean cried, clinging on to him. "I'll pack you in my suitcase!" he said, and she nodded, thinking this sounded like a great idea.

Irma was quiet.

There were still boxes to unpack so they kept at it. They started to pile things up for Julian, all the best things they found. They didn't know what he'd need. How much he would be able to take.

Marty untied a garbage bag that was mostly full of shoes. He dragged it over to the stage (they'd found it was easier to sort them on there) and began to line them up. He liked things in order so he sorted them by color, mixing pink high-heeled shoes with hot pink sneakers, and artily painted boots with colorful rope sandals. The children soon messed it up, all of them wanting to try shoes on. Maud (who had long since discarded her high heels) found herself a pair of dark purple ballet slippers. Pulling them on, she danced around on the stage, stepping between all the shoes. Bean, always following, looked around until she found some ballet slippers as well and danced and danced.

There were lots of broken shoes, mismatched pairs, and shoes so filthy no one would ever wear them. They would save buckles, buttons and heel bits; Marty specialized in this. He picked up an almost-new pair of good boots.

"Julian! These would fit you."

"They would," Julian said. He sat down and pulled them on. "Perfect."

"Do you know what we found in a boot once?" Maud said. The others gathered around. "We found a diamond ring. Remember? We tested it by scratching the glass over there." Irma looked; there was indeed a large scratch. "And the time we found a roll up of money. And when we found a key."

"We've found so many keys!" Marty said. "Never found the lock to match!" Although sometimes they were the generic style, opening small locks of cabinets. That was useful.

—

Josh was in charge of the clothing, but most of them had to help sort it. There was so much. They knew the sort of thing people wanted, and bags of that (things with fancy labels, things that felt nice to the touch, things with diamonds sewn on) went onto hangers and racks. They sorted into sizes and styles; they never had to wear the same thing twice. Some of it they'd used as bedding, before the mattresses arrived, and even now they'd lifted their beds off the floor with old dresses and trousers. Some of the good stuff they saved for themselves, parading around for entertainment.

Julian's suitcase was brown, trunk-like. It had a lock on it but he never bothered with that. He loved folding the clothing, stacking it up neatly. He was always after storage bins, boxes, chests of drawers. He was the one to go to if you needed something warm or something cool to wear.

So Josh was the one who found clothes for Julian to pack. These would be different to "home clothes." He was going to training; he needed to look smart. There were pants and shirts, socks without holes. Two good jackets and one big fluffy one.

Julian fitted it all in; clothes, shoes, a dog leash to remind him of a long-dead pet, some of the jewelry, some of the coins. They didn't know how he would use it or if he would need to, but just in case. He packed in an old watch that didn't work. "This was my father's," he said. "My mum gave it to him. She said that every time it ticked, to think of her and how much she loved him."

"Awww," Irma said. "That's sweet."

—

Maud knew that it was good for Julian to be leaving, but for the moment she didn't want him to go. She sat, staring into the fish tank. She wished the fish were still swimming so she could watch them. But there was only sludge, and bones. She wondered who the fish had been. What color and how big. You couldn't tell from the bones.

That could be any fish in there.

Bean came and sat by her with a big pile of old birthday cards. Her job was to tear them in half, so that the old greetings were removed and they could all write on them for Julian. Long ago the habit became to have birthday parties instead of farewell parties. No one remembered how it started, but, as they told Irma, they were starting a new life so it kind of made sense.

The torn off bits would go down into the parking garage into the paper recycling. They were all scared of the recycling pile in the parking garage. Much as they loved stories, the ones about that massive pile were too frightening, about someone falling in and being drowned there, all eaten up by whatever ate up the paper, turned into sludge like the sludge in the bottom of the fish tank.

Underneath the decades of paper lay a river of this sludge, and even a drop on your skin would work its way to the bone.

—

Julian appeared in the doorway, dressed in the "stepping out" outfit Josh had chosen for him, inspired by an old fashion magazine. He wore a beige turtleneck jumper, with a navy blue jacket. He held a striped scarf.

"You look great!" Irma said. "Very grown up. But your hair is a mess!" It really was long, and stringy on the ends.

"You need a haircut," Maud said. She loved giving haircuts. The hairdresser (Curl Up and Dye, it was called) still had aprons and sharp scissors, so they made their way there.

As *Hard Times* played, Maud made Julian sit in the chair, where he fidgeted, bored as he often was, but she joked with him and got him to tell stories, and when she was done he cried. "I look so good," he said. "I actually look good."

Izzy went to the kitchen to bake some cookies. They had enough That's the Way the Cookie Crumbles supplies to last a lifetime, as long as they had tinned milk or water for powdered milk. Izzy stirred in an extra handful of chocolate chips saved for special occasions, and set the oven going. She never questioned where the power came from; none of them did. They accepted the fact they had light and heat, that music played throughout the day. She pulled the trays out, burning herself as she always did. Her fingers, hands and forearms were crisscrossed with fine lines, remnants of past burns.

Julian leaned in the doorway. "Are those all for me?" Izzy thought he was getting fat and told him so, but he just laughed and shoved three cookies in his mouth at once. She laughed, and he did, sputtering crumbs over the floor. The ants and the cockroaches would clean that up.

Bean ate as many cookies as she could before someone stopped her. She liked sausages and cookies, not much else. She hated beans. She did some horrendous farts, though.

—

They traipsed up to the roof. Julian peered into the distance, one hand shading his eyes. "I see the future," he said. No one paid him attention, so he said it louder, then they listened. "I can see a new delivery of sweet things, a great big tin of fudge. I can see the water out there, and I'm swimming in it and you all are, too. You all get sent to school in the same place, and we all go swimming whenever we feel like it."

This sounded too good for words. "But seriously, I will find a way to send a message or something. Keep checking the café. I might be able to send a message about where we can all meet."

"In the trees," Kate said. "Way out there. Where those lovely flowers are growing." All the trees in the distance had large flowers, hanging down.

"You can send us a message, Julian. When you're in school."

Irma said, "Don't get your hopes up, though. I don't want you to be disappointed. He might not be able to."

———

They saw a small cloud of dust before they saw the car itself. It hadn't rained in a long time, months, and the ground outside was dry and cracked. Even someone going by foot could raise a small dust storm.

Julian had grown noticeably stronger over the last few months. Carrying his suitcase in one arm, Bean in the other, he walked to the door. Irma wondered again why they hadn't decided to pretend Julian was the boss when she arrived, given he was that bit older than Maud. But watching him now, she could see he found it hard to stay focused, would be distracted easily. Maud stayed on the job better. And he wouldn't have wanted it, anyway. They all thought Maud was the better actor.

The front doors rattled. No one could ever figure out how to open them from the outside so the children had to let people in.

It was two tall people, a man and a woman. She was dressed in black, with tight pants and a fitted jacket. Underneath was some kind of filmy garment, as if she'd forgotten to change out of her nightclothes.

The man was shorter, dressed in soft purple pants and matching warm top. He looked like a cuddly bear, like the ones in the old toy shop with a message on their tummies "I Wuv You" or "You're the Bearst."

The man clapped his hands and bounced on his toes. "You guys! It looks great in here. Even better than last time."

Maud said, "Last time?" and Julian whispered, yeah, remember Brent?" but she didn't, which was bad. She hoped she wouldn't forget Julian like that. You shouldn't forget people. It left a little blank space in your brain like the ones her parents left. She remembered Rachel, at least, but a different pair of people had collected her.

"How are you, Big Fella?" the man said. Maud and Julian exchanged glances. These officials couldn't really tell one from the other. They were so dumb.

The woman said, "Hello, Julian, got your things?"

He had his suitcase and he lifted it to show her. Izzy gave him a few more cookies, wrapped in a tea towel, and he stuffed those into his jacket pocket.

—

Everybody went to the high tower to watch him go. Up there were vast windows where they could watch comings and goings. They looked out at the rubble, the piles from the demolished buildings. Wondered if there was anything good to be found, anything worth collecting. Should they go to look? With wheelbarrows or old shopping trolleys? Irma told them she saw piles of boxes, things half-buried. She said, who knows what could be out there.

Kate noted down which song was playing when Julian left (*I Just Wanna Sleep*). They didn't know the actual names of any of them, but they could hum the tune and they all knew, or could sing, the first few lines or the words that got repeated sometimes. Kate kept the list in a notebook. It wasn't a reliable way to tell time or witness the passage of time, or perhaps it was.

Kate hummed his song. Everybody was crying, all of the children. They'd watched the car take Julian away and now he wasn't here. It felt like the car had disappeared into a hole or something. Behind the buildings. Irma explained there was more beyond.

Maud couldn't remember feeling as bad when Rachel left, but perhaps they did and she'd just forgotten.

"We'll never see him again," Marty said. "He probably already doesn't even remember what we look like."

That made them all cry even harder.

Irma poured herself a drink. Many drinks. Then gathered up more bottles to take with her.

As they walked back down all the stairs, everyone was crying.

"I miss him already," Bean said, and they all agreed, crying harder. Carlo refused to walk anymore, stopping in the stairwell and weeping.

Irma would say later to Robbo, "It threw me. I honestly didn't think I'd care so much about these kids. But they were really sad; it was heartbreaking."

Irma felt helpless, then she said, "How about if we write him a letter? We could all do that! That way he'll be able to read our letters and remember us easily." She led them to the post office. She hadn't been in there but knew there were many mail bags. She'd been intending to check it out, see if there was anything worth opening and keeping.

A motivational sign over the door said, "We are our brother/sister's keeper." As they entered, the children fell quiet. Irma had noticed they did this. They spoke mostly in whispers or very quiet voices anyway, but in places like the post office, they became almost silent. There were places that quietened their voices. Possibly people died there. And ghosts deadened noise; they changed the atmosphere so noise didn't carry. Ghosts didn't like loud noises or laughter and they hated children. So everyone tried to be quiet near them.

"Okay! Let's get started!" Irma laid out paper and pens. Many of them couldn't write so they drew pictures. Marty said, "Let's write to our parents as well!" and she didn't stop them, but it almost broke her, seeing such hope, such belief their letters would be seen. They had an innocence about them she didn't want to shatter. They wouldn't believe her if she told them; they'd just think she was crazy. Her own parents had died when she was twenty-two, both of them killed in the liquor store during a holdup. Wrong place, wrong time, people said, as if that made any difference. Irma hadn't even thought about the possibility that one of these children could be the offspring of the people who murdered her parents. They'd be grandchildren, perhaps. When her parents had died and she had to clear out the house, she'd found things that still chilled her to this day. Still made her angry. Even thinking about it, even playing at post office now made her feel sick to the stomach and furious. They'd kept any and every important thing that had come into the house secret from her. Most of it was online in those days, of course, but there were official letters, there were love letters, there were notes from grandparents and gifts still wrapped that she had never received. Why her parents had hated her so much, to do that to her she would never know. It's not like they left a note explaining themselves. It was just one of those things they'd done to her. One of the things that made her who she was.

Everybody folded their letters into envelopes and without thinking, Irma began to address them all: The Factories, with a question mark because she didn't know which jail each person was in.

Most of them lost interest then and wandered off after ceremoniously mailing their letters in the post box, leaving Maud and Irma to explore. "Kate loves the chemist but I love the post office!" Maud said. "I love it here!" Together they went through some of the old mailbags, filled with letters. Irma showed Maud how to squeeze them, feel for things inside.

They found a stack of parcels and decided to take them all. It would cheer everyone up, even if there were only socks inside, or someone's dirty washing being mailed home, or whatever. Irma had investigated the area earlier and knew the possibilities. It wasn't hoarding, she told herself, not if she was just stacking and sorting, or asking the children to stack and sort. And it wasn't stealing. All of this was abandoned. The senders and recipients likely dead; at the very least no longer interested in the contents. Julian had told her not to take anything, although why it was up to him, she didn't know. He'd set himself up as the monitor of belongings, or something.

—

There was a section called the "Dead Letter Office." Someone, the last worker to leave perhaps, had added the words "this whole place is a" to the Dead Letter Office sign.

Maud didn't want her to go in there. "It's haunted," she said with great certainty. "It's full of bones. There are bones in there and bodies," Maud said, nodding. She sat down amongst a great stack of letters. "You can go if you want. I'm going to stay here for a while. It's peaceful."

"Apart from the ghost?"

"The ghost is only in there." Maud indicated the Dead Letter Office. She looked at the letters. "How should I sort them?"

Irma could barely remember. She pointed out the postal codes. "Start with those," she said. "Sort by number."

Maud sighed, deeply satisfied.

Irma would have to check out the Dead Letter Office later.

Chapter Seven

Maud was in a deep sleep when a great rumble, a crashing, woke her up. She grunted and turned back over in bed; it was a delivery, she thought. There would be nothing urgent in that delivery. Piles of junk no one else wanted that they would sort and use and try to sell. By the sounds of it, there were weeks of work in the delivery, so a few more hours sleep wouldn't hurt.

She was woken again by a tapping at her feet. It was Bean.

"They sent me a friend!" she squealed, her voice so high Maud's ears hurt. "A dear little friend with her own suitcase!"

It was true. Standing near the entrance, where the massive fallen Christmas tree rested, was a young child. They hadn't had anyone new in months at least; before this one, it'd been three around Maud's age, who were still settling in.

A large pink suitcase reached the child's shoulders, bulging with belongings.

Bean whispered, "Ooh! Nice suitcase!" Bean's suitcase was plaid, very large but with small tears. "I wish mine was nice."

"Leave her alone," Maud told her. She went to the child and asked for a name.

"Sally," she said.

"Come and play, Sally!" Bean said, but Sally hid behind her suitcase

"Take her into the supermarket and find a treat," Maud said. There weren't a lot of treats left but they tried to restock when they could. The two girls skipped away.

Maud checked the tag on Sally's suitcase and added a pin on the map of Australia someone had long ago pinned to the noticeboard. She didn't really know where she was pinning. It didn't seem to matter. She tied a piece of string from that pin over to the Directory Map of the shopping center, connecting Sally's place with a specialty pen store.

They all had their own pins, if they could remember where they were from. One of the few rules of the Emporium was *don't move the pins*, because it was easy to forget their origins. Maud didn't remember anymore unless she looked at her pin.

Every now and then, one who could write would make a list, but not everyone could read it.

I can't feel nothing played and Maud got on with the job.

—

Over the next while, they sorted the delivery. More came the next day, and more, but they worked methodically, slowly, because they would never, ever get to the end of the junk, so there was no point trying too hard. They never rushed. They liked to look at everything and tell stories, and they tried to fill their suitcases with things that might have been theirs.

They ate box noodles, because a delivery had come in and they all loved them.

They sorted wineglasses into boxes, because requests came through for these. Two hundred champagne glasses, one hundred brandy balloons. They had pictures reminding them of what each glass looked like. They'd get the glasses back in the same boxes, most of them broken. Broken glass went into the parking garage, dropped through the hole in the corner. The old manager used to threaten to throw the kids down there, but since he was gone, no one had feared anything at all. No one went down there. It was like an old game called Jenga, the manager had said. If you pulled one bit out, everything would fall. And the paper recycling pile was down there; no one wanted to go near that.

They could keep whatever wasn't on the lists. The so-called "high value" items were pretty much worthless to Maud and the other children. What was of value to them were the items that made them think of a time before the Emporium. They talked a lot about those other lives, although the real memories were fuzzier now. They had to remind each other of the details.

Each time they added an item to their suitcase, a story was added to their past lives. Maud picked up a pair of red shoes. They were leather, small, to fit a five-year-old, perhaps. If she closed her eyes, she could remember riding a bike, dragging her feet along, her mother yelling at her to *lift your feet, lift your feet*.

"Those are my shoes!" Josh said, thrusting them onto his feet and spinning around like a ballerina until he fell over, making them all laugh. His suitcase was a big red one, pale and faded now, but with three deep pockets on the outside full of comics and newspaper clippings. "I swear these were mine," he said. It was all an invented mythology anyway; she would find another pair of shoes to tell a story about.

Three large cartons of cereal had come in. Breakfast for the next couple of months would be chocolate cereal, barely out of date. What they didn't eat would go out to the birds on the roof, and the carboard flattened and stored in the old paper shop.

Some of the boxes were labeled: Mum's sideboard, top shelf. Susie's toys. David's cars and trains. Grandma's back cupboard (wrapped). Carlo found a set of ten silver apostle spoons that Irma claimed as hers. She understood how it worked now; if you had a story, you could keep the item. She said, "That was from my christening. I had a godmother who no one spoke to, but she always sent presents. No one wanted to use these spoons because they thought she might have dipped them in poison. But I always loved them."

Maud nodded, and Irma tucked the spoons into a pocket. She'd find a good hiding place for them later. She'd taken to stacking things in the empty shop next to the chemist, wanting to keep the chemist clear for work, and for times away from the children. She had a fold out bed in there for quiet naps in the dark.

Grandma's back cupboard box was full of tacky items from around the world. They sometimes had a call for this stuff but mostly it was rubbish and no one wanted to claim it. Snow domes, decorative plaques, dolls in national costume, spoons, plates. All of it covered with the names of places they didn't know, and pictures of things they didn't recognize. Still, they sorted it by name and boxed it up. Someone might like it.

Sally had gathered a pile of the dolls, lining them up. "You got those when you were born!" Irma said. "Your godmother gave them to you." Even as she said it, she worried about the similarity with Sally's real story. The children didn't care, though. They found a small lunch box for the dolls to sleep in, and Sally was happy for hours after that.

They found a briefcase initialed ESB. There were piles of papers inside, all stamped "top secret" or "of utmost importance or in-extreme-confidence." They piled the paper up to go into the parking garage.

Kate's suitcase was blue vinyl, in perfect condition. She was very selective about what she placed in it. A very special book. A perfect shell. A small drinking glass. A pair of reading glasses, ornate and set with shining stones.

—

Sally cried herself to sleep every night for a lot of nights, but as memory of life outside the Emporium faded, she settled down and became as happy as the rest of them. She loved chocolate cereal and would eat nothing but. She still cried every now and then, but they realized she was crying because she wasn't lonely anymore. "My house was so quiet," she told them. "And no one went to school, and no one was allowed to play with each other."

The children were never lonely. Sally cried sometimes just hearing voices. She clung to Maud often, like a little monkey, causing Bean to be a bit jealous. Irma tried to take her on occasion, but she really wasn't interested; she could sense, as they all did, that Irma was more interested in herself than in them.

—

There were hundreds of books in this delivery. They'd use them to stack against the walls for insulation. For making cubby houses. They'd tuck books into alcoves to keep the creepy crawlies from coming through. Books were also the best thing for the fire pit they had on the roof. Kate was in charge of looking after that. Books burnt slowly and didn't pour out fumes.

They didn't burn the art books, or the beautiful picture books. They didn't burn the many pieces of artwork that came to them either; these they hung on the walls, more insulation, layer upon layer of pastorals, portraits, still lifes, beach scenes, marine scenes, huge great sailing ships so cleverly painted the sails seemed to flap in the wind.

They sorted through the sheets and pillows, looking for more blankets. The ones they found were musty and clammy, mostly, but they found if they hung them on the pipes that radiated heat through most of the building, that smell would sizzle out.

They found more bedding in the day care center. There were

lots of snacks in there too, just like Julian had told them, and using his hand-drawn map, they found a stash of chocolate eggs that were still pretty fresh.

—

Kate found a pair of shoes with wheels on them.

"Roller skates!" Irma told them. "You put them on and it's almost like you're flying." She had a memory of a first kiss at a roller rink but it wasn't hers, it was her mothers.

"They were yours when you were a little girl," Maud said. "See that mark underneath? That was so your sister couldn't say they were hers."

It seemed real when Maud said it.

Kate strapped them on. She clung to the walls and to the other children, grabbed onto the fake plants, held onto the backs of chairs, all the while laughing her head off.

"We have a few more pairs around somewhere," Izzy said. "In the sporting goods store." No one liked to venture there much. The smell of old rubber, leather and plastic, and the resulting smell of the metal, made it unpleasant. They told each other a team of footballers' ghosts lived there, kids who died in a bus crash on the way to a match.

The sporting goods store was on the second floor, in a back corner. Irma hadn't seen much of this area before and took it all in. There was a shoe shop, smelling like fresh leather, a delightful smell. A gift shop, mostly stripped, but with a few items left on the shelf. And "We buy gold." She doubted there was anything left in there, but she'd check it out later.

"We're still making lists of all this stuff," Maud told her. "In case people want it." The gift store had a fake fireplace, oddly, and a grandfather clock that was clearly made of carboard.

The sporting goods shop was a delight. It was still pretty well-stocked; people weren't so keen on do it yourself sports these days. Thinking that she could convince some of the delivery drivers to stay for a bit if she entertained them (and in the back of her mind she was planning a party), she collected things that they could play with. She found a soft ball and bat set (Nerf Fun, it was called) and a game of quoits, and there was plenty more she could come back for.

The roller skates were piled in a corner, in a bit of a mess. "We keep adding them when we find them," Maud said. "No one's ordered any yet, but you watch, I bet they do now."

There were enough pairs for all of those who'd followed along. Bean and Sally both cried; their feet were too small. But Maud, Izzy, Irma, Carlo, Josh and Marty all joined Kate. They wheeled around the shop, screeching with laughter, falling over, pulling themselves up, falling over again.

Then Marty rolled out the door of the shop. The passageway out the front was much more slippery, and he headed toward the stairs, much faster than he'd planned. He squealed, a high-pitched sound that had the others trying to race after him but falling over themselves. Irma tore her roller skates off and joined the chase, only to see him slip backward and land with a crack on the back of his head.

"Kate! Run down and get my bag! Maud! Takes his skates off." Marty wasn't responding. When she held his eyelids open, the whites of his eyes showed. All her old training kicked in. She'd done part of a medical degree before shifting to nursing; it was her nursing stuff that helped her here. She'd always been good at this. She'd just been sidetracked by life.

———

Irma felt more attached to the children after this. They changed in the way they looked at her; they trusted her now. They loved her, she thought, or at the very least admired her and were grateful to her. Marty had a headache and a massive bandage around his head, but he was apart from that okay. She stopped in at Young World to find gifts for them all, knowing in her heart they had all they needed. She found them clean socks, packets of hand-kerchiefs, scarves. She made a pot of spaghetti sauce with lots of hidden vegetables. They all ate it, although they made it clear they preferred Izzy's cooking.

———

The delivery bell rang. Most of the drivers didn't bother; they just left the stuff on the dock, or piled up outside the walls. So Irma knew it was her favorite, the one called Robbo. and who she rather liked. It had taken her a while to realize there were a few of them; they all looked quite similar. He was in the Children's Services truck and by now she had realized it was the children providing the service rather than the other way around.

Everything was laid out on the deck. Garbage bags full, boxes, crates, and one white Styrofoam box, addressed to the Dead Letter Office.

Irma wanted to look in, but the driver stopped her. "Best not to know some things," he said. He offered her a cigarette. She saw then that he'd clearly been in a fight. His face was bruised and two of his fingers bandaged. A partially healed cut split his cheek. Irma touched it gently.

"Some arsehole," he said. "Jumped me out of the blue. They got him, though. He's in the Factory, will be there for a while."

They stood together, smoking. One of the children appeared in the doorway and Robbo tried to hide his cigarette, but Irma said, "They don't care. It's not like these kids'll ask questions. I love them to bits, but it freaks me out a bit that they don't ask any questions.

"Maybe they can't see the point in knowing stuff. Maybe they'd rather not know."

"But they talk about their parents; they just don't know anything about them. They're always talking about them being at work, without really knowing what that means." She pointed to buildings in the distance. "Like, that's where they are. Right? In the Factories. And they think being here is all about how old they are. Not about their parents and what they owe society."

"Some people deserve to be in there," he said. He took another drag of his cigarette and winced as if his cut lip gave him pain.

"Sooo?" she said.

"Misunderstanding," he said. "Wrong place, wrong time, wrong assumption about what I was doing."

Bean and Sally appeared beside them. "There you are!" Bean said. "Hiding!" Maud came up behind them.

"It's all about keeping them safe, right?" Robbo said quietly.

Maud remembered something of life out there. The sense of a "lack of safety." Whereas here she felt secure. Even with the younger boys battling it out to be "the boss," with Julian gone, they were easily reminded of the other life, and of the importance of looking out for each other.

———

After Robbo left, Irma watched the children unpack. The Styrofoam box had gone straight to the post office. She'd look at that later.

They unpacked a box of out-of-date breakfast bars they had received in exchange for a crate of flattened drink cans. The bars were full of marshmallows and chocolate, and while the nutrition panel claimed they covered 5% of daily needs, they also covered 95% of salt and sugar limits.

The children loved them.

Irma felt sleepy and half-drunk. Watching them, she wondered if they understood what they were doing. She'd packed up her grandmother's house and the contrast here, of these children unpacking a stranger's belongings and claiming stories, was so very different she wondered if they saw the metaphor of unpacking a life, of naming items in order to own them.

Maud saw a shoebox, battered but intact, and claimed it. It was unlikely to hold actual shoes but you never knew. Mind you there were plenty upstairs in the shoe shop. A small percentage you had to match up, but most were already in pairs. Maud and Josh liked pairing the shoes with outfits. She said, "Josh! Maybe we'll find an animal print pair in here to go with the coat you found!" It was a magnificent coat, soft, long, sleek. Josh had it hanging on a mannequin near the stage.

"I hope not," Josh said, but he smiled.

Inside the shoebox was a teacup set, carefully wrapped in yellowing tissue paper. Cup, saucer, plate, not chipped, barely used, but very old.

"Oh, look!" Maud said. She turned the cup (cream, with a dark green stripe around the rim) over in her hands. She pretended to sip delicately from it. "This belonged to my grandmother. One day I went to visit her and we sat in the car and watched people play football and drank tea from these tea cups." She thought for a moment. "I drank Milo, she drank tea. But then something happened to her and she dropped her tea onto her lap and burnt herself and died."

Josh made a sad face, although he was clearly more focused on unpacking. Maud could picture the scene in her head but the memory seemed wrong, because of the light. Her brain kept shifting it to the Emporium but she knew she'd been outside once.

Carlo dug down into a pillowcase that had pictures of cartoon animals (a lion grooming his mane with an enormous comb, an elephant with loops of string tied around its toes, a leopard in running shoes). "Ooh, I found something for Sally." It was a small metal cup, designed for a young child, with a big handle and the etching of a teddy bear.

"Here you go," he said, handing it to Sally.

Sally stared blankly.

"It was a present from the people next door," Maud said. She was the best at getting stories started. "They gave it to you when you turned one. It used to belong to their little boy but he died."

"How?" Sally asked, entranced.

Maud held the cup. "Not poison," she said. "It was a terrible accident. He was playing on the roof and fell off. He thought he could fly. He jumped and he landed on the big tree in your back-yard. It was a . . ." Maud closed her eyes to picture it. "It was a tree covered with yellow flowers. He broke some of the branches and died, and all of the flowers from then on were red, the same color as blood."

Kate showed Sally how to pack the cup into her suitcase. "You can tell the story next time." She lifted a pair of binoculars out of the suitcase and handed them to Sally, who lifted them to her eyes.

"We can use them next time we're on the roof, to look a long way away," Irma said.

Josh found a small pencil case, with drawings of rockets in a childish hand. "Don't you remember?" Maud said. Most of the stories started that way. She led Josh to his own story. "Don't you remember?"

He opened the case to find a pile of blunt colored pencils. "I made a map with these. A map of the Emporium."

"Was it? But the blue is nearly gone. You drew a lot of sky. Or water."

"Water," he said. "I drew a map of the ocean, with lots of islands." He looked around, as if trying to find the map. "We used to sail our boats to all the islands and spend a night on each one. The worst one was full of birds. They hated us camping. They were only quiet at night, and even then we heard them whispering."

"That was probably ghosts," Maud said. In the rare times

when everything was quiet (air conditioner off, momentary music lull between cycles, everyone else asleep) whisperings could be heard.

Irma found a bag of jewelry and set it aside to check later and stack with her other finds. She knew she wouldn't be able to take it all, but she wanted as many options as possible. She sat there in the semidark and felt a sense of loneliness drop over her. She craved adult company. She craved action and flirtation. She craved physical contact with an adult male.

She went back to where the children were and told Maud, "You know what? I think I'll throw a party."

They shifted dozens of clothing bags. Josh would go through them over the next few days. He had fifteen dress mannequins lined up (he was terrified of the day someone would put an order in for them) and he loved to dress them. He tipped out one of the bags, hoping for a treasure.

"Oh!" Maud said. She reached into the pile. "Look!" She lifted up a bright scarf, all purples and pinks, with pictures of flamingoes reflected on the water. "Have you seen another like this?"

"It must be Rachel's!" Josh said. "Do you think she sent it to you somehow?" They both looked at the scarf, mystified, before Maud tied it around her neck.

"I love it so much," she said, almost whispering in awe.

"Rachel sent us her things!" Kate said. They all decided that Rachel's things returning to them was a message from her to them that everything would be okay. They decided she'd moved up in the world. She could unpack her suitcase and her backpack because she was staying in the same place for a while. They sometimes unpacked their suitcases but no one liked to be unprepared. They all wanted to be ready to go at a moment's notice.

They decided that Julian would send them a message too.

Sally found a packet of black markers. Squatting, she began to draw on herself, and Bean sat next to her to watch. "My dad had some like this," Sally said.

"And the man, too," Bean said. They called all of the delivery drivers "man."

Sally covered her arms and legs with drawings of flowers. "I love them," she said. The others all joined her, drawing on each other and themselves. Maud drew Julian flying, and also a picture of a cat, with little footprints left behind all up her arm.

Sally drew flowers on everybody. Irma said, "If you really love flowers, maybe you can look after our little flower tower on the roof? The birds love it."

Sally shook her head, but Bean said, "It's so cool! Can we both?" and Maud got them set up. Josh found them matching overalls, and Maud found them a small watering can each. They raided the florist, which had a small greenhouse filled with dead flowers and plants.

Irma said, "When I have my party, you girls can be in charge of getting me some flowers to put on the table!"

Chapter Eight

There was a lot to do. After sending out some invitations, Irma started her preparations.

It was past midnight. Music played: it never stopped. *We play these parlor games. You say you love me.* With most of the lights off, the atrium took on a silvery glow and in her fancy she saw fairies dancing in the corner and flying through the air, racing around as the children did by day.

She realized it wasn't fairies at all but some of the older boys throwing balls around and other things as well.

With Julian gone, some of the boys thought they could step into his shoes, although Julian was never in charge, he was just calm and clever and helped to solve things. There were four or five of them, she thought, although it was hard to see in the low light. They'd all taken their shirts off and were circling each other. One brandished a baseball bat, another what looked like a mannequin arm. She would need to take control of them sooner rather than later, but she wasn't sure how. And it was entrancing, watching them. How did they know this stuff? Was it instinctive, or did they have some memory of time outside the shopping center? Of adults in their lives taking part in this violent circling.

Then it was on, all five of them hitting and kicking, still quiet, somehow not disturbing the peace as much as they should.

They were agitated and at this stage only hurting each other, so she didn't intervene, and they ran out of steam very quickly.

The next day, she gathered those boys together. She'd recognized one, and he quickly told her the names of the others. She took them up to the tower and filled them with junk food; chicken nuggets cooked in the microwave, cheese twists, potato chips, candy canes. She pointed out into the distance to the trees, and the pods hanging off them.

"Do you know what they are?" she said. "Any ideas?" None of them wanted to guess. "It's people hanged. People like you, like any of you, hanged for violence. Remember the other day, when the driver came all bashed up?" They nodded, and she pointed out. "He's hanging out there. The guy that did it to him. Hanging out there with all the others. There's one main thing this society hates, boys. It's violence. Battle it out with a game of some kind. Best for all involved."

—

Irma was on a roll, feeding the children. She cooked up a big feast, more chicken nuggets, chips, some zucchini fritters she found stashed at the back of the freezer. She laid out nuts and energy bars. She fed them then asked them to help her clean up. "Let's make a good impression. Let's show these people how well we can look after our own place. Then they might leave everyone here." She gave them all gloves and asked them to clear up the broken glass around the windows. So many broken windows, all the way up the tower. The gaps were covered with clear plastic in most places, so the light still got in, but it was less than perfect. "Be careful!" she told them. They threw some of the glass into the parking garage, but some of it they tossed out windows, in an attempt to deter visitors. Irma didn't approve of that but they didn't care.

Buckets sat over the floors, gathering drips of water. Another drowned mouse floated in one and the water in the others was discolored and smelled bad. Irma tipped them out herself. She wasn't squeamish, after all her years working as a nurse.

—

After the cleanup, they were all exhausted. They sat up in their beds eating snacks, so tired they could barely manage even that. The lights were bright that day for some reason, so some of them made little tents over their beds. It was never completely dark in the shopping center. Maud wrote a letter to Julian and snuck out to mail it.

—

Preparing for the party was one of the best days any of them had ever had. They wanted to dress up (encouraged by Irma, who just wanted them not to annoy her) so they raided Cool Jewels and the formal wear shop. They all dressed in clothes too big for them; Josh tried to get them to change but no one would. The girls put gowns on over their other clothes, the boys, big jackets. They chose the most colorful jewelry. Irma noted none of it was of value. Most of that had gone. But the costume pieces were fun and who knew? Maybe they would be worth something. Certainly some of the pieces were rare.

"This is my mother's handbag," Carlo said. This seemed unlikely; it was a massive green thing Irma doubted anybody had ever used. "She used to carry my dad's dinner in here when he worked . . ." He had to think. "When he worked on the buildings. He worked so hard he never stopped to eat so my mother would come with food for him. In here. You can see crumbs at the bottom." He opened the bag wide for them to see and while there were no visible crumbs, all of them could imagine such. Everyone wanted handbags then, and that was fun too.

They showed Irma the makeup collection, and how they shaved off the lipsticks so they were as good as new. They tried on all the perfumes (some quite genuinely having memories of these scents) and they did their hair.

They wore hats and gloves. Irma wore black gloves with white stitching. Matching black hat with a black rose. Josh said she looked like a model. Maud thought she looked more like a killer, like a woman out of one of their true crime magazines.

They had a whole wall of pictures cut from magazines for a game they played called "Killer or Actor." They'd mix up the true crime and the Hollywood pictures, and you had to guess which. It was disturbing to Irma, because some of them even had family members in these pictures. Julian's father was literally famous for what he'd done, but because Julian was unnamed in the story (the magazine called him "the boy, the spitting image of his father") they didn't know.

Marty said, "You should play it at your party too." The children only vaguely remembered birthday parties but they knew there were always games.

"We might," Irma said. She wanted a few of them to act as waiters. "I'll give lollies to the people who do it."

"Ooh pick me! I want to be the waiter," Bean said.

"It really will be fun," Irma said.

She'd asked Robbo to bring food in. Izzy would do the warming up, using the bar microwave.

—

Irma hadn't worn high heels in a while. She liked it. She liked the extra height and the way it made her legs feel. She looked at herself in a mottled window in a dressing room and felt like something was missing. She looked unfinished, lacking class. She wanted to look as if she was in control.

She walked downstairs to the mannequins, lined up in their fancy gear, and she shucked the fur coat off the shoulders of one of them. She slipped her arms into the sleeves. They felt cool, not clammy like a lot of the clothing, and the weight of the animal on her shoulders gave her a sense of power.

—

Then it was time to wait on the dock. Maud came with her, Kate as well, and Carlo joined them. They tidied up a bit while they waited and they sang, *Tell me what you're doing on the other side* and *We are family*, words taken in by osmosis by multiple playings.

They heard Robbo's truck before they saw it. It rumbled, and there was a rocketing noise as he drove over the increasingly-ruined parking lot. He backed onto the deck and parked. Slamming his door, he walked around to greet them. His hair was damp and neatly combed and he wore a nice shirt. He took Irma into a big bear hug, lifting her off her feet, saying, "Nice coat." Irma spun around, showing it off.

There was a banging on the truck's roller door, and he said, "Your guests are here," as he lifted it, revealing a dozen or so people. One of them was Pat, her transport driver. That caused a flutter in her blood.

They all carried boxes and bags of food.

It was bright out there and they squinted. For a minute Maud thought one of them was Julian; he had the same loping walk and similar dirty blond hair. They were about the same age, Maud thought, and she was about to call his name when the guy lifted his head and she saw it was not Julian at all but someone entirely different and older. "That's Jinks," Pat said. "Good mate of mine."

"I think we should call him Not-Julian. Because he looks like Julian," Maud said, and so his name was set.

Not-Julian said, "Man, there are some serious wrecks of cars out there. Anybody claim them? I reckon I could make one go."

No one answered him.

They were drinking something out of bottles, *"Champagne for everyone,"* someone said, but it clearly wasn't champagne. They handed Irma a bottle and she took a sip.

"That's bloody awful! Come on. The booze in the bar is shit, but not that shit."

In the back of the truck were three polystyrene boxes, marked DLO for Dead Letter Office. Usually Robbo would take these himself to the post office, where Irma would quietly look through them for the good stuff. She'd found nothing of real value so far, but perhaps these boxes would bring some joy.

"Kids, you take them, okay? We've got some partying to do," Robbo said, and the group of adults cheered. They noisily traipsed through the doors, leaving Maud and the others behind.

"One box each," Maud said, and they carried them away.

—

Irma led the way upstairs to the bar. She felt full of bubbles, light on her feet, her head airy, free from worry. "If you get lost, walk to No Spitting and walk up the escalator. Turn left and walk to Every Dream Has a Chance to Live and up that hallway is the lift to the eighth floor." The adults noticed the moss and the mold. They spoke of their own memories of shopping centers of their youth; of first kisses, of stealing magazines, of a first job. They admired the art on the walls, and the rare examples of graffiti. Irma had to hurry them along; she wanted a drink.

They walked past the real estate office, with peeling photos of properties in the windows. The slogan of the office said, "Everybody deserves a castle." Pat and Irma stood together. She had a moment of pure longing; an impossible dream, a moment of absolute loss.

She wasn't alone. One of the others said, "Can you imagine? It seems impossible, right?"

They walked past the wishing well. Not-Julian knelt down and peered in. There was still water in there, opaque and stagnant. "Are there any coins left?"

Irma said, "Long since scavenged. And that water'll rot your fingernails off." If there was any money left in there it was hers, not this guy's.

Robbo lifted him up by his shirt collar. "Let's move on. That drink is calling me." They walked past a lineup of mannequins and half the adults jumped. One of the women squealed. "Who the fuck is that?"

Maud and the other children had finished their work in the Dead Letter Office and had joined the party. Maud laughed as if to say *These adults are not too smart. But fascinating to watch.*

They passed no smoking signs, keep door closed signs, do not loiter, dispose of rubbish thoughtfully, de-fibrillation machine here, fire hose here. Not-Julian tried to pry one of the signs off. Irma felt irritated, something she hadn't felt in a long time. "Why don't you have a drink from the bubbler?" she said. Maud opened her mouth, but Irma winked at her.

Not-Julian had no interest in water anyway.

They reached a sign saying, in gold, ornate lettering, "Top of the Town Nightclub and Bar (women drink free) Eighth Floor"

Not-Julian pushed the lift button.

"Sorry, none of the lifts work," Irma said, although the indicator light came on. "And if they work, we can't always trust the electricity supply. We just don't know when it'll cut out. There's someone literally in one of the lifts. Not this one. But you know, they just got stuck there and there was no one to get them out."

"Yeah?" Not-Julian said. The lifts doors opened, and he got in. No one joined him. "See you there," he said, as the doors shut.

Irma and the others walked up the stairs. The bar was empty when they got there, puffed out. They watched as the lift indicator traveled up, down, up down, up, and as it reached the eighth floor again, Robbo levered the door open, and there Not-Julian was, laughing.

———

The bar itself was light, with wraparound windows which had fewer cobwebs and less dust than on the lower floors. Irma had dragged all the bar tables together, lovely things inset with colored bottles and pieces of curious toys and games. She'd found the nicest dinner plates, and there were unlimited choices for wineglasses, if not a wide variety of drinks.

"It looks beautiful!" one of the women said. They all set out the food and Irma poured them drinks. There was some wine, but a lot of advocaat, cherry liqueur, Fejoia vodka and other over-flavored drinks.

On the walls, most of the art remained. It was cheap reproductions of classic paintings, mostly. Someone had a vision at one stage: mostly paintings of isolated trees, forests, backyard vistas. Contrasting these with the trees in the distance, Irma could see what the vision was.

The party ate and drank. Maud and most of the other children helped, hung around the edges. No one noticed them. They were fascinated by the aimlessness, the apparent pointlessness, of what they were watching. Sally in particular was entranced, leaning up against the legs of the adults, wanting them to notice her. None of them did.

"So!" one said. "Did you all hear about the jailbreak? You know how close I live? I could have been raped if they'd succeeded."

Not-Julian laughed. "I can give you better action than that. What's with women wanting to be raped all the time? I'd never do that. I'll never need to." He really was pleased with himself.

Pat shook his head, but he seemed amused, and in that moment Irma found the man far less attractive. She'd still have sex with him, sure. But she'd gone off him.

Standing at the window, Pat looked into the distance. "Hope they got all them jailbreakers. That's a few less shitty people on the planet, so that's good."

"Keep it quiet," Irma said. She had forgotten the children were there but didn't want words to carry. She lowered her voice, so Maud crept closer. "We had the son of one of them here."

No one was interested in that, so Irma said, "Who wants to come to the roof? View is even better up there."

They all walked up to the roof, carrying their drinks and bottles, laughing. The air up there was very still. There was no wind, although it could appear at any time. It was early evening, balmy and perfect. In the distance, lights went out then flickered on and off as they watched.

"Lucky you're not in the lift," Robbo said to Not-Julian.

Irma had the children set up nerf guns, and roller skates. There was a high wall around the roof; you'd have to try very hard to fall off.

None of them knew how to roller-skate, so there were multiple bangs and cuts. Irma gave Kate the key to the chemist. "Go get my bag of things. And extra bandages and you know that red bottle. And let's go back to the bar, everyone," Irma said.

———

They moved the tables aside so there was room for dancing. The floor was filthy; stains everywhere, including two large ones that looked like bloodstains. It was hard to drown out the music already playing so they danced to that, *We Like it Like That* and *You Gotta Dance for Me.*

The children joined in at the edges, enjoying the wild movements. All except Sally, who stood, staring at the stains.

"What's up with her?" someone asked.

"She hasn't been here long. I guess she remembers stuff from before," Irma said. She looked around. "Children! It's late. Time to be."

They trooped out, except for Maud, who hid behind the bar. She didn't want to miss this. There was going to be news, information. She was going to learn something.

"Jeez, is that who she is? Is she like under witness protection or something?" Pat said. He had his hand on Irma's thigh, his forefinger gently circling.

"I guess," Irma said. They all talked over each other then, but what Maud picked up was this: that Sally's father had kept a series of corpses in a locked room in their house and that Sally had done the same but with animals, a whole collection of them under her bed.

Not-Julian laughed. "It's bullshit, of course. The bit about the kid. I mean, right?"

They ignored him, asking more questions. Enjoying the attention,

Irma said, "We had Julian Grande here as well. His dad was Marcus Grande."

"Oh, crap! Jesus. That poor kid." And again, they all talked over each other, but what Maud heard was this: That Julian's father had killed his siblings (she couldn't understand how many of them there were) and his mother and that Julian had only survived because his dad called him Mirror Image, as if Julian was identical and it would have been like killing himself.

Irma and Pat started dancing, and the others, too.

Not-Julian came to the bar for more alcohol and saw Maud crouching there. The conversation had turned to things Maud didn't understand and she wanted to sneak out but didn't know how. Not-Julian grinned at her. He reached over for more bottles of strange colored alcohol and walked back over to the group. They were all collapsed on couches now, screeching with laughter and making other odd noises. "I'm gonna have an explore downstairs," he said. No one responded.

He guided Maud out. None of the other adults noticed or cared. Maud shook her head at the lift so they took the stairs.

"Thanks," she said.

"They're all pretty awful," Not-Julian said.

"Irma is nice. She's nicer than the last manager we had. Do you think they know about my parents too? If I asked?"

He shook his head. "They won't say. But look. Look. Don't tell them I said this. But I saw what was in those boxes. I'll admit it; I wanted to thieve something. I couldn't do it, though. I'm not that bad. Every last one holds the belongings of someone who died in jail."

He gave her a strange salute and took off.

—

The other adults appeared over the next hour, stumbling, sleepy, no longer full of stories or joy. They left, all in the back of the truck again, including Not-Julian who carried a big pillowcase full of stuff no one asked him about. Irma went to lie down and the children cleaned up, throwing all the dishes and other rubbish down the elevator shaft. Sally seemed shell-shocked, so Maud took her to the salon and gave her a haircut, which seemed to settle her. They moved their lips to the words of the song, singing *I gotta good feeling*, all the oohs and aahs.

Chapter Nine

By Kate's estimation, 360 cycles of songs played before they received Julian's belongings back in a file box.

The delivery alarm went off and they all gathered by the dock. They heard the beep of a truck backing up and Kate opened the roller doors. Robbo jumped down from the driver's side and gestured. "Got myself a helper."

It was Not-Julian.

The smell of the truck wasn't good. Old sweat, old food, old sneakers. There was the smell of smoke, too, underlying it all.

Irma and Robbo kissed each other to the horror of the children.

"Fire at the jail," Not-Julian said, wanting to be the one with the news. He began unloading the plastic bags and boxes. "In the food hall. Terrible. They were all trapped." His eyes were wide. He found this exciting. "They're not even sure how many dead. A dozen at least. But that's life, right? And better them than us, I say. Good riddance to bad rubbish. Hey, and ask him what happened to the guy that beat him up." He gestured to Robbo, then mimicked a hanged man, head hanging at an awful angle. "Good stuff!"

There were a dozen boxes for the Dead Letter Office. Maud made sure she took one of them, then stayed behind after the others left. "I love the post office," she told Irma. Irma was distracted anyway, with Robbo there. Not-Julian winked at her. "Don't forget what I said," he whispered.

———

In the post office, Maud lifted the lid off the first box. Robbo had told them they had to keep them for a few months, then they could sort them, but Maud wanted to see for herself. Inside was a stack of file boxes, some light, some so full they didn't close properly. All carried a number. She picked up 6-358-Alpha

Inside, she found a man's watch, some notes and coins, a set of keys with a key ring that was also a bottle opener. She found a small notebook with names and notations inside, a folded, stained pair of socks, a toothbrush and a light metal ashtray.

She took out all the file boxes and stacked them. She opened them one by one until she reached the one that made her recoil. Sitting in that one was a lunchbox with Stan Stedman written on the bottom. There were no cookies inside, but in the file box she found a dog leash and an old watch. It was his father's, he'd said. He'd said that the ticks had reminded his mum of how much his dad had loved her.

Maud couldn't quite comprehend what this meant, at an intellectual level, but tears came, because she really did know that this meant Julian had died in the food hall fire at the jail, and she really couldn't cope.

She stood at the doorway of the Post Office. Below, everyone was busy, unpacking, sorting, shouting at a good find.

"Where's Irma?" she called out, but no one knew.

She called others to open boxes, too. She said, "Look for anything familiar, and show everyone what you find."

Bean found a soft toy that she swore was her mother's. And truly, it did have the same look about it as Bean, and it wore a tiny red and purple scarf to match the one that Bean wore sometimes. Pinned to it was a fascinating brooch made out of half a walnut shell. Maud felt cold, chilled to the bone. What did this mean? Did Bean's mother die in the fire alongside Julian? She couldn't bear to think of it. She just couldn't.

It was Carlo who found Maud's father's box. She knew it was his; wasn't that a photo of her, an actual photo, not a lie? Wasn't that his mug that he never let anyone else touch, with TOUCH MY COFFEE AND YOU DIE and a tiny, cute cat on it.

Maud tried to feel something, summoning up misty memories of long ago, shells on the beach, digging into the delicate soles of her feet, her father way ahead, belting into the water with a great excited "whoop."

She pictured him easily, and her mother, too, although she didn't like to think of either of them. It welled up in her then, and in the others, too, and by the time Irma got to them they were all a mess of hysterical tears.

The younger children really didn't understand. Bean certainly didn't, although she carried the soft toy everywhere. Even Josh and Carlo struggled with the concept. Maud felt utterly alone and strange, as if she was dreaming a reality that didn't exist for the others. Josh was shell-shocked, immobile. For him it was the realization that no one was coming for him. For any of them. No parent would collect them. They all had their suitcases packed ready to go but they were going nowhere. It didn't matter. They'd keep collecting. Keep telling stories.

That was all they had.

"I hope Julian got his letters at least," Maud said, but then she knew; she knew. She opened up the mailbox where they had naively posted the letters and of course they were in there, all the letters to Julian and years of other letters that would never be collected or delivered. An animal had died in the box and there were bones and filth, and she hoped that Julian . . . she didn't want to think about Julian anymore, or about her father.

———

And then Irma found a red envelope delivered to the café.

———

The red envelope brought news for Maud and Bean and three others. They knew their jailed parents had died in the fire. Irma thought about hiding it from them but what was the point in that? She'd just be stealing their goodbye time, nothing else. Music played; so often it seemed to fit and Maud didn't know why. *People come and some people go* would be her song now.

Chapter Ten

Bean was excited, with Sally saying, "You're going to school!"

Irma sat with Maud.

"We're not going to school, are we?"

Irma wouldn't answer.

Kate pulled out a box of decorations. "Let's have the best birthday party ever!"

Josh said, "And let's find you the best clothes ever!"

Bean didn't know the truth but Maud did. But still she told stories about all the things. Carlo and the others were crying. "Who's going to tell the stories when you're gone?" Carlo said.

"You can all tell the stories! Just think about the people. And keep reading the magazines for ideas. You can describe one of those beautiful big houses and think about all the things inside."

Bean seemed bewildered. "Is my mum going to be there?" Kate had found her a new suitcase, a bright pink shiny one, and she mostly filled it with stuffed toys. No matter how much they tried to convince her to include clothing and valuables, she refused.

Maud packed all the valuables she could fit. Irma watched her admiringly. "Nothing sentimental for you?"

"None of it really is my story. Except for these." She added her father's belongings. Because Bean refused to pack them in her own case, Maud packed Bean's mother's items; the brooch made out of a walnut shell, and a locket. Bean would want them one day. Bean had not let go of the Beanie baby.

Maud packed the broken watch face from her father's box. She felt subdued, sluggish. "Will I need this for school?" she said to Irma. "But I don't think it's school."

Maud started to shake. "You knew, and you let Julian go?"

"I didn't know. I don't know for sure. I don't." But Irma knew that she wasn't ready to fight the system then. And deep down, Julian had annoyed her because he'd made a big deal of her drinking. She hated that. She didn't care that his father was a drunk; she wasn't a drunk. She wondered if one of the reasons these children invented their pasts was because their realities were too awful to remember.

Maud said, "We can't let Bean go. How can we?"

Irma thought of Not-Julian saying "good riddance to bad rubbish." She remembered those children in jail; some of them had protectors. Many didn't.

"Come walk with me," Irma said, and she and Maud walked arm in arm, doing laps of the shopping center. Irma could feel Maud vibrating. She was terrified and still a child.

"We can't let Bean go," Maud said again. Then, "I don't want to go. I don't want to die in a fire. I want my dad. I don't want to go. I want to stay here."

"I wish you could," Irma said. Already in the back of her mind she had an idea. She'd had it for a while, she realized, gathering clues and thoughts and visual cues. She led Maud to the furniture store.

"I don't want a nap," Maud said.

Irma showed her the fish tank.

"That just makes me sadder," Maud said. "I can't stand it."

"But the thing is," Irma said, "remember? We can't tell one fish from another. And these people, they can't tell you kids apart with your flesh on. They won't be able to tell you apart when you're just bones. They won't. We can try, at least. We can do that."

Chapter Eleven

They went first to the elevator that led to the parking garage. This was the one Robbo had told her definitely had a dead body in it. The children agreed; it was a customer who wouldn't leave, who wanted to steal everything, and they got stuck in the lift and no one ever thought of them again. They hadn't seen the ghost, but Robbo said he knew someone who had. The ghost would ooze out, calling help me, help me.

Irma got Carlo to help her get the doors open. He really was the most unflappable child. And there was a skeleton in there, some flesh still clinging. The smell filled the whole floor, something like old shoes, almost. There was no ghost. Irma, thick gloves on, rolled the bones onto a bed sheet and dragged it out onto the floor.

Next, she checked the freezer in the café, but there was nothing in there but sludge, regardless of the sign.

Then, with Maud, she ventured out in between the abandoned and ruined cars on the dark side to see if there were any bodies. She found one and stopped looking. It was picked clean by birds and bugs.

She found three or four dead dogs and rolled them up in a sheet, too. The more bones the better. She dragged them all to the stairwell that led to the parking garage. The stairs leading down were made of concrete, covered in green moss. The paper mountain shifted and sighed. She didn't think she needed to be too careful, but still she walked all the way to the bottom and placed the bones on top of a steel sheet. She wanted them to be found, or at least some of them. The paper mountain filled an entire third of the parking garage.

Chapter Twelve

The parking garage was full of very rusty furniture. Of the ghosts of old signs. Of old cars, parked randomly. The lines of human habitation could be seen in the exposed pipes and wires in the ceiling.

Whispering.

Abandoned things always cluster together. Cash registers, chairs, stools, crates, telephones, bookcases, racks, desks. They cluster even if no one chooses to put them that way. Things were stacked as if people thought they'd be coming back. Weird tanks, weird doors, amazing light fittings, all piled and stacked together. Skeletons of tables that looked like spiders.

There was a stuffed monkey, which Irma took for Bean. She piled suitcases along with the bones, cases filled with random belongings.

Then she set the paper mountain alight.

The fire blazed. No fire alarms went off; there was no longer any such thing. Irma went to the roof in an attempt to SOS signal, but nothing was big enough. In the distance, a car rattled along.

She was waiting on the dock in a state of practiced hysteria when they arrived. It was the same people who had taken Julian, but the man had a bright green suit on this time. Irma threw herself into his arms.

"Oh god, help us, help us. They've set fire to themselves, they've killed themselves, it's all my fault."

"I'm sure it isn't," he said, although the woman looked very uncertain of this. "Show us," he said. "This is Julie and Anne we're talking about? Known as Maud and Bean?" He named the three others who had been listed in the red envelope as well.

"Yes! Yes!" Irma hurried them. Smoke billowed out of the stairwell, and they could feel the heat.

"It isn't safe," the woman said. "No use risking our lives." She looked at her notebook. "Wasted trip." She shuffled through her carry folder. "Here, for you to file a report. And of course you'll be removed from the job for lack of appropriate care. These things do happen in all of our facilities, but they can be avoided." From the corner of her eye, Irma glimpsed the mannequin that held the magnificent fur coat. "Oh," she said.

Clever Kate, noticing, shook it off the mannequin and came up to Irma with it. "This is for the rubbish."

"Would you mind tossing this out for us on your way out?" Irma said to the woman. It was a risk; distraction was good, bribery was not.

The woman was too stupid to realize she was being bribed.

"Still, we should see," the man said. He and Carlo went downstairs and returned with a pile of charred bones, which they dropped at Irma's feet like they were dogs returning sticks.

Izzy baked cookies and cakes in a frenzy. They all clustered in the kitchen and ate tray after tray, Irma and the man. The stylish woman, safe inside her fur coat, asked Izzy her name. Irma had already told them not to answer truthfully, so Izzy said *Maria.*

"Do you want to see my garden on the roof?" Sally said. They have to stay out there. They die if I take them inside."

"You've built a good life here," the man said.

Chapter Thirteen

Irma received her notice a week later. It was in a blue envelope, not a red one, which was a relief. Maud and Bean (Lisa and Snag, Irma reminded herself. They are Lisa and Snag now) got on with business.

The envelope gave her notice of dismissal on grounds of incompetency. It didn't matter; she'd been told she was shit before and had bounced back. The notice gave her a date of departure, and said: *after this time-date you will be charged for accommodation at the highest possible rate.*

That made her laugh.

She tried to notice everything about her as she packed gold and silver and all the good jewelry she could get her hands on, all the paper notes. She noticed the massage chairs, never to be used again, and the small detail of the air vents, artistic and ignored. She noticed the "back in 5 minutes" sign on the book shop, and the dead plants in the hairdresser. She wanted to remember it all.

She packed her bag quietly, not able to face anybody. She couldn't cope. She understood now why the previous manager had run off without saying goodbye. It wasn't because he didn't care, it was because he did. It was too hard. And made harder because she knew that while she'd saved Maud and Bean (Lisa and Snag) the same future lay ahead of everyone else, and she was powerless to stop it.

—

It was Robbo who came to collect her, in a car. "You've been crying," he said.

"Oh god," she said. "Oh god," and he drew her into his arms. "It's Sally, mostly. I think I've saved Bean, at least for a while, but Sally . . ."

Maud watched them.

"We should take them," Robbo said.

"All of them?"

He laughed. "Just the little ones. Sally and Bean. They're like sisters. And Jesus. Jesus. What they'd do to Sally. They fucken HATE her."

—

Lisa and the other children went up to the very high tower to watch them leave. Lisa had a wig on and wore dark clothes. She looked different enough. It didn't matter.

They watched as the car drove away, past Factory, and Emporium, and Factory, and Emporium, and Factory, and Emporium, and Factory, and Emporium, until it disappeared into the trees.

MANDALA

CAT SPARKS

You didn't live here when the first corals sprouted. Lots of words bandied about, but coral's the name that stuck. Heaters cranked up to eleven on account of unseasonable cold. Pale, clear skies and gentle breezes ruffling through the plane trees' red and golden leaves. Woodsmoke hanging heavy scented. Parrots jostling magpies in our turquoise enamel birdbath. Midafternoons, the valley falls to shadow and that crepe myrtle used to stand beside the Pearson's place—you know it? Course you don't, your lot came second wave, storming along the highway up from Civic. Couple of shadowed hours later, the land around that tree has changed. Half dug up, without a sound, so I'm stickybeaking over the broken fence. Come twilight, Marston Place has totally dissolved. Most of Chisholm too as it turns out.

Should have kept an eye on those birds steering clear of Fadden Pines, like they could sense the danger creeping through. Even the sulphur-crested cockies—and you know they'll mess with anything—or eat it. Folks with houses fronting onto Coyne Street evacuated at high speed. Didn't have much choice—aside for the stubborn, digging their heels in deep, reckoning on the government to sort things. Government or the military. Somebody would come. Sooner or later. That's what governments are for, right?

My neighbor's always saying *come on, you know how it is*. So world weary, pulls this face, been through and out the wringer a thousand times. We argue the merits of civilization. Ancestors famed for fighting beasts, shitty weather and each other. Disease and famine, all that Bible-thumping fire. She sucks up yap from every shock jock tinfoil hat whackjob conspiracist: sentient bioceramics—give me a break. *DeepStateChemTrailBigPharmBioHack*. All fake news, Beth, I tell her, over and over. No one knows the truth and that means *you*.

She takes a deep, long drag on her cigarette. Tells us what she's telling everyone, how she picked up smoking the day this guy drove up from Melbourne, his dusty sports wagon stuffed with Marlborough Reds. How she figured, why not, what with the world half gone to hell. Do people even get cancer anymore? Can't remember last time she even heard that word. She reckons that Pearson girl did all right for herself. A family higher up the hill made room for her in their garage. Lotta that going on back then, total strangers opening up their doors. When disasters hit, reckon some folks take the opportunity to wipe the slate. But that coral . . . my neighbor takes another deep, long drag. Don't you go believing all that tree hugging Mamma-Gaia deep ecology. That coral killed itself plenty of people. The kind of folks get mourned when they go missing. That coral wiped them right clean off the face.

Lucky me has cousins further up. From the Temple (yeah, that's what everybody calls it) Mel has a sweeping view of furrows, swathes and grooves the corals carve into the valley's hard clay soil. Mesmerizing with slow progressions. Little by little she says she senses the shape of its intent. Everything happens for a reason says the sticker on her car. Ran out of petrol late last year, but that doesn't mean those words won't go the distance.

Mel never took to the late infusion of alien farm hypotheses. Nothing fell out of the sky. If coral wanted us penned like cattle, we'd be meat by now. She's talking along the lines of *Singularity*— read about it on her phone before the wifi shat itself. How machines beget machines beget machines, et cetera. Shares these thoughts with those who climb Macarthur Hill in search of truth and solace. We've always honored gods with monuments, she says, right after the speech about how the hill was named after the Missus, not her wool industry baron husband John. Course, it was unceded

Ngunnawal land before the settlers. Monuments. Reckon that's what the coral's building? Memorials to the vanishing human race.

Meanwhile, her friend Sandy weaves mandalas from brightly colored shredded plastic. Things that kind of look like eyes, which is probably how the blessing custom started. Sandy never claims otherworldly powers for her art, but pretty things remind her of her mum and the weaving kit she scored some Christmas back. They made dozens to trim the tree for all Decembers after. Sandy's weaving provided idle hands with busy work back when the Temple community was still small. People brought her cans of food in exchange to sit and watch. Some stayed watching through second and third wave evacuations—before we knew the coral was unstoppable. Before we saw what happens if you touch it. Hill sitters waiting for weaponry and violence to manifest. Will never happen, Sandy says. Because those things—those corals—aren't like us.

Lurid rectangles dangle in the lazy breeze, turning, twisting, spinning in updraft. Fierce sunlight reveals jagged plastic edges and cheap wool patches where the dye has faded. Sandy smiles when Tariq tells us folks are pinning mandalas to their door frames. *Amulets* is the word he uses. Wards against coral spreading up the hill. Not her business if folks use art to make themselves feel safer. She never claimed mandalas work like that.

From Wanniassa's highest point, the valley's unrecognizable. No colors, just a paste of dirty white protruding random prongs and stumps. Kill mechanisms prove unsuccessful: brilliant pebbles spew kinetic froth. Tossed a few barrels of napalm just for luck. Still waiting for the promised spaced based interceptors. Plan is to hike across the thickened scrub to cross Long Gully Road and then through Isaac's Pines beyond the ridge. Scrivener's Creek should still have water, not far from a clump of foreign embassies. Venezuela, Ghana and Qatar; empty now, the diplomats airlifted. Might be safe in there a little while. Last thing glimpsed before we leave, a flock of screeching sulphur-cresteds, swooping low across the valley floor, alighting on a rack of coral spears.

Old man Pearson needs a rest. We could all do with a break but he's eighty-something and can't walk any further. He's plonked himself down on a log and started scratching patterns in the dirt. Stumbling the past two miles so I'm carrying his pack as well as mine. Nobody says anything when I take it off his bony shoulder, but it's clear what everyone is thinking. Here and now is the place to do it, even if they haven't got the guts to say it, in this ragged clearing peppered thick with brown and olive. The old guy smiles at everything. Got no clue about the shit gone down. Keeps calling me Sarah—reckon Sarah must have been his daughter and maybe Sarah's out there somewhere waiting. I don't mind being Sarah for a little while. Old guy used to be some kind of artist. Got a sketchbook in his pocket, yellowed pages filled with pencil roughs and washy landscapes. Some of them are pretty good. Berry Island 1 Feb 1982. Ramsgate 9 August 1983. Pinkish gray, yellowish tinge, deep mauve pool, blue box, telegraph pole. Tamworth. Mascot. I wasn't born in 1983 but maybe Sarah was. *Would you look at that*, he says, pointing to what resembles funny writing on a log. Not words, just trails of long-dead bugs chewing their way through hardy bark. Old guy's attention has already shifted: light glazing edges of a clump of drooping amber leaves. *Marvelous*, he exclaims and yeah, definitely, he thinks I'm Sarah and no way am I going to contradict.

The footsteps come before I'm ready. I wave to let the others know I'm on it. *Dad, I've got to go,* I tell him. Forty miles through ragged scrub ahead crawling with things we don't have names for. *Marvelous*, he says, his eyes all water, pale and blue like skies now lost to time.

Nobody's gonna wait so I can bury the old guy, but I manage a covering of leaves while the light's still good. Sketchbook tucked into my pocket because you never know, I might run into Sarah out there some day.

GARDENS OF EARTHLY DELIGHT
CAT SPARKS

"Them two in the corner. The ones wrapped up in silver. Those would make a lovely pair of elves."

The broker squints through the floating detention center's musty ambience, searching through the mess of huddled forms. Forty bodies jammed into each cage, barely stirring from heat stress and exhaustion. "Might do," he says, sniffing loudly, wiping his nose on his damp stained sleeve. "How much?"

The guard names a figure and the broker laughs. "They're flotsam off the Risen Sea, not royalty or richling lah-de-dahs! I'll give you sixty for the both, providing they don't got nothing worse than scabies."

"Eighty," says the guard, crossing his arms. "Their bloods are clean. My cages are the cleanest on this barge!"

"So you reckon," says the broker, patting down his pockets for his purse. "Seventy—and that's my final. Take it or you can bugger off."

The men bump elbows to seal the deal and a fold of grimy notes passes hand to hand. The guard unclips a torch from his belt, light-spears the huddled forms until they squirm. "You two—get yerselves moving if you know what's good for ya,"

Thermal blankets shiver, disgorging tangled arms and legs. Thin brown bodies shielding eyes from the bright beam, nudging their way to the cage's single door. Stepping around the ones who can't or won't budge.

Silver scrunches as the boy clasps the blanket against his chest.

"Ed here's got an *employment opportunity*," says the guard.

"What kind?" says the girl.

"Well, aren't we the picky ones. A one-way ticket out of this shithole and 'asides—you won't be getting nothing better. Barge can only hold so many. Pass this up and you'll end up wherever yer sent."

He sniffs . . . *wherever yer sent* being well understood as code for *over the side.* The fetid harbor holds a lot of secrets.

Crinkling thermal masks, covert whispers. "We stay together," the girl states. "We must not be separated."

The guard dips the beam, slings a glance at the broker who nods enthusiastically. "Oh yeah, they're definitely a set. No question. Madame will take 'em both, for sure. No worries."

He leans closer. "Madame takes her job real serious. Reckon she used to be one of your lot. She'll see you straight and have yer back. Takes a hefty cut of coin but she's worth it all."

The guard waves over armed reinforcements before punching in a complicated door code. Dulled detainees groan and shift, taking an interest in proceedings, rattling wires and slinging slurs and insults.

The guard grabs the girl's thin arm to yank her through the doorway. The boy leaps after, abandoning the blanket to a sea of grabbing hands as the heavy steel cage door is slammed and bolted.

—

Madame raises an eyebrow when she learns how far the twins have come. Nobody travels far these days. Not like in the Before time when people wandered free and easy to far-off lands with names and edges, their borders crossed with a minimum of fuss and barter.

She frowns but doesn't contradict. Madame Bastarache didn't get to be uncontested Grandam of Calvaria Estate for decades without knowing when and why to listen.

"Give us yer names, then."

"I'm Pearl," says the girl, standing straight, "and he is Kash."

"You'll make a simply adorable faery duo, sister Pearl and brother Kash. Is faeries what you had in mind?" Madame eyes them over, her eyelids thickly painted petal pink. "You're skinny enough for faeries, tis for sure. Course you know you'll have to stay that way. And then there'll be the wing implants. Some folks don't take too well to that kind of thing."

"We will take to it," says Pearl.

Kash nods.

Madame beams, rouged cheeks shimmering with glitter. "Glad to hear it. Faeries are a sensible option on account of the *social distance*. You won't ever have to get too near." She leans in closer, nods with her chin at the vast and lavish Manor House nestled regally within a semicircle of poplars. "Manor children observe you dancing in the distance. Flitting through sunset dappled foliage." She raises her hands and waggles sausage fingers. "You can both dance, can't you? Never mind if you can't, we can sort you out."

"I dance," said Kash.

"Excellent!" says Madame, clasping hands together at her bosom.

"The wing thing—will it hurt?"

"Full anesthetic privileges," boasts Madame. "Never less than the best for my faery treasures. Plus, lefty food, so you won't have to starve yourselves for those willowy figures."

A crowd gathers, a hodgepodge mix of tall and short, fat and squat, hooked noses, flappy ears and tizzy hair.

Kash opens his mouth but before he can speak, he's drowned out by a voice from up the back. A soft voice calling "Tell 'em about the children!"

Pearl panics as a wave of titters ripple through the gathering.

"Hush now, Marlene," says Madame, "There'll be plenty of time for that once we've gotten these new folks signed and sealed."

Kash grips Pearl's arm. She pats his hand. "And we will be working alongside other faery folk?"

"But of course!" Madame places two curled fingers in her mouth and whistles, long and sharp. "Nettle dear, take our two new lovely treasures—remind me of your names again, my sweets."

"Pearl and Kash and we need to stay together—no matter what. Our home was—"

"This is your home now, darlings, and together always you shall stay! I'll make sure we note that in the Book."

The crowd parts amidst much shuffling and sniffling. A girl

emerges, garbed in a confectionary of lace and chiffon; mincing steps, careful not to trip. She winks at Pearl. "Youse can call me Nettie. Reckon ya wanna walk or take the carriage?"

Says Madame, "May I recommend a casual stroll around the lake past the weeping willows. Take in the sights and get suitably acquainted."

More muttering and mumbling as the crowd disperses.

"The old bag never lets me take the carriage," says Nettie once they are safely out of earshot. "She should try walking in these stupid shoes."

"So gorgeous," says Kash.

"The fuckers pinch," says Nettie, "not to mention shatter easy on account of them being glass. I still got scars from falling off the last pair." She tugs at her hem to expose the damage. Kash bends for a closer look, but Pearl can't take her eyes off the immense, luxurious garden vista wrapped around them like a cloak. Deep green as far as she can see, dotted with ornate fountains. Sculpted boxwood hedges, cypress trees reaching heavenward, like arrows. Occasional crumbling ruins out of place amongst such symmetry and balance.

An old man in long white robes ambles across the lawn with the aid of a gnarled staff. Vanishes into a distant copse. The lawns are amazing. Everything in this place is amazing.

"First thing to know, don't mind the animals," says Nettie once they've left the crowd behind. "Not a one of 'em's for real. Not dangerous, all totally built for show."

"Not real how?"

"Mechanicals," she continues, "but you could never tell from looking. They stink every bit as much as the real thing."

The twins nod, because if it's one thing they are familiar with, it's the stench of starving, feral beasts with matted fur and dirty claws coming at you once the lights are out.

But the animals gamboling on the lawns are different to anything they've seen; so sleek and healthy, clean and beautiful. They pause to admire two mighty loping creatures. Freeze as one tags the heels of the other till they tumble in a playful heap.

Nettie laughs. "Like kittens, really, only bigger. Black one's jaguar, the stripes is called a tiger."

"But not real?" says Pearl.

"Hell no," says Nettie, slapping the air. "But they'll still run a mile if you try to pat them. Authentic programming in memory of the beasts that once were living. Lots of things are memorial in this place."

Kash wants to speak but Pearl gives him a nudge. First thing's figuring where they stand. Who to trust and who must be avoided.

The list of things she wants to ask grows with every step. Lefty food? And what about the children—are they dangerous? She's known children who would shiv you with a shard of glass for half a moldy crust, but Calvaria does not seem like that kind of place.

Nettie wipes her nose on her wrist. "Spose she'll want me to rattle the entirety." Takes a deep gulp of air before beginning.

"Calvaria's what they call *Italianate*. You know: topiary, obelisks, orbs, columns, cones and domes. Focal points to lead the eye, providing balance and a sense of *drama*." Nettie strikes a theatrical pose and rolls her eyes. "Whole thing's inspired by the Greeks and Romans. One pinched it off the other—I can never remember which way round it goes."

Calvaria is the neatest place Pearl has ever seen, all clean, geometric shapes and lines. Climbing roses and lilypond terraces. Marble lion's head fountains spewing crystal water.

"And Madame Bastarache," asks Pearl, "is she *Italianate* as well?"

Nettie giggles. "Lotta rumors going round about where she's from and what she might be hiding under those skirts—*if you know what I mean*."

Pearl doesn't know, but nods. "What did Madame mean about the children?"

"Nasty little shits," says Nettie. "Don't go near them tis my best advice."

Nettie's limp becomes more pronounced as they continue. But Pearl is too distracted by a fortune's worth of lemon trees with overladen branches to ask why. *Fallen lemons unclaimed on the grass.* Bunny rabbits, plump and fluffy, unconcerned by people walking near.

After an hour spent crossing vast swathes of verdant, spongy lawn and a thousand wonders, including hedge mazes and sky glistening with unnatural sheen, and miniature versions of famous structures from old magazines: Arc de Triomphe, Acropolis of Athens, Rome Colosseum, the twins are shown to a little cottage nestled amongst others. Each one different, every garden blooming with curling fronds and pudgy blossoms, thick, fleshy leaves, creeping vines in shades of green with silver-gray stripes.

"All yours," says Nettie. "I'll leave youse both to settle in and tomorrow we'll get started on the training." She spins on translucent heels and heads back along the leaf-strewn path, pausing after a few steps. "One more thing," she calls over her shoulder, "mind you don't get up to anything you don't want *that lot* knowing about." She nods in the direction of Calvaria's Manor House, gives a cheery little wave and totters off.

Peapod cottage says the engraved plaque cemented to the ivy-covered wall. Small, but neat. Less pokey than it seems from the outside. The kitchen table has places set for two. A fruit basket, fresh baked loaf and cheese.

Kash lunges, tears off chunks to stuff into his mouth.

"Hell's sake . . . use the knife!" Pearl's mouth waters as she sits and reaches for the cheese. Their last meal had been two days back. Watery gruel bulked up with insect protein.

"This can't be real," she says with her mouth full. "Gotta be a catch. There has to be."

"Wing implants."

She nods, cringing.

"And tigers. Maybe we turn out to be their dinner."

"This *lefty* food is tasty."

"Maybe it turns into poison in our stomachs?"

Pearl shakes her head. "But why bother? They paid for us, they must want us for something." She casts her eye over the kitchen: grainy burled wood with earthy mottling. Smooth floors of ivory painted brick. A hearth, blue and white patterned wall tiles. Dangling copper-bottomed pots and pans.

A well-thumbed book with a bright yellow cover sits, partly obscured by the basket's rattan bulk. She tugs it free and flips through tatty pages.

"Whassat?"

"*The Types of International Folktales: A Classification and*

Bibliography." She holds the page up close to her face. "Print's too small. Smells musty."

"Like a catalogue of faeries and stuff?"

"Not really. There's no pictures."

He shrugs. "Somebody ripped them out, maybe?"

Closer examination reveals jagged tears in several places. She closes the book and puts it back on the table. "Kash—the mansion song we followed could *only* be about Calvaria." She closes her eyes and sings:

"When we gaze in silent rapture,
On our many mansions fair;
We shall know how sweet the promise
Of a home, forever there."

She opens her eyes. "Finney's favorite song. Remember?"

Kash nods, his mouth too full for speaking.

After slaking their thirsts with jug after jug of water, the twins discover two identical bedrooms snuggled side by side. They take the smaller, falling asleep as soon as their heads hit pillows.

———

"There's a room for each—youse get that, right?" says Nettie, standing at the foot of the bed, a wad of papers clutched against her chest. "I knocked but youse were totally dead to the world."

Pearl and Kash exchange groggy glances.

"Isn't another family moving in?" says Pearl.

Nettie snorts. "Calvaria Estate is a unionized workspace—no overstuffed migrant shantytown bullshit here. A house per family, a private room for every employee. Locks if you want 'em. Madame is very strict."

Pearl clears her throat as she clambers to her feet. "Has to be a catch. Nothing comes for free in this mean old world."

Nettie shrugs. "Catch is you gotta dance where and when she says and follow the health and safety guidelines."

"Meaning?"

Nettie leans in closer. "Meaning you gotta follow *all the rules*. Don't go places you're not supposed to go. No poking noses where they don't belong. And where they don't belong the most is the

Manor House and anywhere near the bratty *richling* spawn. We might be sprouting the wings and horns, but those folks are the freaks—trust me."

Richlings. A familiar concept, even if the names differ from place to place: the bling-bling bourgee booshi-boo; uberiche and stanky caked casholes. What remains of every country has them. Every city, every settlement one step up from camp or slum. Lucky ones who've managed to secure a bit of breathing room. Only not like this. Pearl has never seen anything like Calvaria. So much space and so much green. Even the light itself is kind, so unlike the scorching scour of the open sea.

Pearl trails Nettie into the kitchen, blinks at the extra food the girl has brought. Nettie activates the hotplate to brew coffee.

"We've been following the songs," says Pearl, transfixed by a mound of strawberries. "Songs passed along from cousins, strangers, friends. Whispers traveling all the way across the Risen Sea, hollered boat to boat and raft to raft. Everyone knows someone knowing someone knowing someone, but no one we met ever found the mansions."

Nettie shrugs, her attention on the coffee, rich aroma scenting the whole room.

"Calvaria's what it looks like," she says, "a big old garden filled with mechanicals and blinged up, modded faery folks. Sign the contracts and you'll be sweet for life."

"And if we don't sign?"

Nettie shrugs as she dribbles coffee into turquoise ceramic mugs. "Folks like us don't get second chances," she says. "Do youse take sugar?"

"We're signing," says Pearl."

"OK then," says Nettie, "so what's the problem?"

"No problem," says Pearl firmly. "No problem whatsoever."

Kash, having drained most of his cup already, rifles through Nettie's basket to see what other treats might be in store.

—

Air thrums with the starts and fits of musical rehearsal. Horns and strings and drums and flutes all vying for attention.

"Come on, Pearl—there's nothing to it. This tech's as sharp as razors. Watch me." Kash steps aside and gulps a breath, flings his arms out as if conducting a symphony. Surrounding air explodes in a bouquet of vibrant pinks and blues and yellows shimmering with gossamer and glitter. He pirouettes, twirls and poses, apparently multilayered wings subtly adjusting to each movement. "Bit of a trick to it, but you catch on quick."

Kash slows to watch as Pearl closes her eyes and throws out her hands in a clumsy flap, almost tripping over her own feet as a blaze of holographic color envelopes her like fire.

"You got it! Careful—wings will settle down as they take shape."

Within moments she's strutting with confidence. "They're holographic! Weightless. I can change colors just by thinking!"

"Well duh," calls out Nettie from a grotto festooned with small pink blossoms. "What did you think they were gonna stick in your back? Leather flaps? Supposed to be a faery, not a pterodactyl."

Pearl pauses. "I'm still . . . We're still . . . Wait on . . . uh oh!"

Nettie laughs and slaps the air as Pearl tumbles. "Should have warned youse about overclocking. Takes a while to get your balance. Richlings love to see us falling on our arses, but best leave the laughs to the hinkey punks and spunkies. Boggles and leprechauns get away with messing up, but our kind gotta be getting the steps right."

"Or what?" Pearl asks uneasily.

Nettie pulls a face. "Or Madame makes ya line with all the other double left footed stumblebums tripping over each other on that overgrown basketball court behind the oaks. Drills you like a sergeant major till every move is perfect! Seriously, ya got better stuff to do."

A vibrant, startling blast fills the air—trumpets and other assorted brassy reverberations.

"The grand parade!"

"I'm not ready," stammers Pearl, wide-eyed, getting up and dusting herself off.

"Sure you are—you got the hang! Stick to the middle and copy me. You'll be right."

Whip cracks split the air, while a powerful horse drawn coach thunders toward them, all creaks and rattles and splintered fury. The driver doesn't appear to have a head. The contraption slows, dust subsiding as the parade starts taking shape and form. Scenes from the well-thumbed catalogue on their kitchen table spring to life:

A brace of dandies in fine green brocade jackets; hags with their unbound hair all dressed in white—red eyes from dramatic weeping and wailing.

Little boggles, all pointed knees and ears and elbows, flicking elongated tails, sniffing the wind in hope of murderous scents. Green ladies apparently fashioned from thick twists and coils of ivy.

"Come on then youse two—what are ya waiting fer?"

Pearl yelps as Kash grabs her hand and yanks her toward the rapidly thickening throng. Faery folk and other kinds emerging from their secret places to join the parade.

"But I'm not ready. I don't know how to dance!"

"Copy me," shouts her brother, words drowned by strumming harps and beating drums in a range of shapes and sizes. She almost trips over a tiny wrinkle-faced man brandishing a shoe in one hand, hammer in the other.

And Pearl can't help but laugh out loud at hairy stomping hobgoblins and white waistcoated piskies with green stockings and pointed shoes, following brazen Cernunnos, horned god of the wildwood who leads a white horse with a silver bridle.

The parade picks up momentum, lumbering and meandering across dewy grass, coiling toward the Manor House and then away like a whiskey sodden serpent. Never getting too near, nor far, nor out of reach. Figures glimpsed in the top-floor windows, faces pressed up close against the glass.

The troupe do not perform for their own amusement. Big stone balconies and gray steps slowly fill with onlookers in elegant attire. Men and ladies, poker-faced, stiff jackets laden with sparkling jewels. Small children in pinafores with bright bows and shiny shoes. Waiters in their black-and-whites serve refreshments on silver platters, bowing before proffering their trays.

Kash waves along with other exuberant faeries, performing dramatic curtsies and blowing kisses as flower-scented confetti plumes and flutters, mixed with petals, leaves and butterflies.

Richling children watch the passing parade in stillness and silence. Not running, jumping, squealing or reacting. Only staring.

"That was weird," Pearl says to Nettie once the parade's tail has curved on past and the performers break away to attend to personal assignments. "Are the lords and ladies of the Manor always so—"

"Frosty?" Nettie cackles with raucous laughter. "They was positively joyful today. Ya wanna catch 'em when they're in a mood!"

"But those children . . ."

"Don't even look at 'em," says Nettie, tugging a waft of diaphanous fabric free from a rose bush snag. "That's us done for the day then," she adds. "Dunno about youse, but I'll be getting out of this kit and clobber."

Pearl deactivates her wings, scanning for Kash amongst the scattering parade. One moment there, the next one vanished. If she's lucky, he'll turn up sprawled under a willow, entwined with a couple of beautiful, silk-haired boys. If she's lucky. If he hasn't pushed his luck already.

A rainbow blur streaks through the air, then *bounces off* the sky. "Wait—what was that?"

"Stupid bird," says Nettie, glancing up.

"It bounced . . ."

"Well duh. Must have gotten its circuits fried." Nettie checks for Madame before easing out of her shoes. "Like I told ya, they're not real. Mechanicals, same as the tiger."

The bird dips and turns, aims for open sky only to bounce off the invisible barrier again.

"But birds aren't extinct," says Pearl. "We had pigeons in the camps. Seagulls too and noisy miners. Gulls used to fight over scraps with rats."

"Yeah yeah, but all the pretty birds have gone—check that one out. Totally manufactured. Look at the stupid bobbles on its head!"

"Used to catch the birds and eat them. Rats too. Anything we could get hold of."

"Sounds gross," says Nettie distractedly. "Your brother seems to be finding his feet."

"That's my Kash. Nothing bothers him for long. If there's a way in anywhere, he'll find it."

"Yeah, better mind he doesn't go hooking up with wrong sorts."

"Wrong like how?"

"Wrong like not supposed to be here. Which is pretty darn

wrong if Madame finds out. Check the manual in yer kitchen. Anything not listed there's forbidden."

"I found it."

"Well, then ya know what's what."

"It's kind of wordy."

"True," agrees Nettie. "Short version: pretty much anything from European folklore passes. Everything else, steer way clear."

Nettie skips off before she has to answer any more of Pearl's annoying questions.

———

Pearl's flipping through *The Types of International Folktales: A Classification and Bibliography* back at Peapod House when Kash eventually rocks up. Wings deactivated, deep green smudges on his pants.

He slings her one of those looks she's become accustomed to since they crossed the Risen Sea, presses an index finger against his lips, points to an ornate, iron wrought light fitting, leads her by the wrist outside into the neat little garden. He sashays, pointing here and there: a peculiar bloom, a stone rabbit, a water sprinkler. "Whole house is bugged," he whispers, "and probably some of these trees. Artificial, loads of them, monitoring all kinds of stuff."

She follows him to a bubbling brook where they plonk down on the grass. Opens her mouth to speak but he cuts her off. "You'll never believe half of what goes on in this place."

"Kash, we have to be careful. At least until we know who and what we're dealing with. I found out a few useful things. Like what the Manor family's called. There's two in there: Ahujas and Eadburgs. Owned these grounds since way before the wars. Generations hooking up to keep their fortunes close. Right back through and beyond all the way to the old-world wars! Spilled a lot of blood to keep it, too."

"Old news," says Kash. "Plaques set into the steps say all that shit."

"What—those big gray ones out front? After the parade? What were you doing sneaking up there? What if you'd got caught?"

"Chill out, sis. Sneaking up to the stairs and back is a rite of passage in this place. One of them, anyways."

"One of them? What comes after the stairs?"

He grins. "Other rites. Other passages."

"Shut up, Kash. I don't want to hear it. We've come so far. Don't you go putting our safety on the line."

He shrugs. "A bit of fun is all. It's what this place is all about."

"For richling families, maybe. Stankys don't give two shits about us. We're decorations. Lawn ornaments. Useless trinkets to impress other stanky folks. Uberiche wars is what it's all about. Nettie reckons richling families have their own drone armies. Robot soldiers, autonomous tanks. Fighting each other cos there's nothing better to do. The ones not rich enough to go to space."

Pearl gestures skyward, takes a deep breath. "They're disgusting. Could be feeding starving people, fixing the world back how it used to be. Bringing back the animals. I hate them."

"Don't say that. They're our rice and roti."

"Monsters is what they are."

"And now we're monsters too," he says, "fed special food to keep us skinny, sprouting holographic wings. Small price to pay, if you ask me."

"So long as this is all we end up paying."

Kash shrugs. "Pixies can get us anything we need. Coffee and real chocolate! Banana syrup and cling peaches!" He stands and twirls as his wings unfurl and illuminate.

"Kash—we've got a good thing going. Don't go fucking it up for us—OK?"

"I'm not fucking anything!" he says, raising both hands. "Not yet anyways," he winks, then starts back to the cottage.

She shakes her head, but follows. "This place is straight out of our dreams. Lovely gardens way beyond the Risen Sea. All those folks who managed to get out? Remember Kip and Shay and Finney sneaking off into darkness? Promising to send for us if they made it somewhere safe? Not a peep from any of them—not a single one. I know they would have messaged if they could."

Kash shrugs off the suggestion. "Doesn't mean they didn't make it. Maybe they just forgot about their old lives."

He's not listening. Kash stands in front of an antique full-length mirror holding a beaded dress against his chest. Tossing his head when hair falls in his eyes. Cleanest hair he's had since they were kids.

"You don't forget your people," she says. "Not ever."

"I haven't forgotten," he says, shifting his weight to reach for another heavily beaded dress.

Pearl leaves him to it. No point arguing, because despite being twins, they are nothing alike. Kash is afraid of everything right up until the moment he isn't. She's always had to be the adult. The one to take control and make decisions. All the hard stuff, it always falls to her. They'd both be dead already, and he knows it. But the second they're halfway safe, even if only for a day, Kash shoots off like a rocket or evaporates like dew. See him now and then he's gone, embedded firm and snug into the nearest cranny: drug den, play pen, done and dusted, niche, all trussed and busted. Boy's all for hearty partying until the very last. She admires him in a secret way she's not prepared to share because she can't stop worrying about what happens in the moment after, where their next meal or bed or boat is coming from.

She's staring at the sturdy beams holding the ceiling high when the front door slams. Kash slipping out into the dusk. Bread uneaten on the table, him already trusting it to be there when he returns.

Pearl's mind floods with guiding songs; all about the summer-land of bliss. Songs making her believe in life and lands beyond the stinking barges, baking sands and Risen Sea.

> O wand'rers of earth oppressed with care,
> There are many mansions up there;
> You're welcome to come with us and share
> In those many mansions up there.

Mansions peopled with silent, staring *uberiche*, at war with each other over slights a century past, or further. Have they any concept of the world she and Kash barely clawed free of?

She will make Kash understand. They'll live their lives in Peapod Cottage dressing up and blending in, living small, their safety snug within Madame Bastarache's fat and calloused hands.

—

Pearl's half asleep when the rain begins, wakes sharply when it ceases. Throws back covers without thinking, dreaming till her feet sink softly in damp grass. Droplets sprinkle on her shoulders, bled from deep green heart-shaped leaves. Oblivious to cold when the world's all apple blossom, streaky pink and speckled white, silver-barked and double bloomed with ruffled petals.

One lone druid, white robes muddied at the hem, shambles past one of several ruined towers, stabbing the sodden turf with his gnarly staff.

She stays under the safety of the dripping willow screen, wondering what she'll do if he looks back. He doesn't stop or turn or even pause, keeps on moving till swallowed by foliage.

She pauses, enjoys the luscious scents of broken turf and worm churned mud. Life pulsing; chips and cricks of unseen insects, rustling leaves and the warble-whit of birds.

Hair damp from willow drips, she abandons sanctuary to track the druid's passage, arms scratched by slapping branches, trails twist and wind like trickle streams—and there it is, a cottage, like their Peapod, but more higgledy and crooked, burdened with thick ivy and small roses.

Musty scents waft from within; sharp tangs of herbs and spices unfamiliar. Peeps and screeches, a mix of high and low tones.

Tentative steps, careful not to tread on snapping twigs. Prepared to flee at the first curse hurled in anger.

No roost of pigeons cooing softly in dim and misty half-light. Instead, a well-worn chair like those used by security guards monitoring flickering brick-sized screens, its backrest draped with a moth-eaten crochet jumper. Old-fashioned headset—the kind covering both ears. Cracked brown plastic boxes embedded with lights and gauges. A transmitter: humming, droning, throbbing, occasionally spitting out a garbled line or two in crackling static.

No songs here, only strings of numbers, spoken in richling tone, all static crackled. "One. Seven. Three. One. One. Nine."

A childish voice once the crackling subsides. "Zwei. Sechs. Drei. Drei. Elf. Neun. Neun."

Chimes from an old-world clock, followed by music, sweeping and surging, high to low pitch, thick and garbled as if underwater. Tones to make her skin crawl. Pearl backs out before the druid finds her. She'll tell Kash and they'll come back in daylight.

Halfway home, and there's the druid, harmless in the open, bathed in gloaming. Perhaps he's blind, navigating familiar paths and passageways, feeling ruts and furrows beneath well-worn leather shoes, tapping compacted earth and squelching grass.

Her faery slippers flit like gusts of leaves. Pausing whenever he plants his staff and cocks his head to sniff the breeze. Leading her down a winding path shaded by dappled leaves and moss enveloped branches. One final turn into a clearing lit by stabs of silvery starlight. At its center, a wall from a long-demolished cottage, gnarly trees and shrubs grow close, yet keep their distance from the grim and ancient stone.

The druid places his palm upon the wall, eyes closed as he mumbles incantations, then shuffles off, scattering dead leaves with the hem of his dragging robe.

For sure he's blind, but she waits until he's gone. So much more than a wall; a shrine encrusted thick with mementoes. Tattered cards and faded photos. Strips of cloth and dangling chains. Letters with all the words rained off. Blank-faced dolls and teddy bears nailed through.

A wall of secrets, loves and loss. Betrayals and Hell knows what else—things she doesn't *want* to know. But then she spies something familiar, something to make breath lodge in her throat. A locket pinned atop a faded yellow card printed with *Come to the Sunshine Belt*. Breaks a nail wrenching it free, clutches it tightly in her palm. A glance over her shoulder, but the druid is long gone, and the hedge gargoyles remain indifferent.

———

White Rabbit is what they call the smoke-filled mossy grotto where faery folk spend their downtime. Pearl's heart hammers as she enters. "Take a look," she says to Kash, dangling the locket before ganja-glassy eyes.

He sits up, snatches it. "Finney's. From his mum. Was his sister's only—"

"Only she got killed and yeah, if his beloved locket made it this far, so did Finney. He's here somewhere, or once was."

"Where did—"

"I'll show you. Was pinned to a memorial wall."

One of the hubbly bubbly smokers—a pixie lounging upon a

mushroom shaped divan—coughs up a lungful of pungent smoke as he struggles up to sitting. "Stay away from those mazes, man. They lead straight to all kinds of crazy—"

"Our friend was here," Pearl snaps. "We have to find him."

Both Pearl and Kash glare at the mushroom pixie, who shrugs as he continues dragging on his pipe.

Pearl feels her face flush crimson. "We lost everything," she tells him. "Everyone."

Kash loops his arm through hers and drags her out of White Rabbit, back into the crisp, evening air. Whispers, "I met this guy who might know something".

"About Finney?"

"About the comings and goings in this garden and all the other gardens of earthly delights."

"Earthly what? What other gardens?"

"Come with me late tonight and you gotta promise not to make a scene. Want folks to talk, you gotta shut up and listen."

Kash is blessed with the gift of blending into background scenery, becoming an integral part of whatever's burbling and fermenting beneath the surface.

"Kash, if he's here then—"

"Then we'll find him." Kash gives his sister's hand a friendly squeeze. "Trust me."

———

"Don't stare," Kash warns as they approach one of the forbidden follies huddled like a sleeping beast in darkness. "Wanna see something amazing?"

She stops. "I'm not going anywhere near the Manor House—and that's final!"

"Nowhere near the house, I promise. And we won't be breaking any rules. Well, not many and it won't only be the two of us."

"Kash . . ."

"Shhh."

"What are the follies for?"

"Follies aren't *for* anything. They're decorations. This one's supposed to be Castillo de Kukulcán from Chichén Itzá—see the steps?"

She's never heard of such a place, but he's already clambering up the streaked gray stone. She places each foot carefully. No handholds. Heights scare her, but when it comes to Finney, she's up for taking chances.

Six grinning faces waiting when she reaches the topmost perch. A bottle of wine passes hand to hand.

"Just in time for the show!"

"What show?" Accepts the bottle as it's thrust her way. Takes a small sip, knowing Kash is watching.

More people bump and jostle across the chill stone surface, squeezing into available spaces, cheering loudly at spectacular explosions, none of which seem to be doing actual damage.

"Budge up, gorgeous!"

She moves out of instinct. The speaker grins, flicks his gaze to one of the others. "Oh my god, what are the Eadies packing this time?"

"Couple of Pukguksong-2s" replies someone further along, binoculars pressed tight.

"Get outta town—where they gonna go scoring valuable antiques like—"

"Shit, will you look at them fly!"

Sky explodes in a flurry of electric rainbows; jagged stabs and sparkling arcs smudged and streaked across the bruised and clouded haze.

"Can't smash the force shields," explains Kash, "but doesn't stop them trying."

A million questions, but now is not the time. Pearl waits, stealing glances. Familiar forms and faces, but many she swears she's never seen before in Calvaria's Grande Parade. The grounds must be larger than she thought.

The overhead war reaches its peak, fracturing into harmless fireworks. Spectators bump and shift. Kash nudges and a new boy squeezes between them. Can't make out his face beneath the hoodie until a lemony starburst splatterpaints the sky.

"Skink," says Kash, "meet my sister Pearl."

Skink nods.

She nods back, trying not to gawk at his lizard skin, all rough and ridged, like bark. Large bright orange circles around his eyes. No nose, no ears.

"We're enemies," Skink says with a voice as gravelly as his skin. "I'm not supposed to be here."

Kash laughs and pulls a spliff out of his jacket pocket. "Lotta folks not supposed to be where they wash up," he says, lighting the tip with the battered zippo she recalls him trading from a Somali deckhand—one of the dozen or so times his intuition saved their lives in transit.

"What—you're from another garden?"

Skink nods as he takes the spliff, puffs upon it with thin lizard lips. "And we're totally whupping your arses with superior ordnance," he says.

Kash laughs. "In your cold-blooded dreams my horny bro . . ."

Pearl frowns. "You're *hiding* in Calvaria? Are there others?"

Skink's reptilian eyes swivel toward Kash, then back to Pearl. "Kash already asked me. Sorry, but I've not seen your friend."

Undeterred, Pearl pulls the locket from her pocket, dangles it up close for Skink to see. "Found this pinned to—"

Skink wraps his bobbly fingers around the trinket, tucks it back inside her pocket in one swift, fluid motion. "Best be keeping it to yourself. Never know who's watching."

She leans in closer. "Tell me about that wall. The one with all the old stuff stuck all over it."

Kash presses his thigh against Skink's. "Come on, bro," he says softly. "What's the big secret? What do we need to watch out for?"

Skink clears his throat with a muffled croak. "Wall's a memorial to the ones who disappear."

"Disappear?" say the twins in unison.

"Those Manor House children," Skink says, uncomfortably. "Thing is," he adds, "they're not children. Not really. They're *development delayed.*"

The twins fall silent, so Skink continues. "As in, the parents pay for special treatments to suppress aging and maturation."

A point-eared faery barges in, hijacking the conversation. "Ain't right nor natural, for certain." She waves her silken arm in a sweeping gesture. "Ain't none of what we're doing here true natural, of course, the difference being how you and me what works here, we sign up for what we get. Professionals is what we are."

She jabs Skink with a bony finger. "We're earning decent livings, whereas those overcooked little richling brats, they don't get a say in nothing, sometimes till they're way up in their thirties. Forties even if you believe the stories—not that I do. Not all of 'em. Some says parents want to keep 'em cute and small and safe from all the harms of Earth."

The faery shuffles closer, fixes her birdlike eyes on Pearl. "Forty years—just imagine—stuck in a body looks like ten, dressed up like a doll and likewise treated—so what if they'll be kicking on a couple extra centuries, that's no way to treat a human being. And it makes them mean and sharp and cruel way more than brats of a natural kind. Take my word for it, you wanna keep your distance!"

A hush falls over the gathering. They've all heard this story before, thinks Pearl. *So why has no one thought to mention it?*

"Where do the children take the disappeared?"

"Into the Manor House," calls a solid voice from further along the wall.

"Stay out of the mazes," says another. "Sometimes there's traps. Sometimes there's hunting parties."

Pearl recalls the faces staring out from the high windows. The ones who never smile back when she waves.

"Don't get taken," says Skink, swigging from his near empty hip flask. "Your Madame's crafty, but her clout only extends throughout Calvaria. Beyond the hedges, you're in no-man's-land."

Murmuring and muttering. Seems everyone has a story.

"What about the druid?" says Pearl. "He goes wandering every-where. I've seen him."

"That mad old druid's been here longer than anyone," says Skink. "Longer than the Madame before your Madame. Story says the children kept him prisoner in a cage for twenty years. Cut up his brain and let him go, eventually, so the goblins reckon. Not sure if it's true or not. All the goblins here are full of shit."

———

Next Grande Parade performance is thick with cucumber-nosed trolls, their tails long, hair lank and filthy, jewel boxes clutched against their chests. A brace of uldras riding Labradors and naked laumes tangled up in weaving. A Welsh hag faery and a couple of water nymphs, skin drying in the blousy breeze.

Pearl clocks other creatures embedded in the motion. Things

she's certain are not listed in *The Types of International Folktales: A Classification and Bibliography.*

When the parade is done, Kash drags her aside. "Wanna see something amazing? He drags her across a lawn and then another, over the gently rolling hillock to a point under a shady tree offering a good, clear view of the Manor House's west aspect. Large white framed windows look over the grounds of the estate.

"I'm not going closer," Pearl says. "Not after what Skink told us."

"Relax—you don't have to move from this spot." He unshoulders the brass telescope he's been sporting lately, slung beside his decorative pouch of herbs and jeweled curved blade. Yanks it to its full length and aims it at the windows. "Third one along. Hang on, I need to adjust the focal length."

She shifts uneasily. "I don't like this. We shouldn't be spying—"

"There he is!" exclaims Kash. "Looking out." He lowers the telescope and passes it across. "See for yourself."

She takes the brass contraption from his hand and aims.

"I can't see . . . no, wait . . . Oh my god!"

She freezes, staring. Finally, she lowers the telescope. "That's Finney."

Kash grins. "Sure is."

"But it can't be."

"Why can't it be—he's standing right there!"

"But he would have sent for us."

"Pearl, we were homeless. How were messages supposed to find us?"

She presses the telescope against his chest. "We need to stand where he can see us."

He slings it across his shoulder. "What we need is get inside the house."

"No!"

He points to the window. "Finney's alive and now it's us who's got to get him a message."

Pearl stares at the big white window until horns sound for afternoon dance rehearsal.

—

The radio room, as Pearl has come to call the druid's grotto, has a chill to it a few degrees below the garden's shady understories.

A cold and musty, forgotten corner filled with faded, half-grasped memories.

The druid's seated, back facing the door, surrounding air humming with blends of electricity and white noise. Sound as undercoat for other messages. Formless, timeless whisperings searching for somewhere safe to settle.

He hums along to the song he's sending out into the ether. One she's heard so many times about the summer-land of bliss. About the land beyond where there's no night. Songs luring innocents from land onto the Risen Sea, most never to be heard from again.

"You've got no right," she says loudly.

He doesn't respond so she shakes him by the shoulder.

The druid ignores her, focused on his broadcast, mouthing words soundlessly.

"Tell me how to get inside the Manor House. My friend Finney's in there. Do you know him?"

The druid says nothing.

"Look at me when I'm talking to you!"

Tired old wheels screech in protest as she wrenches the chair around. The druid gazes up with pale rheumy eyes. His lips still moving, thick tears streaking down sallow cheeks.

Pearl stares back at the old broken man, his robes filthy, hems blackened with soil. She groans and shoves the chair away. The druid sits for a while, staring at nothing.

Eventually, he staggers to his feet and ambles off into twilight, stumbling and unsteady. Shuffling through his nightly rounds with Pearl keeping a wary distance, wondering who else might be watching.

Temperature abruptly drops. Looking up, nothing to see but oppressive hedgerows neatly clipped. The druid's song gets fainter. She hurries to keep pace. Too easy to get lost in the sea of mazes bleeding into other mazes with patterns only discernible from high. Which has to be the point, but it's too late now, she's made her choice, that druid's going to help her, like it or not.

A blast of icy wind stirs up swirls of browned and yellowed leaves. Skies contaminated with the purplish bruise of Calvaria's defensive shield. Hedgerows replaced with a stretch of open garden. Sleeping lions and blank-faced statues.

No sign of the druid, but ahead at fifty paces stands a sturdy slab of vine encrusted Manor House wall. Antique stone, solid and unmoving, a relic of the old slow years before technology swelled and surged and broke the world. Vines probably older than she is, growing strong. She's climbing hand over hand as the sky explodes with the now familiar phantasmagoria of pyrotechnic frenzy. *To have so much and even think about destroying it.* Pretend warfare, intentional developmental delay. For what? The tarnished, rotting ruins of a gilded cage? The face of a boy half turned into a lizard?

The higher she climbs, the colder the wind snatching at her flimsy faery threads. Flinching at detonations—everything in this confection of illusions feels so real. Are the vines bearing her weight synthetic? Thoughts vanish as the marble balustrade is within reach. She clings tightly until the sun-bright fireworks disintegrate, then clambers up and over the side before the next one blooms. Crouches on the cold stone, gargoyle still, in case anyone is watching.

Dusty stone littered with lost leaves. Rusty window locks choked with age. She crawls up close, steals a peek through grimy glass. Inside, a vast and empty room. Shadow-brown furniture. Leaden chandeliers.

The stiff, jammed handle eventually turns. Wood shudders against her shoulder, then she slips inside. Musty scents enveloping; antique woods no longer growing wild. Darkness fading as her eyes adjust. Dusty drapes have her itching to sneeze. She buries her face in her elbow till it passes. Heavy furniture. A piano. Paintings of people in frilly cuffs and ridiculous ballooning skirts.

Pearl moves away from the window and kaleidoscopic skies. This room is only half a room. A half-partitioned doorway beckons.

Treading softly—used to stealth, having crept across a thousand floors in search of life-sustaining morsels. Only from those with a bit to spare. The kinds of lies she's had to tell herself.

But this is different. She's not stealing. Pearl's reclaiming moments and memories stolen from her and Kash and millions like them.

Through the half-partition, another lighter room with grander windows. More detail in the painted lords and ladies, floral patterned rugs and carved armrests.

Starbursts filtering through glass: burnt umber, ochre and sienna revealing a silhouette of charcoal deep. A man in a jacket with his back to her. It's him for certain. She doesn't even need to see his face.

"Finney."

Soft, but loud enough.

He tilts his head. "Don't come any closer."

"Finney! I knew it was you! It's Pearl. Kash made it too. Come on—we can find a place to hide you in Calvaria!"

Glassed skies beyond him shiver with kinetic luminosity. "Too late," he says.

"Nonsense—let me help you. Come on!"

Finney turns, takes a few steps, his movement accompanied by a peculiar sound. Familiar, but out of context. She can't place it.

The fiery sky begins to ebb and fade. As he moves into a dusty shard of light, her breath sticks in her throat. Finney is only human from the waist up, his torso grafted onto the body of an animal, perhaps a goat or miniature horse. Hooves clopping on bare floorboards. His back fitted with a child-sized saddle.

"You never should have come here," Finney says as a final missile scars the smoke-stained sky.

—

When Madame talks, everybody stops to listen. That's the law in Calvaria's magnificent faery kingdom because Madame is the one who gets things done. The one who connects the dots and mends the bridges when mistakes are made—and they so often are. Calvaria Estate is more complicated than it looks.

She wears a grim expression, but her eyes are flushed with kindness. News of trespass and apprehension travels fast within closed wall estates. A throng of Grande Parade regulars are gathered to learn what will happen to the twins.

"Those wicked, wicked little children," Madame says. "Should have introduced you properly to Marlene when you arrived. Things might have gone a different way." She sniffs. "Poor girl was a faery too—and a pretty little thing—but we had to have her overhauled. Did the best we could with what the children left, but the *limitations*, as you can see."

Sidestepping and rustling as the crowd disgorges Marlene: a sluglike creature with a human face and caterpillar hands, shuffling forward, cherry lips pressed together in a thin line of disapproval.

"What's done is done," Madame continues, "and there's no going back from it. No use crying over spilt milk. I've never been one for saying 'I told you so.' *The Types of International Folktales: A Classification and Bibliography* is supposed to be a closed book, but a promise is a promise, and I will never go against my word. You two will get a page in the next edition."

At Madame's feet, a plaid blanket conceals a quivering shape.

"On the bright side, your contracts hold up watertight. This is your home now, like I promised. You will never leave and—as requested—you two will never be separated."

She nods at a hairy hobgoblin, who bends to snatch the blanket away. The crowd gasps at what lies underneath.

"Although," Madame adds, "I'm not sure what we should call you. Kashpearl? Pearlkash? Neither sounds quite right. Happy for you darlings to come up with a new name for the register. The goblin builders are hard at work on Peapod Cottage as we speak, combining your two bedrooms into one."

The double-headed creature thrashes, not yet possessing full bodily control. The crowd shuffles back to give it room

"You have my word, I'll never sell you on to Prince Balthazar's Menagerie of Oriental Curiosity and Wonder, or Mammadou Wynae's Carnivale of Biological Rarities."

Madame seems very pleased with herself until the creature lets loose an ear shattering howl, its voices different timbres and out of synch, yet achieving powerful volume.

"Back to work then, my faery treasures. Word from the house is the Nobs are expecting new choreography for a victory dance!"

When the last of the baby trolls has shuffled off and the nixies have swept leaf litter from the floor, Madame hitches her trailing skirts, mind already distracted by other things.

She pauses to inspect a white robed shape slouched against a drystone wall. "What is this dreadful mannequin doing here? Pumpkin? Nettle? Have a couple of boggles come and clean this mess away immediately. Those dreadful brats abandoning their broken toys all over my nice, neat gardens."

Madame steps over a gnarled staff attached to a pale arm sticking out of a pile of dirty linens, hems thickly encrusted with mud. A headless torso, the neck stump dense with coils and springs and tatty fiber-optic cable.

Behind a low hedge, a boggle squeals, holding high his prize—a druid's head, features expressionless, glass eyes aimed at the blue dome sky.

Note: Lyrics quoted from *Many Mansions Up There* by R.F. Lehman, Public Domain

AIR, WATER AND THE GROVE
KAARON WARREN

We've got food for *seven* days. Water for twelve. Because sometimes the Saturnalia doesn't end when it should. It's hard for people to settle, after. Mid-slash, mid-fuck, mid-theft. Do you just stop, then carry on with your suburban life? Leave things half done? Most people prefer to see it through. Take the extra hour or two. Chase away the doldrums for a bit longer.

We've stocked up on hydrogen peroxide and oxalic acid. There are going to be a lot of bloodstains and they'll be coming in after with their bundles of clothes, "Oh, I had an accident," is a good one. Or "I was helping an injured person," is another, not one of them wanting to admit what they've been a part of.

Seven days where nobody works. Nothing is open. There are no arrests, although crime occurs, it does, I've had friends murdered. I've lost worldly possessions. But you're not going to be arrested, not during Saturnalia.

We'll be called out to deal with carpets and mattresses. We've stocked up on pepsin powder for those, and we'll charge for travel. It's a good business, stain removal. Especially after Saturnalia. I hate having to go into people's homes, though. Other homes are dirty and they reek and I don't feel safe there. You never know what people will do, what they consider normal, in their own homes. I've had clients stand naked watching me. I've had food offered that I wouldn't feed a dog or a goat. I always need a shower after being in a stranger's home.

Though people are mostly dull these days. They care less than they used to. They're tired and old. I know I feel older.

We've stocked up on sodium percarbonate. That's good for chocolate stains and there will be plenty of those. People think they are original, as if they're the only ones to cover themselves in the stuff. I say, "Seen it before. Seen it plenty."

I'm lining up my stocks, counting the bottles, when my son says, "I'm not staying home this year." He's twenty-one and perhaps I can't keep him safe anymore. "This year, I'm going to be a part of it. I'll help you with the clothes when I get back."

"You should stay at home." I try not to cry. I don't want to make him feel guilty. That is never a good reason to do anything. "We can watch it on TV."

"I want to be the one on TV. Can't I be happy, for a little while?"

"Don't go," I say. "I'll make you a steak dinner tonight. And tomorrow night a chicken dinner. I'll cook you your favorite food every night for a month." He nods, and he eats two steak dinners, but when I check his room at midnight he is gone.

He's slow, though, and loud, so I hear him stumbling to the front door, kicking the umbrella stand as he does every single time, and knocking the Saturn Tree we keep high, under a light, as he does every time as well.

What can I do? Tie him down? Join him to commit our own Saturnalian acts, in our own home?

Maybe it is time to let him free.

He fumbles with the door locks, as he always does, forgetting which turns which way, and how many turns, and whether or not he's already turned one or the other. He looks almost like a shadow in the dark, not a real person at all.

I don't say, "This is why you have to stay home," because it's my fault he's that way.

I'm the one who did it to him.

—

It's been twenty-three years since the return of the *Tarvos*. Can you call it a return, if the ship never made it back whole? I was only four when it set out amidst a wild fanfare, because they like to make a fuss, don't they? The rocket scientists. As if they are the ones who'll save us all. They're still like it, years on. Discovering new planets. "Earth-like" ones, and you find out it's all bullshit. You know? What they mean is Earth ten million years ago when the only things here were crawly little worms or something.

Speaking of which, there will be dirt to get out. Some of them get buried, up to their necks. They showed it on the TV last year. Being used as a toilet, one of them. If those clothes had come in, I would have burnt them and paid the difference.

I was nine by the time the Tarvos reached Saturn. Those pictures of the swirling north pole made me dizzy, that's mostly what I remember.

Most people were more interested in watching it suck in samples of the icy particles orbiting the planet.

We've stocked up on bottles of filtered water. The drycleaners' greatest trick is that air and water are the best cleaners, at the end of the day. We can charge what we like, but our basics costs can be minimal.

I was fourteen when the *Tarvos* returned; I remember that clearly. All the adults so excited by the return of the thing, the rest of us not caring all that much. Happy that they were distracted so they'd leave us alone, and we could party. Skip school without anyone noticing.

But we were all out there, watching the sky for a glimpse, when it blew up.

They calculated wrong, or something. Didn't think the ice would be as heavy as it was. It's all about the micro millimeters, isn't it? And they get it wrong.

—

We've stocked up on methylated spirits, and we've got plenty of clean absorbent paper. Candle wax stains are always a problem. People get carried away, and there's spillage. There are fires, too, but that's not up to us. Other people manage that. Or don't.

They love the fireworks, don't they? And the fires, they don't care about safety or property. They'll set things on fire purposely, to see them burn. In the shade of the Saturn Trees, all of it seems to make sense. Is it because of the *Tarvos*? How it burnt on entry, exploded in the night sky like fireworks?

Six crew onboard (and the ones with children mattered more, according to the media), all of them now with streets named after them. Suburbs.

It felt like rain but the drops were solid and stayed heavy on your skin if you left them. I wiped all the drops off but some clung to my hair, and my ears, and in my eyebrows.

People dragged their children inside, because there were parts raining down as well. There were deaths, though not in our neighborhood. I heard one girl my age was pierced through the heart by a shard of metal.

Workers in Bangkok offices, Singapore noodle houses, sheep farms. Miners dredging gold and oil and zinc. All of them went out and stood in it. Most of them felt it.

The ice particles, melted. The pieces of ship. The other pieces. Those poor astronauts.

The astrologers told us they predicted it. That this was bound to happen, it was fate. Saturn was in the eighth house and that meant horrible death.

"For who?" people like my dad asked. "What, all of us?"

"Prepare for the grave," the astrologers said.

Wasn't long before many of us wished we'd been one of those early ones. Knocked down flat by debris. Gone in a flash.

We all feel the melancholy. The taller the trees grow, the more the melancholy sinks into us.

We're all whirled up into Saturn's dark heart now.

———

The ice, the ship, the others. All of this rained upon us. The ancient alchemists were partly right; for them, Saturn designated lead. They believed the planet was made of lead. And these water droplets, when they were tested?

Traces of lead. Surprised them all, the so-called smart ones. They hadn't thought that.

Once the particles touched ground, they crystallized. It was beautiful to watch; we all thought so. Especially once they started to grow.

In the forests. In backyards. In bowls set as centerpieces. On roofs and walls, on the heads of statues, in footpath-cracks and sewers.

So many crystal trees.

Each of them growing up, up, toward Saturn.

My father worried that the magnetism would shift the earth off its axis, but he didn't finish school. I told him lead isn't magnetic.

It looks like silver, he said. He was one of many who broke pieces off, grew more trees.

Share the wealth, he said. The beautiful crystals shouldn't only be for the rich, he said, and they weren't.

The richest people in the world used to be the ones who owned the land that provided the metal. People like me didn't get a look in. But now we all have our own trees; they grow anywhere.

Air quality testing showed that the Saturn Trees were not only beautiful, but healthful; they attracted lead particles, literally sucking lead out of the atmosphere.

Places whose high lead content led to birth defects and early death grew more and more of them. We all did. All you needed was a small piece. Every home soon filled with the air-purifying trees. Every school. Every hospital.

Some trees grew tall as houses.

Some trees grew fat.

The trees were so beautiful you wanted to watch them all the time, and people did.

It seemed the trees absorbed light as well as lead because the world seemed duller, anywhere the trees grew.

They bore no fruit.

Not at first.

Saturn is time. Saturn is the Bringer of Age. Saturn is the bringer of melancholy and dismay. We didn't notice the effect; the tiredness, the melancholy. The graveness.

We didn't notice.

Not at first.

———

I scoop up the shards my son's clumsiness knocked off and drop them onto the upper branches of our Saturn Tree. If I had the patience I could sit and watch them being absorbed. It's hypnotic. It would distract me from thinking of him, out there amongst it. There are no good people this week. No one who will look after him, bring him home to me.

I wasn't allowed out during the first Saturnalia. I stayed at home, listened to the dogs howl. By the time I was 16, though, they were mandatory and I was out amongst it. Blind drunk most of the time. Those crystals! And no regret the next day because who remembered anything? It's why we don't know who his dad is. Could be one of many. I don't blame any of them. I don't feel used by any of them. It's how it was, how it still is.

I don't like having methylated spirits in the house. The alcohol smell of it takes me back. I've not touched a drink since the day he was born and we knew. We could see what he was. So many of them like that; damaged by the booze we'd drunk during Saturnalia and beyond. We didn't know. We didn't think. All we knew was that the crystals, dissolved in alcohol, provided an almost instant high and somehow negated the hangovers. Sparkle, we called it. They still call it. I spent a month in a state of numb euphoria; I didn't care when Saturnalia started or finished.

He came out smelling of booze. I swear it. Not that sweet baby smell they are supposed to have. And his tiny eyes, his flattened cheekbones.

"We're seeing a lot of these," they told me gravely at the time, as if that made it better. Holding that tiny baby, his tiny head, and they say no one was to blame. Because no one wanted the Saturnalias stopped; they still don't.

My son; what worries me most is what happens when I die. But I probably won't die before him. He's clumsy, so accident prone. His liver is shit and he's impulsive. I can't see him lasting too long. If he survives this Saturnalia, out there with the lunatics (not lunatics though. We're not talking about the moon. The Saturnine) then perhaps he'll be safe for another year.

He should be safe, and return to me and our quiet, clean life. He can help me move some heavy furniture around. It's a good time for change, after Saturnalia. Good time to pretend things are different.

If he comes home in time he can eat with me, but I don't mind eating alone. It's a quick clean up. No spillage.

We are in the Saturnian days, my father used to say. He liked to quote from things he didn't understand. "The days of dullness, when everything is venal," he'd say, nodding as if we should know what he was talking about.

I feel dull. We all feel dull, but they numb that with alcohol. Drugs. Sparkle. With sex and dancing, throwing themselves to the ground in a passion they do not feel. These times are when Saturn is unbound. When we are all so grave on the inside, if you cut us we'd bleed tears.

My father always did call me fanciful. But I loved the classic story of the god Saturn, bound with woolen strips beneath the city of Rome to stop him leaving, unbound only during Saturnalia. I think Saturn is with us now, unbound because we worship him with our dullness, our melancholy.

Satin stains badly and is difficult to clean. I can do it, though, if you give me the time, some cool water and some delicate soap.

I hope my son comes home unbloodied.

I hope he kills no one.

—

He is back. He leaps and jumps about like a frog in a box; I've never seen him energized before. His clothing is in disarray, stained, his hair is shaved on one side, his face cut, his chin dark, his arms bruised, his legs bleeding. He talks without taking a breather for an hour or more, while I clean his cuts, feed him and give him tall, cold, sugary drinks. I sponge the stains with cool salted water, then rinse a dozen times with clean water. The rest I remove with hydrogen peroxide.

Dark days follow. After the excitement fades and the ordinary returns, the melancholy seems more intense. As if Saturn is angry that the revels have ended, and is exerting his power, laying his lead-weight against us. Some communities leave up the banners and bright ribbons, but they fade with the sun and become sadder than anything. I could wash them in vinegar but that wouldn't be enough.

I try to help my son. I put him to work, because work distracts, and I need him to keep up. We took in more purple stains than usual; he told me they were passing around a grape drink that tasted like medicine but that numbed the entire body. I tried to find this drink, to give him a taste, cheer him up but there were no supplies in town.

He carries a tiny Saturn's Tree with him everywhere, carefully, as if it was a full cup of tea.

Then a customer tells him about the grove.

"The greatest Saturn Trees you'll ever see!" she says. "And you walk in amongst them and can feel your blood racing, your heart so solid and strong, and you smile, and you should hear the laughter in there. Strangers all together as one. It's beautiful."

I think of our own Saturn Tree, how even standing next to it makes my mouth droop, and my eyelids heavy.

"That doesn't sound right," I say. The customer laughs.

"It's not really for people like you." She actually winks at my son, and he winks back, as if he knows what she is talking about.

He leaves with her. I tell her that he needs help and she laughs at me again, as if I am making things up, have invented all the hours I spent cleaning him up, trying to teach him.

He isn't gone long. He comes back quiet, but he seems happier.

"It's so beautiful there. The sky looks bluer than it does here. But she was wrong, that woman. It is for people like you. It's for everyone. Next time, can you take me?"

"Maybe," I say, the universal, eternally polite parental No.

—

Ninety-seven customers later, he goes out and doesn't return. I know where he's gone; I only wonder how he traveled. I call him. He says, "Come and see, Mum. You'll love it, you really will. I'll meet you at the entrance."

He sounds so bright I wonder if something has changed within him.

I set some clothes to spin and close the shop.

The streets are quiet with the Saturnalia well over. There is a low hum, a low moaning, I think, but I see that people are humming and I realize it is music.

I drive to Saturn's Grove. The sign is cracked, tired-looking; the o looks like an a.

From the moment I enter, I am filled with a sense of my own worthlessness. Pointlessness. I am uninteresting. Unlovable. I think the customer was right; this place is not for me.

There are hundreds of metallic trees, growing as tall as redwoods, wide as sequoias. I can barely see the top of them.

I find my son, his arms stretched around the base of one of them.

"Isn't it beautiful?" he says. He's never cared about anything before, beyond food. He reaches his hands up to swing on one shining branch. He winces, pulls away, and I see that his skin has reddened.

At the base of many of the trees are clothes. Perfectly good, most of them.

"What are these?" I say, smiling. I think *He brought me here to collect the clothes. It is kind of him, bringing me here.*

"People don't want them anymore," my son says. So I start to gather them up, to take home and clean. At least washing clothes gives me a kind of purpose. I feel giddy if I look up, so I look mostly at the clothes on the ground.

"We'll be able to get most of these stains out easily," I say. He was right; I do feel delighted now. Excited.

He doesn't answer. I thought he was behind me but no.

He has stripped naked and is already three meters up a tree. I haven't seen him naked since he was fourteen and insisted that he could wash himself. "This is the one. This is my tree."

I look up. "It's very high."

With my head tilted back, I can see that many of the trees have flowers at the top. Some are bulbous. Some brightly colored.

"I thought they didn't flower?"

"That's the others. That's each one who's climbed. As the tree grows, they reach closer to Saturn."

He drags himself up further.

"Don't go any higher," I say. I fall to my knees. I don't want him up there. "I'll make you any meal you like, just name it. And you don't have to clean the clothes if you don't want to. We'll find you something else. And we'll find you someone nice to be with and don't forget Saturnalia, how much you loved it! Only another ten months and there's another!"

But he climbs up. I watch him and want to follow him, but even the feel of the tree under my palm makes me sick. I sit at the base, waiting for him to come back down again. I can hear him crying.

"Son! Come down! You don't need to feel pain!"

"It's not painful," he calls, but his voice is shaky, withered. "I'll be down soon. Wait there."

I have to trust that he will return. I sort the clothes I've collected by material and color. People watch, asking questions. Distracting me. Until one woman says, "Do you need a hand to get all those things home?"

"I'm waiting for my son. He's climbing up. He'll come down soon."

The woman shakes her head. "Look," she says. She leads me through the trees.

Some have tiny thin trails of blood to the ground, crystallized. "Every last one of them climbed like he did," she says. "Step by step as if there was no other way. This one's my daughter's tree." She stands and puts her hand near a tree that dwarfs many around it. She doesn't touch it.

My son has become one of them.

There are others, lost like me, gazing up and weeping. The woman says to me, "The only certainties in life are air, water and the grave. Saturn's sons, Jupiter, Neptune and Pluto. The only ones he didn't kill. That's all that's real anymore."

"I'm going to get my son down."

I don't want to go up. The thought of it makes me want to cry and never stop.

But my son is up there, and I want to bring him down.

Each step is like climbing on sharpened knives. Blood pouring I don't have the strength. I can't do it.

"He won't come down anyway. There's nothing you can do. Once he's climbed all the way up, it's too late," the woman calls. She tugs at my ankles.

As if to demonstrate, one bright green bead of liquid drips down past my face.

Do I love him enough to die trying to get to him? I climb for another hour, making no progress, slipping backward, dragging the skin from my arms and hands, from my cheek. Then I'm stuck. I can't move up and down. Frozen.

"Stretch your fingers. Spread them. Let go. We'll catch you," they call from below, and I do, and they do.

"It's too late. He's so deep now, you'll never get him out, even if you get him down. They climb up there to die; at least it's a choice. No one has come back down again, not alive." My new friend shakes, rolls her shoulders. "I come back every now and then to take a piece of my daughter's tree," she says. "She's happier now her suffering has ended."

"What about us? What about our suffering?"

She lifts her arms. Smiles. The rest of her is shivering; only her lips are still. She reaches into her bag and offers me a small bottle of vodka. It sparkles. I shake my head at her; not that.

I cry then. I've always known I'll lose him, but I didn't know he'd choose to go. I cry, leaning against his tree, until I realize my tears are being drawn in. Absorbed.

I break a piece of his tree off to bury it. It is stained slightly with his fluids.

I make his grave in a tiny, tiny pot next to my other Saturn's Tree. It will grow if I look after it. Feed it. Water it. It may fruit one day, as do the trees in the grove. We watch them grow, the other grievers and I. I say to them, "Whoever said these trees don't flower? There are our children up there, fruiting." Sometimes one drops and shatters, looking like an arum lily, the corpse kind. Surrounded by crystals worth a lot of money, and I wonder if people will use them, if it will come to that, and what they'd call the drink. A friend brings me some Sparkle, and another does too, and once I remember how good it is, and forget all the rest, things are better.

—

I reopen my shop when I run out of clothes to clean. My job is so instinctive I can do it Sparkled or not.

Air, water, the grave.

And Sparkle.

DREAMS OF HERCULES
CAT SPARKS

Kanye aims his dad's nocs at the big, wide-open sky. Some folks reckon birds are lucky. Birds mean you can make a wish. Kanye always wishes for another Hercules plane. His vision sweeps in a wide arc, past the stackbots in a blur, past the dump and the concrete buildings, comes to rest upon the Hercules's sand-scored wreck. Not much left of it, or all the other good things he remembers back from when his mum was here.

He squints at the sky again. The black smudge in the far-off distance might be another Hercules; so hard to tell, with heat haze blurring the edges. Most Hercules turn out to be scrawny birds—occasionally an eagle, vultures mostly, now and then a lost and battered drone.

Kanye raises the nocs to double-check, holds them steady just in case. So much sky, not much of anything else—*which is how we want it*—his dad reckons. *No one tells us what to do out here in the Woomera Badlands.*

Kanye's boss of the compound while his dad's on R&R. He put Kanye in charge; said they'd only be gone a couple weeks, long enough to get the shit they need, which means he's due back any day now.

Any minute.

His dad knows all there is to know, like programming the stackbots that are building the ziggurats from crushed-up rocket cubes. Kanye's dad and his mates built BigZig where Kanye's sitting now. When they get back, they'll build a tower and maybe a mighty bridge.

When they get back from the Ram-and-Raid.

If the arseholes messing with the 'bots don't break them.

One 'bot's extended arms stack metal cubes like sun-dried bricks while another one injects sharp blasts of spray glue. Gellan's built a second platform up since yesterday. He must have figured how all on his own.

Another 'bot throws rocks at BigZig.

The persistent slam of stones against BigZig's side shreds Kanye's nerves.

"Leave it off!" he hollers down. Gets no answer. Gellan, Slate and their dickhead buddies will keep chucking rocks at BigZig's prison slits until they think of something else to do. Not much happens in Woomera, especially not with his dad on R&R.

Not since that time Kanye tracked along the railway line, dug under the fence and followed the Chinook trail.

That day still makes him want to puke.

He picks at blister scabs along his arms, sniffs and wipes his nose against his hand. Air smells worse than usual, on account of stackbots stirring up thick dust.

Kanye stands to stretch his legs as another stone clangs against BigZig's metal hide.

"Give it a rest, ya morons!" he shouts.

Slate yells back, drops his dacks and bares his pasty arse. Others copy, like they always do.

Stackbots screech with random bursts of groaning, grinding metal. His dad's gonna chuck a fit at all this mess: goats running loose and dogs tearing up the chickens. Nobody gave anyone *permission*, just like the time those guys built a trebuchet and started flinging cubes at the astronauts.

Still, dry air reeks of diesel and burning plastic, bright sun makes his sweaty skin itch bad. Hot air thick with fat blowflies—the only things that ever get fat round here—comes off the garbage, still piled up to mountain height even though the trains stopped coming ages back. Scavengers rooting through the filth rock up regular enough. Kanye's dad doesn't give two shits, so long as they keep away from the big machines.

And BigZig too, goes without saying. His dad says his future's invested heavy in cash-cow reserves there.

Prison slits were cut to let in air for the cash-cow crop. Kanye's only been in once—and not for long. Double dared, he'd entered BigZig, then stumbled out pretending he'd seen stuff.

Corridors stank of shit and piss, and rats ran across his foot. Swore he'd never go back in again.

Kanye watches the stackbot's arm unfurl like a creepy bug antenna. It's not supposed to be doing that. Those drunken arseholes got no fucken clue. He takes a swig of water, warm from his canteen. Flat and stale, it greases his mouth with petrochemical taint.

He can't visit his *secret place* while those drunks are messing with the 'bots, so he aims the nocs at the long, straight stretch of rail. Just checking. Hasn't been a train forever, not since that one piled high with yellow barrels that had propellers stenciled on the sides. No Chinooks either. No shrieking grind of hot metal at velocity; no Black Hawks buzzing high over the tracks. All of them plowing straight through, never stopping, full speed all the way to the astronauts.

———

He's back to scanning the sky for birds when something red-hot snickers past his ear. No wasps left so it can't be one of them. Fingers come back bloody from his head. One of those drunken fucks is *shooting* at him.

Not the first time shit has gotten wild and drunk and random. Gunfights have been on the rise, ever since that army convoy— trapped and herded into the BigZig compound. When his dad gets back Kanye's gonna tell him all about it. Those guys get way too shitfaced to be bosses.

Another bullet scores the ledge. Kanye halts, lost without the Smith & Wesson Uncle Jaxon says he should be packing always. Kanye slings his nocs and canteen, scrabbles on all fours in search of shelter. BigZig's exposed on every side, making him an open, easy target, the only thing protecting him is the fact those arseholes get too pissed to shoot straight.

Snatches of howling laughter carry on the breeze.

"That's not fucken funny," Kanye shouts. Anxious, seeing Gellan's second level near complete. Thick black smoke belches from the place they toss the giant dump truck tires. None of this is supposed to be happening.

Blur of metal, whizzing close to his bleeding ear. He ducks as bullets ricochet off cubes. He trips and scrambles, arms grazed and stinging against sharp edges.

Amidst a sloppy hail of bullets, he rolls and drops down another tier. Landing forces breath out hard. Hip hurts when he tries to get back up.

Bright blood smears and stains his shirt. Everything is happening too fast. Slate keeps firing, hooting and hollering whenever Kanye jumps.

Gotta hide. Guns are going off like crackers, bullets peppering metal all around. Kanye whimpers as a squirt of warm piss dribbles down his leg. Scrambles for the nearest prison slit in BigZig, prays to Hercules for luck, holds his breath, sucks in his gut and wriggles on his belly like a lizard.

Sharp things stab and snag his skin. He makes it through, landing on his hands, curls up tight until the shots subside. Even Slate's not dumb enough to shoot dead air. Kanye sits up, sniveling and tasting sticky dust.

Bright light spears in from outside. Everywhere else is dark. A foul stench—something's died in here. Something big. But everything hurts and all he can do is wipe his nose and work out what the hell to tell his dad. How Gellan thrashed the fuck outta that stackbot, messed it up, shooting guns and people just for kicks. How Slate is getting too big for himself, all the stackies reckon he's crazy, reckon he's dangerous, what with all the home-stilled booze he chugs.

Something stirs in the pool of darkness just beyond the slit window's bright glare. Kanye stops, strains to catch a glimpse. Prays to Hercules it's just a rat, but when it moves again, he knows it isn't.

Cries out as something emerges from the stinking, shadowy, all-encompassing dark. Kicks, propelling his body back until his spine slams against the wall. "Don't hurt me!"

Stays put, stares at the emerging figure. The oldest woman he's ever seen up close. Long fingers, bony like talons. Gray trousers and a shirt that badly needs a scrub.

"Are you ok?" she asks.

"Get away from me!" Tries to inch back on his arse, forgets he's up against the wall. "Touch me and I'll kill ya!"

She smiles. "No you won't. Give us a look at your arms and that ear. Caught yourself a nasty scrape, looks like."

Kanye whimpers; all the fight's spooked out of him.

"I'm Judith," she says softly, kneeling down and reaching for his arm. "Call me Jude—everybody does, or at least they used to."

She curls her fingers around his wrist, prods him gingerly in several places. Checks his other arm and then his ear. "Nothing broken."

Kanye snatches his arm away.

"So, what do they call you?" she asks.

"Shut up. You don't get to talk. My dad's the boss of everything round here." He gestures broadly at the bright and spearing light.

Old woman uses her knuckles to push herself to standing, then steps back, swallowed by the gloom.

Kanye keeps his back against the wall, remembers the words his dad uses—cash-cows—words he's never thought about too close. In his head, he'd pictured actual cows. Wouldn't even call this one a cow, she's skinny as a line of pipe.

"Please," she says, stepping back into the light, "I'm starving. The girl who brings me food hasn't come for two days."

Kanye stares through swirls and plumes of dust.

"Tell me your name," she says.

"You don't get to ask me shit. My dad—"

She clasps her hands and cuts him off. "Of course."

Her pants are gray like the suits on TV. Too big for her bony body. Bare feet. Toenails dirty. Pale blue scarf knotted tight around her neck.

"Your dad's been gone a while, hasn't he?" Holds him with her gaze. "That makes you the man in charge—am I right?"

"Too right." Gets up and brushes dirt off his pants, thickening the dust swirling through the air.

"Things aren't going so well with him away now, are they?" she says. "Can't see much from here, but I hear all sorts."

"Shut up! You don't know anything. You don't know jack shit."

"Thing about ransom prisoners," she says carefully, "is that nobody pays good money for a corpse."

The old woman sways unsteadily. Brings one hand to her head, then hits the floor with a soft thud, stirring up another cloud of dust.

There's a chain around her ankle.

She slumps forward, groaning, head resting in both hands.

"I'm in charge here," Kanye reminds her. "You don't get to tell me what to do. Don't you forget it, old woman."

"I won't," she says softly.

—

Three days Gellan has that stackbot running nonstop. Smoke pours from its grinding, screeching gears. Nobody knows how to shut it down. Gellan lost his shit and attacked it with a Super Dozer, that only made things worse. 'Bots are programmed to protect themselves—anyone with half a brain knows that.

What nobody knows anything about is Kanye's *secret place*. His dad never goes up top of BigZig, never checked how one cube came out dented. A space where special treasures can be stashed. The place Kanye comes to think about his problems.

He built a shelf on two red bricks. On it sits a spotted shell brought from a real live ocean, four brown falcon feathers—each one from a different bird—toy soldiers from some war he's never heard of. A lipstick: stay matte rose & shine. And his favorite thing—the 24-inch, plastic, US Army C-130 Hercules, with its Stars-and-Stripes flag on the tail and muscle-man stickers on both sides. The lipstick and a faded photograph are all he has to remind him of his mum.

The trains are starting up again and he doesn't know what to do. Rumbling and rattling, shivering through his bones. The ache that's been there since *that day*. Dad should be back from R&R already. Should be but he isn't, like a lot of other things that aren't.

Perhaps a lucky bird will guide him, but the sky's as still and flat as always. Time's past needing birds to help him. Kanye knows what has to happen next. He waits a while, then stands and tucks the Smith & Wesson into his dacks, picks up some stuff salvaged from his dad's office. Loads his pack, climbs down to the prison gate, gulps good air before letting himself inside.

Not much light in the passageway. Ignores flies buzzing on dead things in locked cells. Finds his cash-cow hugging her knees in a single shaft of dusty light.

"Brung you some food."

She's not half as old as he first thought. Grunts as she rips the MRE in half and scoops mush into her mouth with both her hands. Like she expects him to change his mind. Like she isn't taking any chances.

Random crashing from outside and bullets plink against Big-Zig's cubed sides.

Fucken tools have started up again.

The woman licks the last smear from the plastic pack and belches.

"You saved my life," she tells him. "And I'm grateful. Really grateful. You have no idea—you really don't."

Kanye sits, placing the gun just beyond the reach of her rusty chain. So she knows he'll use it if he has to.

"Nice boots," she says.

Kanye sits a little straighter. Black crocodile-belly boots cost more than sacks of marijuana. Only worn when he needs extra luck.

"They're all dead, aren't they? The other prisoners," she says.

"Not much value in them," he says, scratching his scabby arms. "Not like you. Slate reckons you're worth heaps."

She tries to clean herself with a corner of her filthy shirt.

"How about more water? Bucket's nearly empty."

He sniffs.

"And how about you tell me your name?" She crosses her legs and folds her arms in her lap. Chain clanks every time she moves.

"What's so great about you anyway?" he says. "Why are *you* worth big bucks? You don't look like a queen or anything."

She pushes greasy hair behind her ear. "You haven't exactly caught me at my best. I'm the Federal Minister for Environment, Infrastructure and Sustainable Futures."

He snorts. "Government, ay? Pack of liars, that's what my dad says. Stole the water, chemtrails through the sky, back-pocket, big-pharma weaponized diseases—AIDS and COVID, Pig Flu, Nypah, Hendra . . . So much bullshit brewed up to poison us."

She bursts out laughing and shakes her head. "Well, you sure have got yourself a bumper crop there. You forgot the aliens,

Bigfoot, mind-control labs and new world orders . . ." The chain clanks as she stretches her legs. "Don't give us government types so much credit for stealth and ingenuity. Keeping secrets from the public is harder than you'd think." She glances around her prison cell, "Although, I don't know. Out here it seems much easier than back home."

She's cut short by a piercing shriek. Not the stackbot—this time something human. The shrieking ends abruptly—which is worse.

Kanye's chest feels hot and tight.

Next comes machine-gun fire, metal slamming hard on metal, howling dogs and roaring engines.

"Name's Kanye," he says.

She leans forward. "Kanye, my government is doing its damnedest to build a future that's safe and sustainable for all. There's been damage done, for sure, in recent years. Big damage, slow responses. Mistakes beyond anyone's control. But that doesn't mean things can't get better. Doesn't mean we should give up on civilization itself."

She leans closer. "Nobody's trying to poison you and your father, Kanye. Help me get away from here. Back to where there's proper food and medicine. Come with me to Sydney and I'll show you."

More rapid fire and a muffled blast, big enough to rattle Big-Zig's walls.

Jude swallows hard. "Your friends are running feral, Kanye. Reckon it's time to take matters into your own hands, you know? Before it's too late. Help me contact my people and they'll pull us both out of here. You saved my life today, so I owe you one."

"No way. When my dad gets back—"

"He's not coming back, Kanye. If he was, he'd be here already—and I think you know it. Get me out of . . . wherever the hell this place is . . . and I'll save us both."

—

"Oh my god—fresh air!" she says. Shuts her eyes and breathes in deep. "But where the hell are we? What's this place called?"

They both duck as stray bullets whizz and plink.

He shrugs. "Woomera."

"*Woomera!*" She slides from a crouch to sitting, rests her

forehead on her palms and the fight kind of goes out of her. "They snatched me from Sydney—how the hell did I end up way out here?"

Both stare at the scene spread out below. Scattered fires burning bright and high, broken-down machinery—some of it house sized, people staggering about and firing. Dogs and goats. A bulldozer attempts to ram its way through the side of a rusted shipping crate.

Kanye clutches his gun against his chest, waves it whenever he speaks, like punctuation. "Fuckers got no fucken idea," he says. "Nobody's doing what they're s'posed to be doing."

She shades her eyes to stare out across the desert. "No wonder nobody's come looking for me. This really is the arse end of nowhere."

"Everyone knows Woomera," he says.

"Not for a bloody long time, they haven't. Got turned into a theme park or a museum or something. Sold off for mining too, maybe." She squints. "I can't quite recall."

"Astronauts know about it."

She almost smiles. "Haven't been astronauts at Woomera for a very long time."

"There's astronauts. I've seen them."

"In fact, there weren't even astronauts at Woomera back in the day. Rockets, yes. Mission controls and plenty of weapons testing, but astronauts no."

"Lady—I know what I saw."

She's not listening. She's squinting at the sky. Nothing to see, not even clouds, but a look on her face like she can see beyond the blue. She scrambles back into a crouch, checks her balance, peeps over the edge.

"Got my gun trained on you so don't go trying any tricksy moves," he says.

"Binoculars." She holds out her hand and he passes them over. She squints through the eyepiece, past the loudly malfunctioning stackbot that's jerking and spasming as it launches another random cube into the low roof of a demountable shed. Past the thick black smoke of the burning garbage heap and out into the desert, scattered with rocks and wrecks and human bones.

A bucket-wheel excavator lies on its side, half-buried under mounds of sand. Like a dinosaur. He used to have a book of dinosaur pictures.

"Hey—what's that wreckage over there. Away from the other junk—is that a plane? Get me there and I can get us the hell away from here," she says.

He stares at her with sullen disbelief. "It's broken. You don't know—"

"Shut up, kid, and listen to me if you want to get out of this place alive. Government satellites pass over this big old dump. Come and help me send a message, or stay up here alone if you'd really rather."

The gun weighs heavy in his hands. Protecting the cash-cow is one thing, taking orders from her is something else. So tired and his head hurts and what if his dad really isn't coming back?

He leads the way along the goat track hacked into BigZig's side. They're three tiers down when the rumbling starts. Horribly familiar. He can't bear to look—perhaps it's coming from the 'bots or from one of those random monster storms. Could be from lots of things, no need to panic.

Jude's face flushes with color as he feels the blood drain out of his.

"Oh my! Kanye—there's a train coming!" She jumps up and down and waves.

His stomach lurches like he's gonna spew. Spins around and slaps at her. "Stop it, ya fucken idiot! It'll see you!"

She's got this dumb look on her face. "Why—what's the matter? A train can take us back to civilization."

Kanye doesn't move, despite the raucous fighting on the ground not far away. He stares fixedly as the train approaches the compound. *It's all happening again.* The train zips through like a dirty bullet and his chest hurts from breathing ragged. He doesn't turn to watch where it is heading.

Jude nudges him as bullets fly. He slaps her hand away and keeps on moving.

"Where's that train heading, Kanye?"

He grips the gun tight like Uncle Jaxon taught him. He runs across a stretch of open concrete strewn with rubble, some of it still smoke-charred and warm. She follows. Air explodes with random weapon fire. Two women wearing knitted hats and oil-stained gloves gawk from beneath a tattered awning, but don't do anything to stop them.

But Jude stumbles to a halt, her bare feet leaving bloody footprints in the dirt. "Hang on! Kanye—it's bloody cold at night. We need supplies."

He waves the gun at a shipping container covered in skull graffiti. Jude ignores the dead man slumped beside it. Makeshift door swings off its hinge as she pushes past. She's banging around in there a few minutes while he's trying not to think about that train.

She comes out swigging from a canteen, wearing a big man's jacket with bulging pockets. Walks like a clown with her skinny ankles stuffed in battered trainers.

"First things first," she says. "Need to get out to that wrecked plane."

"Plane's fucked," he says.

"Doesn't matter."

She takes the lead. He dawdles, kicking stones and bits of metal. Not listening, but she's still talking, banging on about not being where she thought she was.

"Think I've figured out this place," she tells him. "One of those off-the-grid white elephants knocked up during the decade of big fire. A relic of the New Cold War—the kind that doesn't make it into history books. Back then they did what they had to do to make up budget deficits. Sold off slabs of useless, barren land to any bastards keen to pay for it."

Darkness falling, chill nipping at his bones.

"Drug lords, terrorists . . . Wouldn't get away with that today, of course—Jesus. Where did all this twisted metal come from?"

"Rockets," he tells her.

She trips and swears but rights herself. "Well, I suppose there could be old space hardware. Ancient British missiles. Black Knights and Blue Steel . . . that sort of thing. Brits used to test their nukes out here—did you know that? Early days of the space race and all that."

No point in arguing. He pushes on and reaches the smashed-up Hercules ahead of her. Doesn't look like much in the fading light.

"All right, this is far enough. Now we get to work," she says, short of breath, swigs on the canteen again. "Find me a bunch of fist-sized stones and scraps of metal."

He watches Jude trace huge numbers and letters in the sandy dirt with a stick.

"My tag," she tells him, smugly. "Kind of like a secret code. Military algorithms will pick it up via satellite, even if my ministry has written me off for dead. Which they might well have done—a month spells a long time in politics, let alone kidnapping. I'm heavily insured, so *someone* will be pushing for a rescue once my tag is scanned and verified . . ."

Kanye's only half listening and he doesn't look up, and he most definitely doesn't glance to the place where that train was heading. He slams down rock after rock in draining light as another explosion shakes the camp behind them.

His dad will fix it . . . his dad should have fixed it . . . his mum should never have left in that Hercules. If she'd stayed, his dad would never have got so angry. He'd never have shot the plane out of the sky.

"So, I'm guessing you grew up in all this junk," says Jude as she places rocks inside the letters.

He doesn't answer.

"Kanye, what's your dad been doing out here?"

He shakes his head too vigorously, stares at the ground and not her face. Walks away to collect another rock.

"He's been taking care of you—that's something. Loads of kids out there with no mums and dads."

Kanye slams his rock down hard.

"Why don't you tell me about the trains? Where they're from and where they're going? Gotta say, I'm surprised to find a functional line out here."

He stares into darkness. "Used to run through regular. Locked up tight, never stop, just push on through." He slams another rock down on the line.

She places one not far away from his.

"We used to try and guess what was inside," he continues. "Food and stuff, ya know. Good stuff from the coast, maybe. Kind of stuff used to drop out of the sky." He pauses to relive the memory. "Everything was different when I was a kid. Better—ya know?"

Jude nods. "Oh yeah, you got that right."

He searches for another rock.

"So, what happened? You followed the train?"

Kanye nods. Clutching a rock, he flicks his gaze in the direction of the tracks.

"And?"

He smashes the rock down, straightens, dusts his hands on his pants. Swallows. "Astronauts making people push yellow barrels into the ground. Cranes swinging big blocks of cement."

"Astronauts? Are you sure?"

"In space suits. Like on TV." Shakes his head, like he's trying to clear it. "People off those trains were sick. Infected or something. Astronauts kicked 'em over the edge, down there into the pit with all the barrels."

Jude's been hanging on every word, a rock gripped tightly in her hand. She drops it, rummages through the big coat's pockets. Pulls out a torch, slaps it against her palm a few times to get it going.

"I was saving this until we really need it, but . . . oh my god . . ." The beam cuts through darkness, moving as she moves. "Jesus . . . Kanye, those big shapes over there. They aren't junked planes or old British rockets."

She hurries from one mess of metal to the next, like she's looking for something specific. "These look like Dongfeng ICBMs, Kanye. They're not ours—and they definitely shouldn't be here. None of this should be here."

She kills the beam and backs away from the missiles. Stares up at the night sky, as if it might hold answers to her questions.

"My dad says . . ." His words are drowned out by a rising rumble loud enough to shake the ground. Wind tears at their hair and clothing as a long, cold shadow falls across their faces.

The moon hovers, impossibly big and low. Through streaming tears, Kanye's vision skews. Not the moon, but the underbelly of a Hercules. Smudgy images dance across its surface. All gray and white, like dead TV static.

Jude is laughing, waving and jumping, but he can't hear anything she's saying. He clutches the gun against his chest. His lucky boots are white with churned up sand.

Because the Hercules is not a Hercules—it's a Chinook with

tandem rotors, bright lights flooding stronger than the sun. Sets down and the back end opens, spills astronauts pointing guns and barking orders.

Jude is screaming. Kanye backs up until he's pressed against the broken plane that holds his mum's burnt bones. And it's not his uncle's Smith & Wesson clutched against his chest at all, but the plastic Hercules stuffed with special treasures: the seashell, feathers, lipstick, unknown soldiers and faded photo all tossed, tumbled and mashed against each other.

EVERYTHING SO SLOW AND QUIET
KAARON WARREN

Faye rose with the sun, slept with the sun. In the city, they used manufactured light in most of the public buildings and there were some who thrived in that artificiality, but Faye hated the shadows cast. Natural light was beautiful. Sunlight. Moonlight. Twilight. Dawn. Faye liked to walk at these times, gathering anything that caught her eye. There was a simplicity in this collection of castaway items that calmed her.

—

She slung a large hessian bag over her shoulder. When it was full she'd have to lean sideways to balance the weight. She was as light as a bird these days, although she ate well all day, nibbling on nuts. On the poached fish she ate each night. She was never hungry.

—

The sand was damp with the tide receding. She liked this time, the sand pristine, the tidewrack new and waiting for her. A long pale branch, unscarred although marked with strange lines stood sentry at the water's edge; she added it to her shoulder bag. Once around the next curve, she could see ahead to her work.

From this distance it looked like a fist raised in the air; a bit closer and it would be a whale cresting a wave.

She collected pieces of smooth glass, some beautiful, perfect shells, another piece of driftwood. She collected a bone.

Everything washed up on the beach eventually. Bones, skulls, all evidence of a failed world. Street signs, car license plates, huge swathes of plastic. She tended to pile the bones up on the dune line, gathering them in bundles that, in her dreams sometimes, merged, rose, and walked.

She collected a plank of wood, burnt, its bright paint all but blistered off.

—

The whale became a horse as she neared.

—

She sat for a while, gazing at her work. It had withstood a mildly strong wind, as well as sleeting rain, and the beating sun. It had attracted creatures; there were droppings of three or four different animals.

She spent an hour adding the new pieces. The horse was almost done but it looked static, and she wanted it to look like it was galloping, mane streaming, muscles straining. She imagined herself on that horse's back, riding along the water's edge, wind in her hair, the pace of it making her heart thump.

Everything was so slow and quiet. The waves, and the way the air hummed in the heat, and the rustling of the ti trees (and their glorious eucalypt smell) and the shifting of the sand; she could even hear that.

—

On the way back to her hut, she collected more things. Some for firewood, some for the sculpture. She left those on the dune line. She found a small skull, possibly a child's, and she left that there as well, surrounding it with seaweed in a makeshift memorial.

—

In her hut she showered the sand and sweat off and dressed in loose pants and a purple shirt. She kept all her clothes hung on the bushes behind her hut. She'd sometimes rinse them out but found the salt stiffened them and made them uncomfortable, so best leave it to the wind and the rain. It was time to eat then so she boiled a soup of herbs and onions on the small wood barbeque further up the beach. The smell made her remember hunger, if not actually experience it, and that gave her a pang of longing. It had been forever since she felt hunger. She had a collection of old cookbooks, washed up, thick with water, unreadable, but sometimes she flicked through them. They were from another time, when people felt hunger and desire for food. It was strange but at the same time beautiful.

The photographs made her smile. Some were of people on a beach like hers, others were groups of people at tables set bright with things she barely remembered. The photos were barely visible but there. Photographs! How you could capture a moment like that.

She ate standing up. Once she sat down, relaxed, her muscles would seize up and it was hard to get up again.

———

Then she fell ill for a time. She was bound to her hut and the outside drop toilet, unable to make it even as far as her fishing line. She lived off dried fish. She always dried half of her catch, a lesson she'd learned early on, when there were still others to talk to who could teach her how to do it. They used to laugh at a man who starved to death because he dried all his fish for the future; it was such a nonsense to think that far ahead. She did keep a store, though for those times when she was too tired to set the fire, and she was grateful for it now, and for the water tank she kept covered by large leaves. That water was sweet and as pure as it could be without boiling. She couldn't walk to her strawberries and snow peas, which she kept out of sand's way up dozens of steps.

It was the only time she regretted becoming invisible, an unneeded person, past her usefulness date. There was no place for her in society, not even if she wanted to join. No resources were allocated to check on her, help her keep healthy. Even if she could ride her bike the eighty km away to a doctor, she wasn't sure she'd be seen.

Or if anyone was there anymore. The nearest town was deserted, as if they all disappeared. Gases poured up from the center of the earth. You could see where they tried to plug it with outdoor furniture, engines, sacks; anything they could lay their hands on.

This is what inspired her sculpture, last time she'd passed through this ghost town.

———

She was glad that she no longer had cats living with her.

She never got into the habit of feeding them because she was never sure what would happen and didn't want them relying on her. She had seen animals starve before when things changed.

"Be self-sufficient" was another lesson she'd learned early on. Because support could be taken from you at a moment's notice. She'd lost her job and house in the city. Lost her voice. She still never spoke, there was no need to, beyond clicking at the cats. They clicked back at her. They were gone now, though.

———

She recovered; she always did. Much later, when she was better, she would find fish and crabs dead and rotted in the water cages and on the hooks, and that made her cry, for the waste of their lives.

———

She gorged on her strawberries and snow peas, experienced moments of pure joy for the freshness of them.

———

The beach was awash. She moved slowly, not fully recovered, but relishing every step. She found an ancient newspaper, still rolled in plastic. It was swollen, and so old it fell apart like sludge when she unrolled it. Tears came and she realized she was desperate for news of other people. Desperate to know if they were still out there.

———

She walked. She collected everything, keeping some things in her bag, placing others on the dune line. The salt air was tinged with something else, as if even here it was becoming toxic. The sky was purple, tinged with green. Beautiful, really.

Ahead the fist/whale/horse. She stood looking at it, inordinately proud of how real it looked, how beautiful . . .

Someone had added to it.

Had she been delirious, done that in a stupor? But there were things added she'd never use. Man-made items. Strips of metal, beer can plastic holders, ring pulls.

Furious, she went to pull this rubbish off, but then paused. She looked up the beach, in the other direction. The city lay that way, so far distant she wouldn't see it with binoculars or a telescope, but still she fancied she could see a dark cloud hanging over it.

She walked a hundred steps or so then turned back to see what this new artist had done.

It was good. They had added the movement she'd been seeking, and gathered more around, giving an illusion of community around the horse, of a herd unseen but following.

Faye cried. It was beautiful. And it proved her artwork had been seen. That she existed. But then panic took her. If there was someone else, where were they? Did they think it was their horse now?

Faye ran, her legs heavy, her feet lagging in the sand. But, hating herself for being indecisive, she turned back. The other artist hadn't destroyed her work, they'd added to it.

She added her own new pieces. Her eyes watered and she thought she better get indoors. One last touch and she stopped for the day.

She'd come back tomorrow to see if there was anything new.

—

And one day, perhaps, before the world ended, they would meet, and see each other, and talk as they worked together.

DOLL FACE

CAT SPARKS

The kids want to pat the donkey and the donkey doesn't mind. The mums, on the other hand, despise the clanking old contraption, biodiesel dribbling down its legs like clotted blood.

WHATCHA BRUNG US, COME ON, WHATCHA BRUNG!

Aloha Joe raises his arms, pats the air to shush their clamoring.

The little ones like plastic dolls with lurid bubble heads. They reckon that's how people look beyond the Great Divide, all goo-goo eyes and pouting painted lips.

Used to be that way, some of 'em, Joe says, a sort of, kind of truth.

The mums and dads want medicines, but he can't help with that. Instead, he crates in memories, charging through his bulbous, crusty nose and they'd pay without a squeak, only these folks don't have coin or much besides, abandoning such things when they crossed on over.

The Great Divide sounds like a mountain range, but is, in fact, the crumbling ruins of the Dispensary with a portal-gateway fixed.

The Great Divide is no longer great, nor fit for purpose—human-kind or other. Aloha Joe keeps telling, but no one's listening.

Folks once driven through by clavers fearful of their plasticated limbs have come to like it, nestled into cracks and folds, night skies blazon with kinetic borealis, shimmer fields warning of danger spots, elders cussing everyone over what they should and shouldn't eat. Some crawling things look plump and tasty, but if it weren't on the Ark, then it's not safe. Everyone remembers that Granger girl, how they couldn't even bury her remains on account of what she ate still growing fleshy fronds.

What Joe wants most is to scream into their placid, settled faces how they can't stay here and how they oughta run. *Look at the sky, fer fuck's sake—damn thing's literally cracked.* Never mind all the other stuff, how he once went full on face-to-face with a Saint and lived to tell, that Saint staring right back through him—*once they've clocked you, there's no breaking free*—and yet, he's standing here, still full of breath. Upturned mountains, gouged out lakes, skyscrapers smashed back into bricks. Unfolding geologies, geometries expanding and unraveling. How the physics from encyclopedias no longer ticks over, how the sprouting coral's least of all their worries. Every forage run, he swears will be the last, every scavenged slab of rubble a dance with death and other kinds of crazy.

Mums and dads don't want to hear about that.

"Oh my god, is that Crofter Country Harvest?"

"Simpson of England—my grandma had a whole top shelf . . ."

Two women exuberant over a Nallyware kitchen canister; green with white lid, *Rice* in raised white letters.

Vintage Lusterware, Pyrex, Diana, Elektra, Ruby Bohemia, Mingay, Villeroy and Boch, all names like heroes from antiquity instead of fucking cups and saucers, jugs and plates, and how exactly are you all not noticing those sickly scudding clouds, all weft and buckle and the way the horizon bends if you stare too long and hard?

One woman shoves another on her way to a pile of greasy Tupperware.

Aloha Joe breathes deep and sucks his teeth, dislodges a scrap of jerky with his tongue. Tells them all he's looking for his daughter. No one ever challenges him on that. But they chip in.

"Your girl will be older—would you even know her face?"

"She'll be dust and bones if she's anything," he answers. "Was almost in that state when I brung her through. Couldn't have walked herself a single step."

"Something took her?" Big-eyed stares.

He nods carefully. "Something."

A man clasping a Pyrex bowl nods back, understanding.

"Wasn't a Saint, if that's what you're thinking. Weren't many moving around in open air back then. No time for anything that grand to manifest. I only left the girl alone a moment."

Poor Lily, his Lily, a girl so lost, there'll be nothing left to find. Only thing he's truly sure of these days.

———

"Hey Doll Face!"

Wind snatches at his words.

Worse than coral or Tupperware skirmishes stands the old girl's wall, an abomination roughly sized and shaped like an ancient Greyhound bus. A slab of particulate upthrust dead sea life, drifted and crushed beneath layer weights across millennia, eroded by wind and rain and sun: *sediment cemented sentimental.*

Sinead's banging away at it with chisel and hammer, carving nooks and niches from siliceous infill veinlets. *Tap tap tap* till she's scraped space enough to stuff a doll inside each hollow.

Hard to guess what's on her mind, *tap tap tap* below a tepid, sticky sky. That face of hers gives nothing much away, a fact she trades on when she's flush with bouts of *My Way or the Highway*, another of those old-time phrases echoing through cavernous mental spaces. *High life, high and mighty, high rollers, high falutin.* What the fuck did *falutin* ever mean?

Sinead means business. All her ducks stuck in a row, or in this case, dolls. Only ducks this side of the Divide being flat ceramic, all chipped wings and cracks, once were three flying up the mess hall wall.

Sinead's dolls give Aloha Joe the willies, even more than goo-goo eyes and bubble heads. Broken queens and aching princesses granted bespoke chiseled crannies in a gallery growing faster than scurvy weed, but not as fast as corals thrusting spikes and fronds through former human claves. Nothing fucks things faster than that stuff.

Old, old dolls, putty-fleshed and startled; pouting, painted, pocked and frocked. Balding, battered and abandoned, chubby-cheeked and cupid-bowed. Grime smudged, cockeyed, each one sporting worn out, haunted eyes.

Aloha Joe digs them out of abandoned malls and other secret spaces. Sometimes Sinead gives them a rinse and wipe, other times she takes them as they come, crusted with dirt and blood and gods know what—*no use hiding from the truth now is there?*

Joe brings dolls but has long stopped asking questions. Doesn't want to know the answers only gods can speak to. He wants the settlement to listen—folks in 53 used to hang on every word. Once was value seeing places others left behind. Before space started folding in on itself.

"Hey Doll Face. Catch!"

"Doll Face! Long time since anyone's called me that." Sinead half smiles at distant triggers. Straightens as he approaches the driftwood platform she knocked up for tools and nick-nacks. Wipes her damp brow with a wrist, full attention on his hessian sack. He takes his time, drawing out the moment, tugging hard then letting the fabric fall. Holds the content high for her to see.

Hands on her hips. "The fuck is that?"

"What it looks like." He throws.

The chisel falls as she clasps the missile in both hands. "Cute. But what am I s'posed to do with a human skull?"

"Sinead, we need to talk about the Great Divide and how it's stopped dividing there from here."

She sniffs, tosses the skull back, wipes another sweaty trickle, bends to scrabble for the fallen chisel. "So, what's new? Always known coral could push through any time it wanted. Portal-gateway wasn't built to—"

He steps closer, slams his fist on wood. "For starters, that portal-gateway's completely gone."

She pauses. "Like I said, it was just a symbolic—"

"Nothing *symbolic* about a fuckton of newly spewed up coral. Reckon even you gotta see that my way."

He coughs a clot of dust out of his lungs and points. "That skull came from our side, not the other."

She flinches, such a small thing, but he sees it.

"Got your attention now, do I?"

Sinead says nothing.

Joe joins her in silence, letting the moment flow. Decades on the road have taught him not to let frustrations show to these rough-shod plasticated innocents squatting on lands supposedly *terra nullus*, scratching subsistence from indifferent soil, trading with occasional passing randos. He brings them more than he's getting in return, but that arrangement suits. Least he can do—and the most. Aloha Joe doesn't get a lot of offers. Forage doesn't frighten when you know you've passed your own expiry date. He's been a dead man walking since Lily vanished.

Waiting for the *tap tap tap* again before he speaks, voice raised for effect. "New world's catching up with us. Time to try our luck in greener pastures. I've been searching—"

Sinead faces him, chisel gripped hard. ". . . she's not your daughter, Joe, and you oughta stop pretending . . ."

He stiffens, feels his face flush crimson. "You weren't here when—"

"No I weren't. And I'm sure you tried your best. You always do. What happened to that kid was way past your control. Time to settle down and face the fact."

He stares past her at the curdling sky. "Trouble's brewing, Doll Face. Something's gonna happen. Something big."

A big broad smile cracks her plasticated face. "Ya think?"

—

If you're hearing this, doesn't mean I made it out alive. Just means the doorway works both ways, is all.

Aloha Joe's been talking to the dead for half his life. They don't talk back—*Get real, I'm not crazy.* The dead make better listeners than the living. Sometimes listening's all he really needs.

So much hearthside banter about sacred spaces, bullshit soaking deep into his marrow. No one stepping through that portal-gateway uses that *S* word. *Sacred* suggests the hand of god and the coral don't have either: gods or hands, but this is their place all right. He can smell it.

The girl can too, weightless as a desiccated bird, blanket tucked around her like a shroud. What little form she holds shifts slightly in his arms. More movement than she's achieved across the past two years, so her mother told him.

If I make it back, Clave 53, they're gonna want to know.

We. If we make it back.

This place is enough to scare you straight. Too many rectangles. Stuff that looks like nature, but it isn't.

Monster breaks is what *their* structures feel like. Closest thing. Remembering the biggest wave he ever saw. Facing down the early season killer Atlantic swells of Nazarè, eighth wonder of the soon-forgotten world. Trapped in the death zone, heavy water slamming down like concrete. Eighty Ks an hour, feeling nothing but elation and respect.

Keep walking.

Sky's a sickly pastel, no place to stop and rest. No shelter. Not much of anything, air humming with electric fizz. He expected something, definitely more than this.

Places the girl under a tree, or what kind of looks like. Might be something other, but he's not blowing time on details. Harmless, dry and sheltering, unlike everything else on this undulating plain.

At the fringes, coral extrudes in ways impossible to describe. Not structures. Sculptures maybe, punched and twisting upward, refracting light with spiral slashes of a substance smashed some way between concrete, lava, chrome and diamond.

Could be AI art for all he knows.

Lays her down for just a while. No time at all in the grander scheme, needed a piss was all. Landscape gently misted, disappointing after all the ballyhoo and build up. Clavers back in 53 so certain they were walking to their deaths, fresh hells and fury waiting through that Dispensary portal-gateway.

Moonlight shivers on the silent sea . . .

More than anything, he wants to take her surfing. *Ocean's the only place I feel alive.* All the young who've never seen beyond half a rain tank's water in one place. His dreams are crystal pools of azure, champagne-laced salt spume, water horses striking, lapping tides, sandcastles, seagulls coasting updrafts. Every night when he shuts his eyes, yet not a word of it worth sharing. Might as well bang on about the surface of the moon. She'd make no sense of it, the girl and all the rest of them who fell between the cracks of now and yesterday.

One day.

But by time he walks back from emptying his bladder, the girl is gone. No visible tracks, spoor, signs of struggle. Tree's still there and it looks the same, an unmoved assemblage of brittle sticks and bark. Panic wells, but he crushes it back down.

All his fault. She was dead already, but he brought her here. Deader than the seven seas. Him too, probably. Give it time.

Suspicious skies shimmy and pulse to private rhythms.

Wind could have carried her away. Wind or wolves.

He's being watched. Always being watched.

Presses palms to his own plasticated skin but nothing's changed. No mystery runes or sigils manifesting by way of phantasmagorical revelation.

Figures he's got a water bottle's worth of time. Whatever took the girl will take him next.

Broods as gossamer fog thickens, descending gradually over the portal-gateway. The far side's crumbling Dispensary manifests as a wound on this, already starting to scab over.

If he's going back, oughta do it now.

Oughta done a lot of things: *shoulda, woulda, coulda.*

Ruminating options as he blows his last remaining spliff, scored off that swamp witch hawking pumpkins next to Dreamers Gate, false promises laced with PCP and magic mint.

He's puffing blue when the thing appears like a Medjugorje sky virgin blazon with *abundant fruits of grace.*

Mouth hanging open, he gets it now, everything he needs to know: Saints don't march, they shimmer-shiver, surfing through heat haze, light refracting, bouncing all which ways. Nearer than appearing, yet further than you'd reckon, churning air choked with fractured static.

Not his first rodeo—or apparition.

Years spent trading bullshit around Gunning and Collector campfires, plenty accounts of Saints moving through and *buggering up the sky, man.* Those things change sky to soup. What's happening now's the light-on version and he wouldn't call it soup, more like coagulant.

Bullshit encrusts until you don't know how to listen, all campfire stories taken with a pinch, 'specially when it comes to whats and whyfores. Knock knock: *What do you get when you kickspawn intelligences smarter than their creators?* Not much use for whyfores after that.

Near as Aloha Joe can figure, A Saint steps in when the Other takes an interest in the Meat. Coral doesn't register humanity as sentient, just pushes through like we're aggregates in gley.

Some years back, tripping down Psilocybin Sunset Strip with a *salvia divinorum* chaser, he witnessed something unaccountable: windstorm blowing in out of the north—luminous clouds flush with erratic lightning. Burnished bronze entities center front, multifaced and winged, with human hands. Wings melding where they touched, bright fire moving back and forth amongst them. And lightning. Always lightning, intersecting wheels of fearsome crystalline, sparkling like topaz and lapis lazuli, jasper, carnelian and emerald, moving when the windstorm creatures moved. A soundtrack roar of rushing waters, like the violence of an army blended with the radiance of rainbow.

That was not a Saint. He knows that now. That bronze-faced thing was something else entirely.

—

The sky might be cracking but his donkey doesn't care, standing in the open, oblivious to wind doing its worst. Lost its head back out Goulburn way and hasn't minded much of anything since. Aloha Joe gave it the same name as his dog, but time blew on and nowadays he's forgotten both.

Sinead's been *tap tap tapping* a new niche. She brushes the last stone crumbs aside, inserts a doll into its forever home, a blue-eyed thing with tiny teeth, no arms or legs.

Small wonder the old boot doesn't want to shift. Anywhere else, she'd be shot on sight with her face the way the coral made it.

"What's with all the dolls, Sinead. What is it with the fucking dolls?"

She takes her time to steady, jumps down, bends to scratch a handful of soil, rubs it between both palms until they're brown and filthy.

"Don't look like much, but this stuff's thick with nitrogen and phosphate. Mineral nutrients, organic carbon, bulk microbial activity, density, diversity and pH. Water-holding capacity and infiltration—the whole shebang."

She smears dirt down the sides of her pants. "Don't you find it odd how such good soil wound up sustaining our scrubby kitchen gardens out here in the middle of nowhere? When you first came through, only plant standing was a tree, and a dead one at that."

He still pictures that tree with startling clarity.

Hands on her hips. "Meanwhile, back over the Divide, they hit a rich vein of apocalypse: erosion, acidification, glyphosate and neonicotinoids, salinization, sodification, soil carbon loss, contamination from urban and industrial expansion—and that's aside from whatever befell the oceans.

"Guess we got lucky," says Aloha Joe, nodding.

She laughs. "We got *farmed* is what we got." She wipes more dirt down her pants.

"Working our arses off growing edibles, all the while *they've* been growing us in this . . . ant farm. Ever have one of those when you were a kid?"

He stares.

"Me neither, but I had loads of dolls and hopefully you're starting to get my drift. This here's some kind of terrarium. And what I want is to open up a dialogue."

He blinks. "With coral?"

"No, you great dumbarse. Coral's like lantana and scurvy weed, colonizing on autopilot." She inches closer and squints.

"Reckon it's time to talk to *them*. To *it*." She raises both hands, palms open, dirty fingers splayed. "The brains behind the operation. The things got birthed when our grandfolks slacked off paying attention."

"We're infected," he says. "Possessed." Lifts his shirt to reinforce the point—this side of the Divide, no one hides their plastication.

"Call it whatever you want, but it's conversation time," she says. "I wanna talk to the boss. And so did you when you first came through. Harping on about it, singing songs with that shithouse ukulele. Boy, was I glad to see the last of that thing."

Pain is a shortcut to mindfulness . . . he pictures seagulls screaming above crushing waves. "You mean talk to a Saint?" he says eventually.

"Nope, I mean talk to your Lily."

He staggers back a little, like she's slapped him across the face. "What the—"

"Think about it."

He glowers. "I don't think about much else . . . Been searching . . ."

"Course you have . . . far and wide." She makes an expansive gesture. "Searching everywhere but here."

He's eyeing the dolls off, face after face, each expression approved and frozen by some marketing executive in the Wayback When. Same folks who broke the world for all the rest of them.

"Oh, she won't look like Lily anymore," Sinead continues, "And I doubt she'll be a *she*, or even human. She never was your daughter, but you saved her when you brought her through, and she's been saving you every moment since."

Forty-something sets of plastic eyes stare back at him, accusatory.

Chest tightening as his words get stuck and jumbled.

"Aloha Joe, you've forgotten why you crossed the Great Divide, just like you've forgotten *Surfin' Safari* and *Blue Hawaii*."

She steps up closer. "Everything built here started with you. Lily's coming back, and then we're gonna talk."

She takes his hand and guides him over to the driftwood platform. "Got any beers in that sack?"

He sits, staring at his headless mechanical donkey, joints grating as its buffeted by wind. "Dandelion wine," he manages to croak, eventually.

"Close enough."

They share swigs from the brown glass longneck, watching clods of earth race tumbleweeds across the flat.

"Jethro," he says eventually. "My dog's name was Jethro."

"To Jethro, dog and donkey both!" she says, unstoppering a second bottle.

Glass clinks as a patch of sky above them brightens.

IN THE DRAWBACK

KAARON WARREN

If he flared his nostrils and breathed deeply, the drummer boy could catch the deep salt tang of the ocean, its seaweedy stink hinting at vegetation and food. He glanced down to where a group of men were collecting firewood. They worked in silence; no voices reached him. But they were companionable. Compatible. The drummer boy knew that if he joined them, they would be agitated. "Be quiet," they'd say. "Stop your fidgeting," and they'd ask him to fetch something from the caravans, something difficult to find and unneeded.

Sitting on the rocks, he gazed out at the water, far away in the distance. He stared without blinking and chewed on a piece of salt fish until thirst drove him to stand. He blinked then and saw it.

"There's something out there," he said. "Hey! Hey! There's something out there! Something big!" Thomas, down on the beach collecting wood, stopped working and, shielding his eyes, stared out. He stared for some minutes, then shook his head.

"There's nothing there" he shouted through cupped hands. "Maybe a tangle of ropes if you're lucky. Go claim it for yourself, boy, bring it to show us tonight."

The inhabitants of Sunlit Waters rarely looked out to sea. Months could pass without anything being revealed and they grew bored watching the drawback. They had found many treasures in the past; old boats and bone, rubbish, bits and things discarded and lost over the centuries. Once, they had anticipated the revelations and scavenged the goodies, looking for clues to the past.

But the drawback was slow. The drummer boy knew that, yet still he never failed to be amazed by it. "The water will never touch that place again," he'd say to the others. "It won't come back." The men shook their heads, used to it and bored. Decades now, the water had been drawing back. Long enough for it be normal.

The drummer boy walked out on the sand with his sack over his shoulder. He found some smooth glass for Miles's collection, seven plastic lids for Tom. He found a circle of material that he guessed was once the neck of a t-shirt. He filled his bag with little treasures and walked on.

As he approached the pile, his step slowed. It was nothing; he could tell that now. Just a tangle of bottles and the sort of seaweed that looks like human hair. He wrenched the bottles out; everything was useful in some way. They knew that at Sunlit Waters.

There was something smooth, though, right at the water's edge. Smooth and brown, like a rock, but shaped unnaturally even. The drummer boy's bag was heavy and the light was falling, so he left the mystery. He knew it would be revealed when the tide went out.

———

Three of the men had been to the city to shop. There would be a feast tonight. Food was always shared equally, salty food to make them thirsty. They would sit together in the games room and make what conversation they could. There would be no fish, and they would pretend not to hear the crash of the waves, clearer in the night but still far away.

The walls in the games room were covered with mold from the roof down to where the tallest man could reach with a scrubbing brush. From there, mold spread in patches and stripes. The smell of it was dirt and vegetable in one. When the men first entered the room, they breathed though their mouths, but soon grew used to it.

They sat around a massive metal table, circular, scratched and dented. A find from in the drawback.

The drummer boy sat on an upturned boat in the corner and thumped his feet against the wood, thumping thumping until the men turned and noticed him.

"Be quiet, boy," one said.

"There's something out there. I know it. In the drawback. I saw a glimpse of it today."

"Be quiet, boy."

And he was, for a while. The men who'd been to the city spoke of the noise there, the low hum which made them all queasy.

"It's busy, though. Colorful with women. And they laugh in the city. You know, funny ha ha."

"Did any of them speak to you?"

They shook their heads. "They looked at us as if we were crazy," they said. "And their faces are thin, like this." The man sucked in his puffy cheeks and the others laughed.

The drummer boy glanced at their faded clothes, the salt sheen on their skins. Pale eyes in brown faces.

The men drank wine, great mugs of it. The drummer boy found a mug for himself and filled it. He sipped the thick red liquid and felt nothing. He sipped again and again until the numbness set in.

"Look at the boy!" someone said, and they all laughed at him, slumped in his chair dribbling vomit onto his chin.

He lifted his head and saw their faces, disgust showing through the drink.

"I'm not a boy," he mumbled. Thomas spat on the floor.

"You're the closest we've got, so wear it," he said. They all sat back, their feet up to ease swollen legs.

The drummer boy went into a frenzy then, whirling and drumming on every surface he could find; the table, heads, bottles and glass.

"Attaboy," they said, being nice to him, wanting him to keep playing the child because they missed children so much, they missed their little darling over-protected faces.

—

"Hey!" the drummer boy shouted. He started on a run to the cliff's edge, then turned to climb down, slipping and losing his grip in his eagerness. He reached the bottom and ran toward the path through the ti tree shrubs, terrified that whatever he had seen would sink and disappear before he could show the others.

"There's something out there," he shouted.

Everyone was in the caravans. Thomas slammed the door of his, bored with the news. "It's history," he said. "Who cares about what's done?"

Miles had been tending his flowers but grabbed his coat and nodded. "Time was, everyone'd join in," he said. "Time was, you'd be left behind the pack if you didn't hurry."

Fred shouted at them, do it yourself, find it yourself ya buggers.

So Miles and the drummer boy walked alone. The drummer boy knew the sighting was his, once confirmed by Miles. He would receive the greater share of whatever bounty was found. Why else would he sit and watch on that lonely, windy cliff top?

The flat expanse of sand stretched out before them, almost unchanged over many months. Only wind and the occasional scavenger bird digging for worms changed the landscape now. Once the water drew back it did not return.

Far out, near the water's edge, they could see a great mound.

"Is it a ship? It might be ship. It will be full of treasure if it's a ship," Miles said. He loved trinkets and shininess, loved anything that glittered, even if it fell apart in his fingers.

"We won't know until we walk out and see," said the drummer boy.

They walked.

"It's not a ship," the drummer boy said.

"It's a whale," Miles said. They smiled at the thought of a whale, unseen for decades, suddenly showing itself. "A shark, then."

"We'd smell if it was a shark. We'd smell the stink of it and the birds . . ." They glanced up, watching for circling seagulls. There were a small few, as always when people walked. People on the move meant food to a bird.

"Anything dead would stink. It must be some kind of ship. From space. A spaceship that landed and sank and they never got out," Miles said.

They were silent as they approached the giant mound.

It was a man. A huge man, as big as four men. They could see his heels. He was face down.

There was a massive chain around both ankles.

The drummer boy and Miles stared at the man until they shivered. "You run get the others," Miles said.

"You go. They won't believe me."

So Miles went and fetched the men to come before the tide returned and covered the titan to his heels again.

—

They crowded around the huge man. The tide was out to his head, but they knew it was on its way in again. They stepped closer, took off their shoes and rolled their pants up to stand over him and look hard. His clothes were rotten, still damp from being covered.

"It'll be a year before the drawback reveals him," Fred said.

"We can see him when the tide's out," the drummer boy said. "We can get the other caravan parks to help us drag him."

"Let's just leave him for now," Thomas said. "There's no hurry. He's not going anywhere."

"But what if the tide takes him?"

The chain around his ankles, corroded almost to dust, sank into the sand.

"What's at the end of it? It may have been protected by the sand," Fred said, screwing up his eyes.

They brought spades and large digging shells, and slowly removed the sand. It was still very wet, and filled the hole they dug like quicksand. Working quickly, they revealed glimpses of what lay beneath.

"It's a rock. The chain is caught in a rock. They must have used some massive force to press this rock."

"The woman on the hill says once they all were tall. Strong, like this one," said the drummer boy, tapping on the rock with his sticks, tap tap.

They found skeletons about him. Weapons. A buckle.

"Why are they skeletons and he is flesh?" the drummer boy said.

The giant had remarkably little stink about him. It was almost pure brininess, so salty the drummer boy could barely breathe.

"We're not going to be able to turn him on our own," Miles said.

Many years ago, a whale had beached itself and two or three caravan parks had joined to turn, cut and remove the meat. Better to share than to have the carcass left behind. They still had the whalebone cutlery, the needles. They would never kill a whale; they didn't need to kill anything. The shore was always littered with dead fish as the drawback continued. The older men said the fish was saltier now. Chewier. They talked of soft-fleshed fish that melted in your mouth.

The giant's skin was white from being under water.

They poked and prodded, tore off bits of the rotten cloth to use back at the caravan park for stopping drops.

"Someone needs to tell her," said Fred. "She'll want to know."

"I'll do it," said the drummer boy. He didn't mind visiting her on the hill. There was a smell in there the men didn't like. A dried fishiness and they didn't know if it came from her or the things about her

"She'll give you treats tonight and someone will come fetch you in the morning," Thomas said. The men laughed. Tears came to the drummer boy's eyes.

"Baby," sneered Fred. The drummer boy knew he didn't fit in. They wanted him to pretend to be a child but hated him for it. Despised that he made them think of children.

The drummer boy walked back to shore and up the hill to the caravan belonging to the woman, Petra. She wore a floral dress and had him do her hair. "A lady has to look after her hair," she said. The men didn't like to touch it. It was thick and greasy like seaweed, and their fingers felt coated with grease for days.

As he did her hair, the drummer boy told her of their discovery. He said, "They want to wait for the drawback to turn him over."

She shook her head and tiny specks flew off. One landed in the drummer boy's eye. "Nonsense. They'll drag him out. They'll get the neighbors to help and drag him out of the water. What are they waiting for?"

"I think they're frightened of him."

"Well, they should be. They know my stories. The terrible time of ancient dreams. Once there were many people like him. Men and women so tall they used caves high in the cliffs to store their treasures. That table in the games room was a gong," she said. "Can you imagine the size of the mallet? You could dissolve a limb to liquid with one hit. It was used by the giants."

"What happened to them? Did they all die?" the drummer boy asked.

Petra shook her head. "No one knows." She pointed to her most prized cup, a huge thing with a piece like a bite out of the rim. "All we know is, they were here."

The drummer boy had explored some of these caves. He could not reach them all. Inside them he found perfect spheres, papers long past reading, shiny bowls and things that glowed. Petra salvaged nice things, remains of the past she didn't like to use. Mugs on hooks, cracked and yellow. A little stack of books, pages glued together from their time in the sea.

The drummer boy collected remnants of toys. He had the head of a plastic action figure. The axle of a toy car. Seventeen mismatched building blocks.

—

Petra fed him a delicious soup and made him talk about things he didn't want to talk about.

The drummer boy said, "How do you know the past?"

She said, "It's the books and the things we find and the stories I remember. I try to pass the knowledge on but they don't listen. They don't care about the terrible time. They don't want to learn from the past. A great wave begins with a sudden drawback. Something must follow." She muttered, losing her point, and it was frightening to the drummer boy to learn she didn't have all the answers.

All the caravans were falling apart, long past their holiday glory. Rusty. A metal smell about them all. A mustiness. The flooring all white, sanded away by years of walking.

She said, "Did you hear about the fire at Tree Shady Park?" He shook his head, horrified to think of the children who may have died there.

"It's all right. No one died. Places can be reborn, too. They can drown and be reborn. Changed." She squeezed her eyes shut. "You tell Thomas to get the others and drag that thing out of the water."

—

The next morning, the drummer boy told Thomas of Petra's instructions. The men spent half the day discussing how it would be, then sent runners to the other caravan parks to ask for help. They agreed the apex of low tide was the best time.

Thomas said, "Drummer boy, you guard tonight. No one is to begin without we're all here."

They left him a campfire. He boiled a pot of water and dug his fingers in the sand to collect pipis. He cooked them and ate them, hot and tasty, straight from the shell.

He could not remember a time when he felt happier.

He collected a pile of rocks and threw them at the birds swooping down seeking a beakful of meat. Rocks landed with a splash in the water. The ones on sand sank down, and some landed on the giant's back

There was something almost delightful about hearing the bones of this titan clunk, and the drummer let a few more rocks fall until there was a small mound on his back.

He slept, curled sitting up in a ball, and was woken by birds. In the distance he could see the groups walking toward him.

He walked to the water's edge, which pulled rapidly to the shoulders of the giant. The drummer boy washed his face and wet his hair, slicking it back out of his eyes. Then he saw movement.

He turned, thinking one of the men must have run forward.

"We won't begin," the drummer boy said. There was no one there. It must have been a fish, he thought, lifting out of the water, or a low-flying bird.

As the men approached, he quickly removed the rocks nestled on the giant's back. They looked shoddy in the daylight, weak and pathetic, and the drummer boy was not proud of his actions.

As he lifted the last rock off, the giant's shoulder twitched.

The drummer boy shouted and stepped backward. He fell over, landing in the sand and wetting his trousers.

He wriggled backward away from the motionless giant.

"He moved," he shouted to the men. "He moved his shoulder."

They snorted. "He didn't move. He's probably caught a fish in his shirt."

"It's only the parasites. New food for them all. Word will get out and they'll come from everywhere to feast," Tom said.

Miles said. "Time was, we'd shoot those birds."

The giant lay on his stomach, his arms beneath his body. It took the men from three caravan parks in shifts to drag him out and turn him. Others had heard the news and were traveling up and down the coast.

This was something which never happened and it made most

of them uneasy. They were not comfortable with community. Community insisted on modes of behavior, saying the right thing.

Providing for visitors.

—

Thirty men heave-hoed on one side, twenty tugged on the other. The giant's flesh was surprisingly firm, the drummer boy thought. He marched around the grunting men, tapping his slow rhythm as they worked. He felt proud of his drumming. He did not miss a beat, he would not, he would drum and drum and drum while the men toiled to turn the giant over.

Other bodies they'd found were either dissolved to bone, or the flesh turned greenish and jelly-like. Usually you grabbed the arm of a revealed body and your fingers sank to bone. You could slide the meat off the bone and collect it in a bowl. Even the dogs wouldn't eat this sludge, though the woman on the hill swore by its efficacy as fertilizer. She sold the vegetables grown on this stuff (she called it sea sludge) for a higher price, saying it cured ills of the mind. She said that when you defecated next, your shit would contain tiny worms, too small to be seen. These worms drawn down from your brain by the scent of the sea sludge in your belly.

The drummer boy would rather keep his sadness than eat anything grown from that stuff.

The giant's body was not like that. His flesh was firm. The ropes they used dug into his shoulders, and the drummer could see the flesh reddening.

"That can't be right," he said. "His flesh should not change color." The drummer boy drummed one-handed and pointed at the markings on his back. "Why is his skin marked?"

They shook their heads. "Who knows? Let's turn him over then worry about it."

The drummer boy marched around and around. The tide was coming back and would cover the giant to his ankles this time. The men rested and debated whether to come back as the tide drew back.

"If we wait a year the water will draw back, anyway," one said. "There's no hurry."

But as he spoke the carrion birds circled above, rawking down at the people stealing their food.

They set back to work. It was tough going, and they took it in shifts, collecting water and cooking pipis and fish to eat. They all talked, theorized about the man.

"So, did he walk out into the ocean, dragging or carrying his rock, until he could no longer walk?"

"Or did they drop him off a boat and he couldn't move?"

"And who dropped him? And why?"

Finally they had the leverage to turn him over.

"One, two, three," they chanted, and with a strain and a push, he was over.

Water lapped at his hair, softening it into baby fineness. His arms were crossed tightly and he held something there, an armful of something. His wrists were chained. His eyes were closed and his mouth was so tightly pressed he looked like he had no lips. He was terribly scarred, marked.

"His lips are sewn together," someone up that end said. "And his cheeks are puffed out. Has he got jewels in there?"

They had heard tell of people who were buried with their jewels or money in their mouths, their lips sewn shut to scare off thieves.

"Shut up," someone further down said. "Shut up and look at his arms."

The drummer boy pushed through the knees of the men. Some of them were weeping.

"It's children," he said. The giant held, close to his chest like he would not let them go, five small skeletons.

"Children!" the men said. They began to wail with fear and sorrow. "It's children!"

They all stepped back, wondering what to do. Where to go from here. They stared at the children's skeletons.

"They'll need a proper burial," said one. "At least that."

There were nods, agreement. They were good at burials. There were thousands of bones in the dirt behind the caravan park, all carefully laid in a stack and words said over them.

The woman on the hill trundled down on her electric car. When she saw the lips sewn, she spoke. Her eyes were closed, chin to neck, voice muffled.

"They did it at sea. Did it once to the master of a captured ship."

She waved her arm at the sea, as if they would find evidence of this under the waves. "He moaned so much the pirates sewed his lips together and tossed him into the sea."

She tossed her arm and her fingertips flicked at the drummer boy. "Don't you remember we found that boot once, with a needle imbedded?"

This was proof to no one but the drummer boy and the woman. The men hissed, "Shut up! Shut up!"

The giant was covered with sucking, biting things. One burrowed into the eye of his penis, which they could see through his torn pants.

The drummer boy stared at the giant till his eyes watered.

"I saw his finger move," he said.

"Be quiet now, boy," said Fred.

And then they all saw it. One finger flicked stiffly. Then another. Then his shoulders shook.

The men ran, shouting. The drummer boy behind them, not as fast in the sucking wet sand.

They stopped a ways off and stared back.

He couldn't be alive.

They watched as his fingers unclasped. The children's skeletons tumbled about on his chest as he released his grip, and he lifted his great hand and swept the bones off like crumbs. His shoulders shook and the men ran shouting to the cliffs as the giant slowly sat up.

They watched him through binoculars from the cliffs. Petra was there, and the other women, too. He took hours to stand, his movements slow and careful, as if his body reawakened slowly. He seemed so human when he stretched some of the men murmured, "We should talk to him."

Then he lifted his hand to his mouth and touched the stitches there. He looked toward the cliff and began to walk, each huge footstep sinking into the sand and being lifted out with a sucking noise they could hear from the beach. The ancient chain broke away.

He thundered on. He searched the ground as he walked, fingering the stitches.

"What's he looking for?"

"Something sharp."

They moved further back as he approached, wanting to run but wanting to know as well.

Then he reached down and lifted up a shell. He'd found his sharp object.

He was close enough now they could see the barnacles clinging to his ears.

"Stop him," Petra said. Her voice came in gasps. The drummer boy had never seen her scared.

"Who is he?" the drummer boy asked.

She shook her head. "I don't know. I don't know."

"But who sewed his mouth? How?"

She slapped him, the fat fleshiness of her hand softening the blow.

She looked at him sidelong. "I don't know," she said. She began to shake, to quiver, like her body knew what was coming.

Feeling the stitches with one hand, the giant used the sharp with the other and soon his mouth was loose. He bent over and spat a mouthful of rocks to the ground.

He dropped the sharp.

His nose screwed up, his lips kissed out then peeled back in a grimace. His teeth were smaller than they could possibly have imagined; like an adult with baby teeth.

There was the beginning of a sound, a low-pitched noise which made the drummer boy feel sick to his stomach. The giant opened his mouth wider, wider, and his jaw seemed to dislocate itself as he stretched his mouth out so wide they could see deep inside his throat. He began a noise, one long echoing note which shivered the drummer boy to his core.

One man began to cry, then another.

The woman wailed. "We don't want to hear it," but the giant stepped closer, closer, and it filled their world and that of everybody nearby.

To a man they began to weep. The drummer boy was filled with such complete sadness he saw no room for the future, but he was used to sadness. Used to absorbing it, ignoring it.

Miles fell over, dizzy, disoriented. He wailed, "I'm drowning! I'm drowning!" though water was nowhere near. The drummer boy felt his vision blur and he reached for Petra. She was slumped in her electric car, vomit covering her chest.

The giant stood, his head back, mouth open, as men turned to jelly about him. Far out on the waterline, whales beached themselves and those still capable of seeing shouted in surprise at the sight.

The drummer boy heard crashing, cracking, and he saw the cliff collapsing onto a dozen men below.

Men cried salt tears and the drummer boy watched as they staggered toward the water, seeking out the drowning in droves. Thomas led them, striding as if he was in control, but the drummer boy saw him falter in every step. Petra rolled till her wheels stuck then she threw herself down and crawled like a worm out to the water.

How did the ancients stop him? the drummer boy thought. How did they sew his mouth without dying on approach? Did they numb themselves? Sacrifice themselves for the children?

The children. There was a small family of them in Tree Shady Park. The drummer boy's stomach pained him so much he couldn't swallow. He had to spit it on the ground. He wanted to run to the children, gather them up and take them to safety.

The giant wiped spit from his mouth and was silent. He looked around at the deserted beach. The drummer boy thought, He sees me. I should run to warn the children, run my fastest and beat him there.

The giant stepped toward him. The drummer boy thought, no. No. I'll lead him away. I must lead him away.

So he began to run. He ran. The giant stepped after him, walking slowly, each step ten of the drummer boy's.

The drummer boy ran inland, rhythmically, counting the beat in his head as he ran. He knew the giant would catch him. There was no doubt of that. But the further he could lead him away the better he would feel.

He ran for a full day before he sank to the ground in exhaustion.

The giant stepped forward, picked him up and held him close. The tenderness of it crushed the drummer boy's ribs and made him wish for just . . . one . . . more . . . breath.

HACKING SANTORINI
CAT SPARKS

I collect dirty postcards—the dirtier the better. The faded ones with folds and creases, coffee stains and greasy donut smears. My cards have seen a lot of love and can fetch a pretty poem. Pennies and other fiscal residue make great exchange for embroidered lace, cupcakes and mechanical know-how.

Sometimes know-how is handier than poetry. I know how to sail the boat my Gramma crashed into Heraklion not too long after the 88-minute war. Crash landed and stranded as things turned out. Not so bad a place to wind up as many. Not that I've ever been anywhere else, but I've read much of other places, scrawled on postcards sent from Pasadena, Macao and Istanbul. Postcards salvaged from around the globe before the Exclusion Zones started excluding and Heraklion got roughed up and heritage listed.

You name it, reckon I got a card. Evidence exotic places once existed. Best of all are the cards from Santorini, the ones with beautiful blue domes. Sixty-five nautical miles afar says Gramma's stash of rolled and folded maps, only Santorini's own heritage listing means nobody has been near it in living memory.

Except for, that's a dirty lie. My Gramma's boat tossed upon its waves. Close enough to see the gleaming whitewash. But she couldn't land so she took the name of the island for her boat, and I see no point in changing that boat's name now. Santorini speaks to excellence and names are things that get you noticed. Stories too, when you've got to make the best of seventh or eighth hand arte- facts and promises. For instance, Maurice's brass hound dog head mounted coat hook—not much use for coats in these surrounds. Or Genevieve's darling 1940's folk art ice skates—brush painted with a center medallion windmill. And Guadalupe's unforgettable chicken ranch bar spinner brass necklace bottle opener—spin to see who pays for all the drinks! Says she'd trade it for a chicken if such things still existed.

I could go on but a phalanx of Byrons, Plaths and Allendes fast approaches. Fancy folks are my bread and ouzo, aside from *cartes postales*, of course. Postcards always come foremost and first—folks share them when they want to hire my boat and why shouldn't they, being that there's not much else to do on Heraklion between sunup and down?

Seems at first a parade of poets, what with them being so numer- ous, a mix of tall and short and in between, all dressed in white and cream and ivory. Daisy, eggshell, snow and frost, chiffon, porcelain and pearl. Parchment, linen, bone and cream, all frou- froued up and past the nines.

Their couture should have given me a clue: guys and dolls in rosebuds, lace and taffeta. Fussing and flaunting, all tittery and jittery. But me, I'm playing it old school frosty, slouching against the concrete sea wall, waiting for whispered secret codes like *Turkmenistan*, *Nagasaki* or *Rotorua*, name dropping so I know they know about namesakes, keepsakes and significance and whatnot.

Finally, the one with sapphire hair separates from the whole. "We want to get married on Santorini," she tells me, pausing to draw breath. "Marriage is—"

"I know what marriage is." I cut her bridesplaining off because I know everything there is to know about brides and grooms, flower girls and mothers-of. Priests and celebrants, pageboys and designer cakes, groomsmen, candle lighters and *Vratimi*. The kinds of stupid folks did back in the days of connectivity to incite competitiveness and unnecessary complexity.

"Sailboat captains can do the ceremony, yeah?" She looks so young—fourteen or fifteen, born decades after the 88-minute war.

Her stare is hard. Aegean blue and glassy. Like folks reckon the ocean used to be.

"Sure thing," I shrug. "Who's marrying whom?"

She grins. "We're all marrying each other." Hands me a faded, crumpled shape that had clearly once been proper postcard shiny.

Young sapphire hair informs me that her name is Rhizanthella. The one beside her is Goldeneye. I don't ask names for all the others—Captain's all they're going to get from me—but they know all about my Gramma's *Santorini*—and my doggo, Daisychain, who will be coming too—that part is non-negotiable.

The Winedark Soup is what we call the watery smear between Heraklion and Exclusion. Was once called something else, but weren't most things?

I get why kids like Rhiz and Goldie feel so urged to push the barriers, seeing past times as elegant and romantic. Getting married was what everybody did back when. Even folks who had never met before. My Gramma told me all about it. She'd been married loads of times and outlived every one of those long-lost brides.

But *these* brides are the serious kind and will not be trading ceremonials for poetics. They have dug their research deep. The one with the thick moustache hands me a six-pack of religious postcards still sealed in brittle, yellowed plastic with a faded sticker stating *Vatican 60 lira*.

Trying not to look too keen, but I've always been lousy with the bluff. Moustachio knows he has me snared. "Plenty more where they came from," he says with a wink.

Truth is, I've married folks before, only generally one to one or sometimes two. Got myself this little book with all the proper words in. Vilest words to ever splutter, but marrying types always insist on going through the motions.

Shrugging, I say, "Plenty more of what?"

He gives me the knowingest of looks, dips his hand, pulls out his stash and reels me in, with *Travel by Trans Australian Railway; Ireland, land of romance; Michie Tavern, Charlottesville; Fasco Mexico Panoramic Hillside View* and *1964 New York World's Fair Expo Postcard Souvenir Swedenborgian exhibit*.

Excitement sets my heart aflame, but he's not finished yet. Next up reveals an original *Philips' Comparative Wall Atlas South America Climate Summer Map* from 1921.

Seriously now, where did these brides unearth such precious treasures?

Rhizanthella of the sapphire hair pouts, signaling they know they've won me over.

"Genesis or Ecclesiastes?" I mumble, coughing sharp to clear my throat.

She shrugs, so I'm going for E over G, being that those words are kind of filthy when you get under their skin: All about God creating man in his own image, all male, female and blessed and lah-de-dah. Instructing them to get shagging and subdue the Earth, with dominion over everything that moves. Which is, of course, exactly how things played out, long-term, unchecked dominion being what landed us all in this heritage listed, excluded and confined predicament.

No point arguing over spilled histories. I snatch the Vatican cards for my collection—can you believe there's a whole new city I never previously knew existed?

And then we're off as locals meandering the waterfront drop half-mended nets and basket traps, leave racks of drying fishy things and line along the concrete pier to clap and wave and wish us *bon voyage* and *happy trails*, with sun and breeze and wine and songs and the brides do look completely and utterly amazing. A lurid, groaning trifle of structured fashion-forward beaded bodices with restricted boning, clean lines managing to be classic, yet sensual and unique, delicate and romantic with renaissance lace and all the trimmings.

And yeah, it's definitely going to be a job for Ecclesiastes: *Two are better than one, because they have a good return for their labor; If either of them falls down, one can help the other up. But pity anyone who falls and has no one to help them* . . . Numbers in need of upgrading as it goes without saying that if seven lie down together, they will keep very much warmer than only two, reinforcing that one cannot keep properly warm alone.

And the day *is* warm and the sun so lovely, waters calm and smooth and lazy, wind tousling my salty beard and I know I'm one of the lucky ones because although heritage listing is dull and slow and we live off algae pressed and shaped like fish, and nothing ever happens in this fragment of the world, it's a better life than we actually deserve.

—

Daisychain is the best of doggos, acquired from army surplus. Not the prettiest of pooches—a slightly rusty, dynamically stable quadruped military unit shelved (too loud for combat and too picky for reconnaissance), refitted, recalibrated and reclassified as a medical care device before washing upon these shores. Daisychain may well be dented, but he loves me best and that's what matters most.

Air stirs thick with pheromone potpourri as we're casting off from shore, with brides ever elegant and seductive in pastel ombres of buttons, beads, sequins and ribbon; mermaid tulle overlay with ruffles offering a playful commentary, a splash of color infusion tiers and a touch of old-style Hollywood glamour, not to mention those iridescent vintage (obviously) blue-green embroidered Sternocera beetle wings.

They're waiting for me to do my thing. The Winedark Soup lies still so close to shore where safety is assured in shallows. Cloud banks brood along distant horizons, layered dark on dark, a moody, shifting mass of heaving coal from which forked lightning illuminates cracking, fizzing underbellies laced with spidery threads of forked electric sun.

Moustachio offers to take the wheel while I nip below to fetch my admiral's jacket, the one with the bullion embroidery and rank insignia anchor-embossed brass buttons, ribbon bar and breast eagle. The jacket hangs in a slim wooden robe alongside my deep and darkest treasures: a scrimshaw jagging wheel complete with mermaid breasts and tail; a love heart carved from Whitby jet and the assortment of strange pornography I keep in a *Hoyo de Monterrey Jose Gener Excalibur #11* wooden cigar box.

Within the box sit secret postcard remnants of a frightening domain. Dogs and cats stuffed into baskets captioned with *Wish you were here*; the dolphin jumping through a flaming hoop; the woman in dotty bathers posing with a giant bear against red curtains embellished with brassy handguns. Florida—*Drop in anytime*—says the reptile head with enormous spiky teeth, while

Wildlife of the Desert boasts improbably named gamble quail, horned toad, kangaroo rat, kiss bug, centipede, spotted skunk, ring-tailed cat, elf owl, coral snake, side winder, bobcat and others you would never even believe.

Then there's Cove Haven Resort in the Pocono Mountains with a heart-shaped tub in every room; Ghost Riders in The Sky, the gone-but-not-forgotten Twenty Mule Wagon team across a spectacular Death Valley sunset with the Devil's Golf Course in the foreground.

So many cards with old men posing alongside murdered animals, like they were somehow proud of what they'd done. The past is another country is what my Gramma used to say, but I reckon it must have been much, much worse than that.

A sudden lurch slams me hard against the companionway, the rise and fall bow into breaking waves creates a powerful sensation of forward surge. Somehow, against all odds, the wind has found us.

I stuff the porn back in the box and emerge on deck to a blur of brides grasping tight and pulling ropes, fighting gravity and wind, as waves slam fierce against the sides. Wicked gusts spitting mist into our faces, astonished as Goldeneye jumps up to the main mast to reef the sail, rigging singing as water rushes along the hull, sails popping and pulling taut as my *Santorini* heads straight for the belly of the beast.

"Oh hey," waves Rhiz through the foaming spittle.

"What the hell do you crazy brides think you're doing?" I bellow.

"We want to get married on Santorini," she shouts over the ocean roar. "As in, on the actual island, not the boat."

"Over my dead and destituted corpse! Nobody returns from the isle of Santorini!"

"We know that, oh excellent of Admirals. We want to find out why."

My startled, damp stare shifts from face to face. The brides are drenched and enjoying every minute. "Santorini is a smoking crater!" I shout out through my creaking lungs. "The 88-minute war. Everybody knows about these things!"

"Of course we know about the war, dear, lovely Admiral. But you've got a boat and we've got a collective insatiable urge to learn the ever-loving truth."

"The truth of what? What truth is there to learn? The Exclusion Zone . . ."

". . . excludes exactly *what*?"

Thing is, I'm not an idiot. I've looked up *exclusion* many times, firstly in the *Collins English Dictionary Fourth Australian Edition Better by Definition*, with its shiny cover of black and gold. It states exclusion is an act or an instance of excluding or the state of being excluded. Not much help in the grander scheme of things.

"Question is," she continues in a loud and nauseatingly knowing tone, "is the state of being excluded keeping something *out* or keeping something *in*?"

"Santorini is radioactive," I shout back at her, adding a steely glint for emphasis. Which is quite a trick with Winedark spume spraying everywhere.

The fat one with the sideburns rolls her eyes. "No it isn't! No nukes were deployed during the 88-Minute war. That's why the damn thing went on for so long. Surely you've read the *Chronicles of Whatnot and Wherefore* . . ." Pudgy fingers attempt explanatory curlicues in fizzing, salt wracked air.

Above us, dramatic energy discharges flare in shredded indigo sky. "The volcano then. Nea Kameni must have blown its top again."

Sideburns nods wetly. "Plausible." She then leans in close and personal. "But don't you want to find out for yourself?"

"No I don't!" Words blurting far more forcefully than intended, surprising everyone including me. Even Daisychain cocks an ear and tilts his head.

"Just close enough to see if there's smoke," she adds. "If Nea Kameni's belching, we'll get out of there."

"I'm not going," I inform them, crossing sodden admiral arms, "And you can all get off my Gramma's boat now, thank you."

None of them budge. They stare me down while steering the *Santorini* out into forgotten waters. Like they've done such things before. Like somebody has taught them all about it—which is more than anyone ever taught me.

Truth is, I have not the skills to sail this boat across the Exclusion Zone to Santorini. I've never been further than a couple of Ks from Heraklion's rocky shoreline. I am no more a sea captain than this lot are bona fide brides. Gramma's *Santorini* is heaving with impostors.

———

My Gramma taught me lightning strikes are five times hotter than the surface of the sun. With this in mind, we navigate by sextant, compass, paper maps and stars through an exclusion zone as wifi sterilized as every other. We tug and grasp at hardy ropes, fighting fierce wind, gravity and rigging, sails popping and pulling taut. Reefing like our lives are depending on it. Needn't have panicked. These brides know all about the double play of sail and rudder, forward surge and running down the face of waves.

And as winedark soup slops over the deck, it all starts coming back to me in strobing shards and spits and slivers. A voyage under dead of night, ocean waves like thick and blackened blood. Tossed and pitched and rocked and roiled, Gramma's tanned arms straining against the wheel. Thunderous rumbles, random flashes. The slick and oily surface of the deep. Everything so much bigger than I'd ever dreamed of; the boat, the sky, the waves. Rapid dog-leg bolts firing from the base of vast formations, with me a bumbling, clumsy little boy bundled tight in orange polymer; lashed to the mast to stop me sliding overboard while Gramma's shouting words I can barely hear.

Well of course my memory can't catch her words—I was never on the *Santorini*—or any boat during exclusion years. I wasn't even born. I never got to meet my Gramma. But stories, they get under your skin, they sidle up and seep on through and before you know it, you're claiming whole great swathes of half-remembered fancies. Heraklion boasts three Cleopatras, one small gay Napoleon and enough self-righteous Kennedys to inhabit their own island if we could spare one.

Memories are not to be trusted. Nor are digital remains. The 88-minute war messed with our hearts and heads. These days we put our faith in stain on paper. Our library-museum contains so many precious treasures, our paper made from seaweed and driftwood pulp. Ink from bottled squids, charcoal and boot black.

Remembering's what turned us into a nation of poet-gardeners, exclusion zoned and heritage listed, yet here we are on my trusty *Santorini*, slipping in under stealth of day. Crusty old salts back on land are certain old war drones see better in the darkness. Best we can hope for now is obsolescence.

My admiral's jacket's graphite thread count refracts sunlight and radiation. My doggo doesn't need protection—he runs on 100 percent bio-D. The brides have come prepared for anything. A corset bodice is a gorgeous vintage look, pretty bows or knots, cutouts, extremely flattering and the extra exposed skin adds alluring touches, pearls being the ultimate classic feminine detail—subtle yet beautiful embellishments evoking romantic sentiments.

Neither Rhiz nor Goldie listen when I explain exactly what we're going to find on Santorini isle. Bleached donkey bones and crumbling ruins and perhaps a mangled mash of cable cars. Feral cats in disintegrating doorways—haunted beasts, all matt and bone and sinew. The caldera harbor choked with cruise ship skeletons, all sunk and drunk and listing on their sides. A reef comprised of smashed remains of hulls and hulks and fallen Boeing carcasses.

Daisychain's barking up a frenzy and I cling on tight with both hands as memory intrudes of fire raining, people screaming, running with hair aflame. Gramma grips me, won't let go, crushed and mangled by a giant wave. Not my memories. How could anything like that belong to me? Might be my Gramma's boat but I never met her. All I've seen of anywhere is pretty postcards.

Eyes wide open and I can't believe it—no wonder Daisychain can't keep hushed. Laid out ahead is a real-life picture postcard. Skala Pier as good as old, nestled at the feet of impressive cliffs, the curve of donkey steps cut clear. Little boats of red and blue and white. I'm bobbing in a little boat myself, jammed between two bulky brides who don't seem the slightest bit impressed that we are literally entering a postcard, entering memories that can't possibly exist.

"But the 88-minute . . ."

Nobody cares about those minutes in this moment. Brides tumble from the shore boat in a confectionary of white chiffon and lace, dripping water and sloughing rosebuds and sequins.

Faint music wafts from a bistro embedded higher up in the volcano's side. Unfamiliar music that is neither old nor new. Murmuring voices and the clink of knives and forks on china plates. *Nice to meet you. Thank you. Bye bye.*

Santorini, ripped straight from the bluest blue of postcards. A wafting blend of seasoned, grilling fare distracts me from figures in dim corners, hovering.

The donkey trek is beckoning—not taking chances on the clack and shudder of a potentially figmentary cable car fighting gravity up grim volcanic rock the color of sun blasted lichen.

I sweat up pathways lined with spiky cactus, eucalypts and oleanders, perfect as those prewar era dirty postcards. White on white and blue on blue and the sun begins to sink as church bells peal. Hot young things pause, bating breaths and posed for tanned and tattooed boyfriends fumbling with large, expensive cameras. A miserable child throws its regular sunset tantrum as swarthy men heft luggage down the winding, pale gray stairs, white-edged, the solid slap of sandals, passing locals sweeping and fixing and fetching and ferrying, pushing carts and weeding potted gardens.

A welcome splash of bougainvillea as drinks are stolen from passing trays and we merge with random wedding parties, pretty girls attached like limpets to my Admiral arms as fading sunlight dapples cheeks.

Daisychain barks and the girls let go as something emerges from the crowd, at first shapeless, shifting and coalescing, then hardening into solid and unmistakable bride. Not one of mine, this is something new, or perhaps much older as well as blue and borrowed. Brighter than a supernova, entangling me with its searing diamond glare. A being birthed during 88 minutes when humankind let go and dropped the ball.

No words from me. Nor from the bride. Daisychain does all the talking, barking and barking until the moment passes and the entity glides off about its business to the accompaniment of bouzouki, clarinet, lute and mandolin, santur, toubeleki and a flurry of enthusiastic stomping.

And I realize I've been waiting for this moment all my life, suspended in a thousand damaged windows to the past, in garish scenes frozen and manipulated, trapped in laminate, glossed and falsified and static. Whitewashed, airbrushed, Photoshopped, grandslammed and Instagramed, rose-tinted, sunset squinted.

Familiar and comforting sounds envelop: the violent flap and rattle of sun umbrella canvas in stroppy winds and, somewhere in the distance, yelping. Eyes wide open—now what has that damn doggo got himself into this time? Over my shoulder, beyond the flat-roofed houses pressed into volcanic cliffs. Beyond misty blue deceptive Aegean remnants, dotted with white triangle sailboats leaning as bright pink petals scatter on gentle vespers.

Two wedding guests, lithe girls in livid blue, already drunk and separated from their pack. Above their tight-pinned fascinators bob blue and white balloons expelled into the wild, destined for the intestines of sea turtles and whales if only such elaborate creatures still existed.

Tears of laughter, tears of joy and hello, what is happening over there? One blue dome per church or maybe two, three at a pinch and I'm pretty sure that's law—but that one there, by the holy slippers of Saint Spyridon of Tremithus, that church appears to be *encrusted* with blue domes, pulsing and blooming like pustules of far cast cerulean pollen. Whitewashed walls butting against each other, doors and windows merging into tunnels.

And Rhizanthella, she's starting to resemble a tank with human legs and filigree, the bio-ordnance still configuring to her pearl-encrusted form, tugging and stretching, snapping and shifting, folding in upon itself, then outward along new lines.

Furrows ridging deep between my eyebrows. "They're gonna know you're not one of them. That outfit will not fool an artificial mind."

A familiar huffy pout distorts her face. "Who's trying to fool anyone or anything? My repurposed ordnance frock is an expression of solidarity, connectivity and haute couture." She winces as something unseen beneath a polymer chitin layer pinches. Tugs at it till the irritation passes. "Them. It. We are unsure of the correct applicable pronoun, greeting or salutation. Not sure of their status or their numerical identity. Their personhood, so to speak."

Not sure what I'm supposed to say to that, so I keep quiet as she continues. "We just want to talk is all. We—" and she gestures to the brides "—have come to join them."

"Join whom? Who is *them* exactly?"

"The collective entity now known as Santorini, Admiral dearest!"

"Can't be a person and an island both."

"Says who—you? Who made you the boss of regenerating land masses?"

I puff my chest up like one of those birds on the postcard advertising California iceberg lettuce, but she's already turning away as the wedding party ripples at its center mass and an old bird emerges, swaggering into view like one of those vintage cigarette packet cowboys inviting you to come to where the flavor is. She is wire thin with hair like Alpine frost. Thin lips stained flamingo pink.

Daisychain yips and barks and does a midair backflip. Then another and another till he is nothing but a whirring hot metal blur. And I should have been yipping and flipping alongside, because there before us stands, impossibly . . .

"Gramma!" And not a day older than however old she was back when we fought our way across the post-war soup. Except that . . .

"But Gramma—no way . . . How can you be here? And how come I can't remember . . . or maybe I can? I am molecules away from doing backflips of my own. Not the joyous type—the meltdown kind.

"Long story, kid. Turns out I'm older than I look—and so are you. Santorini, however, well now, this island is as young as a spring chicken. Great to see you've taken good care of my dog."

"*Your* dog?"

But by all that is almost holy I can see this fact is true—the doggo and Gramma, well now, they're a team. Daisychain dances around her in a smoosh of figure eights before rolling on her back in a wriggling frenzy.

Gramma bends and crouches down to scratch his tin can belly. "There's a good boy, best boy ever. Thanks for keeping an eye on my precious grandchild."

And I want to ask so many things, but they all get tangled in my throat before the moment slips away entirely.

"This island achieved sentience during the 88-minute war," said Gramma—as if that fact was anywhere near the top of my desperate-to-ask-list. "Must have been well shielded for this spittle-lick of salt and rock to avoid full spectrum wi-fi sterilization."

As I watch our doggo wriggling in the dirt, it all clicks like it's never clicked before. Santorini has regenerated based on a million momentary fragments, postcards all, one form or another. Once a bridal theme park, now a living beast with shifting moods, beyond the captured, trapped and static. Imprisoned memories catapulted, free range to multiply and seed. Pollinating and embedding into pocked volcanic cliffs; gnawed and pushed and jabbed and punctured, flowed like lava, stabbed like steel. Surged and spilled like cactus flowers after a once-in-a century splash of rain.

And how well the shipboard brides are blending, some more dramatically than others, but that's brides for you, so the legends tell us, some being practitioners of stealth rather than flourish. No dress code regulations or traditions exist for interfacing with sentient islands—but looking like you belong here is a start.

And no one wore modular, load bearing tac force haute couture better than Rhyzonthella, who was always safe rather than sorry and looked amazing, blue hair blowing in the wind. But I soon lost her amongst the bustling, narrow streets, amidst manifesting holographic tourists and real-life flesh and blood descendant Greeks who'd never left, despite the manic changes. Who kept on playing, low and quiet, tricks learned withstanding decades of bridal entourage assault in summer months. AI governance seems a trifle in comparison. If governance is the appropriate word (it isn't). For all I know the Greeks are AI too. Never one to quibble over details—and I'm still not.

At the day's end, lurid sunset splashes fuchsia across vague Aegean dregs, when know-how is all very well, but not much good until paired with targeted *know why*. And as for knowing wherefore, well now, that's a different story. Come back and check on that one next millennium.

Because I'm in love with this picture postcard, its vistas swift and inconsistent on the shift, and I can no longer tell my brides from ones with artificial hearts. Boatloads of tourists pull up at the groaning pier and wait for donkeys to take them up the side. Emissaries from other islands, joyous at heritage listing's feisty abolition.

My brides have seen a lot of love and can sing you all about their great escape with the Admiral who braved the Winedark Soup for connectivity with a future not yet written.

Cat Sparks (left), Kaaron Warren (right)

ABOUT THE AUTHORS

CAT SPARKS

Cat Sparks is a multi-award-winning Australian author, editor and artist. Former fiction editor of *Cosmos Magazine*, she also dabbled as a kitchen hand, video store manager, assistant library technician, media monitor, political and archaeological photographer, graphic designer, guest lecturer, festival director, panelist, fiction judge, essayist, creative writing teacher and manager of Agog! Press, which produced ten anthologies of new speculative fiction. In 2012 an Australia Council grant enabled her to study with Margaret Atwood in Key West, Florida. In 2017 she co-edited *Ecopunk! Speculative Tales of Radical Futures* with Liz Grzyb.

Cat has a BA in visual arts (CAI), a postgraduate certificate in editing and publishing (UTS) and a PhD in creative writing (Curtin), the latter concerning the intersection of ecocatastrophe science fiction and contemporary climate fiction.

Cat's debut novel, *Lotus Blue* (Skyhorse, 2017) was shortlisted for the Compton Crook, Aurealis and Ditmar Awards. Her collections, *The Bride Price* (Ticonderoga, 2013) and *Dark Harvest* (Newcon, 2020) were nominated for Aurealis Awards and won Ditmars for Best Collected Work in their respective years.

Eighty of her short stories have been published since the turn of the millennium and her twenty-five awards for writing, editing and art include winning the Peter McNamara Conveners' Award twice. Cat is a climate activist and keen traveler currently obsessed with photographing adorable birds and grungy walls.

KAARON WARREN

Shirley Jackson award-winner Kaaron Warren published her first short story in 1993 and has had fiction in print every year since. She was recently given the Peter McNamara Lifetime Achievement Award and was Guest of Honor at World Fantasy 2018, Stokercon

2019 and Geysercon 2019. She has also been Guest of Honor at Conflux in Canberra and Genrecon in Brisbane.

She has published five multi-award winning novels (*Slights*, *Walking the Tree*, *Mistification*, *The Grief Hole* and *Tide of Stone*) and seven short story collections, including the multi-award winning *Through Splintered Walls*. Her most recent short story collection is *A Primer to Kaaron Warren* from Dark Moon Books. Her most recent novella, *Into Bones Like Oil* (Meerkat Press), was shortlisted for a Shirley Jackson Award and the Bram Stoker Award, winning the Aurealis Award. Her stories have appeared in both Ellen Datlow's and Paula Guran's Year's Best anthologies.

Kaaron has been reading Science Fiction since she plucked the Nebula Award anthologies off her father's bookshelf at around ten. She loves the possibilities Science Fiction presents, as a writer and as a reader. "Air, Water and the Grove," in this collection, won the Aurealis Award for SF, while both "Witnessing" and "68 Days" were shortlisted. Her most recent books include the re-release of her acclaimed novel, *Slights*, (IFWG Australia) *Tool Tales*, a chapbook in collaboration with Ellen Datlow (also IFWG), and Capturing Ghosts, a writing advice chapbook from Brain Jar Press.

Did you enjoy this book?

If so, word-of-mouth recommendations and online reviews are critical to the success of any book, so we hope you'll tell your friends about it and consider leaving a review at your favorite bookseller's or library's website.

Visit us at www.meerkatpress.com for our full catalog.

Meerkat Press
Asheville